praise for
RESCUED DUTY

"Rescued Duty was SO FUN. It was thrilling, exciting, fast pace but most of all touched on topics that left me thinking long after I finished—topics like family, integrity and courage. Thank you Lisa and Laura for such an epic ride!"

—Jefferson Bethke, NYT bestselling author

"Laura Conaway has a way of bringing faith into fiction that transforms the reader's heart as they journey through a suspense that keeps you on the edge of your seat. This diverse romance was full of second chances that were wrapped in the grace of God. Fans of Susan May Warren and Lisa Phillips will delight in this read."

—Toni Shiloh, author of To Catch A Prince

"Full of action, twists and turns, whodunnit, suspense, inspiration, humor, and romance. Excellent story!!"

—Naomi, Goodreads

"Rescued Duty was engaging, fast-paced, and an edge of your seat read with twists and turns, friends to more, misplaced guilt, and faith threads woven in."

—Allyson, Goodreads

RESCUED DUTY

LAST CHANCE
• FIRE AND RESCUE •

RESCUED DUTY

LAURA CONAWAY
LISA PHILLIPS

Rescued Duty: A Last Chance County Novel
Last Chance Fire and Rescue, Book 5
Published by Sunrise Media Group LLC

Paperback ISBN: 978-1-963372-37-3

For more information about Lisa Phillips and Laura Conaway please access the authors' websites at the following addresses: https://www.authorlisaphillips.com https://www.lauraconawayauthor.com

Published in the United States of America.
Cover Design: Ana Grigoriu-Voicu, Books-Design

To the One who has brought me into His forever family
alongside people from every nation, tribe,
language, and tongue.

Soli Deo Gloria.

"But to all who did receive him, who believed in his name,
he gave the right to become children of God,
who were born, not of blood nor of the will of the flesh
nor of the will of man, but of God."

JOHN 1:12-13 ESV

ONE

NAYA MICHÉL MADE IT HER DUTY TO TELL A story and expose the truth. She had a vested interest in each outcome. People's lives hung in the balance. And her job ensured the light shone through. Her latest story as an investigative reporter was proof of that.

Naya's cell phone buzzed, and she fumbled around her desk drawer and swiped to answer. "Hey, friend." Naya propped an elbow on her office desk, then wiggled her computer mouse.

"You ready for your meeting with Drew?" Ingram asked. Naya imagined her best friend sipping her morning tea in her office and perusing the files for the day.

"Nothing like a Monday morning meeting to jump-start the week." Naya hit send on the email with the final article on the McDaniel family, whose son needed a heart transplant. They'd almost been swindled out of a family heirloom pocket watch worth five grand when they'd taken it to a seasonal worker at *Take a Chance* pawn shop. Thankfully, a local had caught wind of the situation and made sure the McDaniels got their money, which had helped pay for their son's life-saving surgery.

"I've been praying," Ingram said.

"Thanks, girl." Naya wiped her clammy hands along her skirt, then straightened the pencil holder and file organizer on her desk. "Someone's got to move up in the ranks around here. This meeting could be my shot."

"God's got this."

One way or another. Naya didn't know what this meeting held, but rumors had been circulating the office that her boss, Drew Warrington, wanted to promote someone to head reporter at the Last Chance Tribune now that the previous head reporter had retired.

"In all things, God works things together for the good of those who love Him." Naya repeated the truth aloud, but it didn't make the unknown easier. If only her heart would catch up.

Naya glanced at the pictures framed on her desk.

A portrait of her family taunted her. They'd posed at the local market in Haiti, squinting against the sun. Her little brother—her best friend. Her parents. All of them now gone.

This one's for you, Dom.

Next to the family photo was an image that brought a smile: Naya and Ingram poking their heads around a palm tree at the beach. A day of sun, finding sand dollars, and a random guy paying for their dinner—although he'd definitely done it to try and get their numbers.

The pictures only told her that the future could bring any set of circumstances.

"Drew always likes what I write."

"Of course he does." Ingram chuckled. "You write with passion. You showcase the truth, not just the dry facts."

"It's what the people want." Naya made sure her stories served the readership of Last Chance County, and she would show her boss he could count on her.

Naya stood up and walked over to the break room. Her fingers shook while she poured herself a cup of her favorite Haitian coffee blend—an ode to her native country in the Caribbean. A place she hadn't ventured back to in eons.

Naya took a sip of coffee.

"If Drew offers me a promotion, I can make sure the truth stays in the light." Naya sucked in a breath. "It's go time."

"Knock 'em dead."

That's exactly what Naya intended to do. Each click of her heels on the hallway sounded in time with her heart.

Naya knocked on Drew's door.

"Come in."

She pushed open the door, and it let out a long creak. Naya rounded the corner but came up short. Seated in a chair across from her boss was fellow reporter—and her ex-boyfriend—Tucker Long. "I'm sorry if I interrupted. I can come back later."

Tucker turned in his seat and smirked. Six months ago, she'd ended their relationship, and he still acted like he had superiority over her. She didn't like the glint in his eyes at all.

"No, no. Please, have a seat. I want you both present for this meeting." Drew tapped a few papers on his desk. He extended his hand to the chair in front of him. The smile on his face accentuated the wrinkles around his eyes, and his gray hair testified to his experience after years of work in the industry as a reporter and editor. Naya intended to impress her boss with her own knowledge and skills.

"Okay." Naya plastered on a smile and took the seat next to Tucker. The chair wobbled on its unsteady legs, and she planted her feet on the ground to keep from swaying. If there had to be an audience, she would take it in stride. No way would she let Tucker intimidate her.

Drew cleared his throat. "I'm sure you're well aware the position for lead investigative reporter needs to be filled since Terry retired. And you two are my best reporters."

Naya sat straight but kept her mouth shut, resisting the urge to correct him that she and Tucker were the *only* two reporters at the Tribune. Given the size of the town and the readership of the paper, there wasn't money for more staff—or better equipment.

"Which makes my job here very difficult. Clearly, I have two great candidates." Drew leaned back in his chair.

"Whatever I have to do, I can show you I have what it takes for the position." Tucker scooted his chair in front of Naya and closer to the desk, then leaned forward.

Naya opened her mouth with a rebuttal, but Drew shooed his hand. "No need. I've already made up my mind on what we're going to do."

"You have?" Naya and Tucker said in unison.

"You each have one week to write a story on the water contamination catastrophe that's all the buzz right now. Whoever's story I like better, that person will receive the promotion."

Tucker sat back and lifted his chin. "Great idea."

"What about bias?" Naya added. Had Drew considered the possibility of the playing field being skewed if either of them tainted the story with a certain view to win this promotion? She would write the truth with a clear call on how it impacted the reader, whereas Tucker would no doubt write whatever he thought would get him the job. "We've always been taught to avoid bringing an agenda when writing a story. How will you ensure you remain objective in your decision and don't let your own bias influence whose article is better?"

Tucker let out a cough. "I have full confidence Drew will be assessing our writing, not us as individuals." He turned to Naya and lifted his brows. "Or our ability to spin a sensational tale that has nothing to do with the truth."

Naya bit her tongue to keep from saying something she'd regret. Even though she'd been hurt and strung along by this man, it didn't mean she had the right to retaliate. Still, she had a responsibility to speak the truth like Jesus—in love. Not out of her fleshly desire. "I guess our stories will speak for themselves." Naya crossed her arms.

"That's a valid question." Drew steepled his fingers on his desk. "You will each submit your story to Kelly, who will remove your name before sending it over to the editorial team who will vote. After they've given their feedback, I'll review the articles."

Naya stood. "Thank you, Drew. I'm honored to submit a story." She'd accept the challenge and give Drew the best story she could write.

Tucker caught up to her in the hall. "If you run out of contacts or need help, let me know. I might be able to give you one or two from the city council."

Of course he'd flaunt his access to the mayor. He'd written a story on the mayor during his campaign four years ago, and now the two were best buddies.

Naya lifted her chin. "I appreciate the offer, but I have my own methods of research. I wish you all the best." She turned her back and stepped into her cubicle.

Rely on him for help? As if.

He'd shown his true colors, and life had taught her the hard way—more than once—that people never did anything just out of the kindness of their hearts.

It proved easier to do things alone and avoid a fallout.

Naya gathered her notepad, recorder, and purse and headed for the door. One week wasn't long.

The clock was ticking toward the deadline, and Tucker would already be on the phone with city hall. She needed to get to the site of the protests that were happening. She could interview people on the scene and have something to write up by the end of the day. He might have connections, but nothing compared to getting firsthand eyewitness accounts from those directly impacted by the situation. That's where important details were that could contribute to the story.

She maneuvered her Impreza into a parallel parking spot two blocks down from the river. Thanks to the sun peeking through the clouds, it wouldn't hurt to log a few extra steps on her smartwatch today.

Chanting was audible, even from this distance, and police cars sat nearby. She made a quick stop in Bridgewater Café for apple cinnamon muffins, then headed to the park.

It had been a week since the protests started.

And two weeks since a medical report had come out with information on individuals being hospitalized. Doctors had found high levels of heavy metals and perfluoroalkyl substances, or PFAS, in those who'd come into the hospital with ulcerative colitis.

Police officers were still stationed by the pedestrian bridge where most of the Green Warriors environmental group congregated. A light breeze swayed the branches of the elm trees that covered the landscape.

Naya zipped up her windbreaker.

The extra hours of daylight were nice, but the beginning of spring still brought with it thawing temperatures.

The river had begun to rise again, and leftover winter debris had made its way into the water source. The environmental group blamed the pollution on poor water quality measures, but nothing had been confirmed yet. No one knew how the water had been contaminated with heavy metals. Right now it was just a whole lot of pointing fingers and people wanting answers.

Which was where she stepped in. People deserved to know the truth, to be empowered, so they could move forward with their lives. She would find the answers for them.

Officer Ramble and Lieutenant Basuto from the Last Chance County Police Department had staked their claims on either side of the sidewalk that led from the park to the bridge and from the bridge to the water. Ramble was maybe a year older than her and wore a mischievous look in his eye. One that would have spelled trouble if she'd accepted his invite to coffee. On the other hand, Basuto was older. Married.

"Long day?" Naya approached Basuto.

"More like long night too. And it's only eleven in the morning." Basuto rubbed his jaw.

"The twins?" Naya asked.

"They don't quite understand what it means to sleep past five."

Naya grimaced. "Ouch. And Sasha?"

"She's a champ. Two more months until the due date."

Naya grinned. "She's a tough one." The few times Naya saw her in the grocery store, the woman knew how to keep order with those kids.

Basuto chuckled. "At least it's peaceful protesting so far today. There're no other civilians we have to keep an eye on over there either." He pointed to the playground, which was void of any children. The cooler temperatures were keeping spring fever at bay for a little while longer.

"Hopefully this will make your shift more manageable." She handed him a muffin.

Basuto's eyes widened and he tore open the wrapper. "This is fantastic," he mumbled in between bites.

Naya laughed. "May I?" She pointed to the bridge. She wanted to get firsthand viewpoints from the protestors. One thing she'd learned over the years—there were always two sides to a story.

"Have at it." Basuto extended his arm. "You know I wouldn't want your job any day."

"It's not so bad. At least I don't have to stand in one place."

He smiled. "True that."

After stopping to hand out the other muffins to the officers, Naya pulled out her pen and paper and made her way up the incline onto the bridge. She went over to a cluster of women among the crowd. "Hi, my name is Naya Michél, and I'm a reporter with the Last Chance Tribune. Can I ask you some questions?"

"Sure, girl. The name's Sylvia." A young woman with a bleach-blonde pixie cut extended her hand, and they shook.

"I'm Veronica." A middle-aged woman with long jet-black hair gave a wave. A sleeve of tattoos covered her forearm. One said *Love our people and earth.*

"What exactly have you been protesting out here?" Naya shook Veronica's hand.

Sylvia pushed hair back from her face. "We've been out here taking a stand for the health of our community and families. Everyone has the right to clean water. Not only the creatures who live in it but the people who drink that water."

Naya hit the record button to capture the whole conversation in case she wasn't able to jot down everything either of the women mentioned. Whether she agreed with the woman or not, she needed to be careful not to weave her personal opinions into the mix of information. Everyone had passions. Often from experiences that fueled their drive for a cause. She just needed to learn what that drive was motivated by. A true desire to better the community, or a personal benefit?

"What prompted you all to start coming out here to take a stand?" Naya jotted down the notes.

Veronica stepped forward and shoved her hands in her pockets. "My aunt is in the hospital with ulcerative colitis and they're doing a biopsy on a lump in her thyroid. Her blood work came back with high levels of heavy metals. She's just one of many who grew up in Last Chance County and are now suffering from long term exposure to chemicals. Of course, people began to ask questions." She huffed. "Everyone deserves a high-quality life. The only way to do that is to take care of our earth. That's when this group, *Save Our Land and Make a Stand*, began to establish action steps."

Sylvia nodded. "If people are sick, the wildlife in our freshwater is suffering too. Someone needs to be held accountable for the lack of water quality measures."

"Do you all have regular meetings?" If Naya conversed with the other group members in a less high-stakes environment, she could get their perspectives too.

"Oh yeah. The second and fourth Tuesday of the month at six thirty in the evening. We meet in Room 4 at the community center. But anyways..." Sylvia shook her head like Naya had discussed a less important issue. "Another report showed high levels of contaminants in the fish in our lakes. That's when we knew this was a bigger issue."

"Who are you hoping will notice these protests? Where do you want to see a change?" Naya flipped the page of her notebook and held her pen ready.

"Ethos Fire Solutions on the west side of town. Rumor has it those people have been dumping their toxic waste into the stream that feeds into the river. Polluting everything in its path from the soil to the water. Isn't that right, Sylvia?"

"You nailed it." Sylvia pumped her fist in the air.

"We even have a group down at the entrance to the plant now protesting. Because what do we want?" Veronica cupped her hands around her mouth.

"Take a stand." People began to shout. "Save our land!"

As if on cue, the entire group began to stomp in unison. The bridge began to shake under their weight, and Naya grabbed the wooden railing for support.

"Have you talked with anyone at Ethos to set up a meeting?" Naya yelled, but Sylvia and Veronica were focused on rousing the crowd. She tapped Sylvia on the shoulder and kept a firm grip on the railing with her other hand.

The woman turned around and glowered. "What?"

"I don't think this is a good idea." Naya pointed to the wooden slats that held them on the bridge. With each stomp, the wood creaked, and some of the warped pieces from years of exposure to the elements began to buckle inward.

"If you're not in the fight with us, you're against us." Sylvia narrowed her gaze and began to jump. "Take a stand!"

Soon the people were no longer stomping. Everyone was jumping.

Naya turned around to steady herself and make her way off the bridge. In her peripheral vision, Basuto and Ramble jogged over to the structure.

Ramble blew his whistle. "That's enough. We need everyone off the bridge."

Instead of complying, the amped-up group raised their voices and whistled back.

Basuto had his hand wrapped around his cuffs and made his way up the left side of the bridge. "Folks! Everyone off this bridge for your own safety!"

Naya slid her hand along the railing and squeezed past a few people. She ducked around signs some of the members thrust in the air. The chanting and jumping continued.

No one was listening.

The bridge gave an audible groan.

Naya stumbled sideways.

Her notepad and recorder flew out of her hand, and she grasped for the other part of the railing. Air whooshed around her. People's screams pounded in her eardrums as the bridge gave way.

Naya's grip on the railing slipped, and she pinched her eyes shut. She was about to fall to her death.

TWO

"STEPHENS. IN MY OFFICE." BRYCE POPPED HIS head into the kitchen at the firehouse. "We need to chat." The man's gruff voice boomed.

Zack's muscles stiffened. Whatever conversation loomed, it would be from boss to employee, not friend to friend.

Zack shoved the rest of his midmorning chocolate donut in his mouth, then set his coffee cup down on the dining table.

Trace, one of the EMTs, slapped him on the shoulder. "Have fun, Trouble."

Zack winced.

The rest of the guys sat around the table. "Who's ready for another round?" Eddie fanned a pack of cards and shuffled the deck.

"I've got a strategy you can't beat." Izan, one of the firefighters, flexed his fingers.

The crew's voices faded, and Zack walked down the hall to Bryce's office. All he wanted was to be part of the team.

Once more, he wasn't included.

He hated being pulled away from the guys. He didn't want to be known as Trouble.

Still, he seemed to have a knack for finding it. Which meant once again, he needed to figure a way out of it. He didn't have to hide that reality. God already knew. And He'd saved Zack from his mistakes. Made him a new creation. He didn't have anything to prove to God, but he sure needed to earn the favor of the squad.

Zack hadn't discovered how to solve that case. It was easier to rappel down the side of a building and save someone's life than it was to insert himself for good as a member of the Last Chance County Fire and Rescue team.

Before he could reach Bryce's office, the alarm echoed in the hall. "Sumner Bridge collapse. Civilians involved. Rescue 5, Truck 14, Ambo 21," the dispatcher read.

Zack's shoulders loosened and he sprinted to the engine bay. The interrogation with his boss would have to wait.

He donned his attire and equipment and hopped up into the truck seconds before Ridge peeled out of the drive. He held his helmet in hand and stared at the picture of his parents wedged inside. A loss he refused to be overtaken by. The reminder propelled him further. He might be loaded down with gear, but the chance to save a life made the burden light.

"Rescue 5 en route. ETA six minutes." Bryce spoke over the radio comms.

A few seconds later, the radio crackled. "Copy. Thirty-plus victims trapped in the river among the collapsed bridge. Officers already on scene."

They pulled up to the edge of the park where half a dozen people waded out of the river, screaming and splashing. The bridge had buckled, the middle section sunk into the river. Civilians still on the unstable structure clawed at the beams, seeking a refuge from the water below.

"Eddie, grab the ropes. I want you and Zack pulling people out." Bryce slammed his door. "Ridge, set up an area for those who need medical assistance."

Zack jogged down to the embankment and took a moment to

assess the area. Those precious seconds of familiarizing himself with his surroundings could mean life or death for anyone involved. Rocks and dirt lined the steep slope that led to the water's edge. Wooden slats from the bridge floated in the water. A few were caught on rocks and jutted straight up.

A woman with jet-black hair grabbed on to someone's arm and helped pull them out of the river. They made their way over to Zack, both sopping wet.

He pointed to Ridge. "Head over to the grass by the swings. Someone will help you."

"Help. My leg's stuck."

"She hit her head!"

"I can't get up. The rocks are too slippery."

Chaos swirled around him, all the voices blending into a wash of noise. *Focus.*

Eddie dashed over to Zack and slapped him on the back. "One at a time. Let's go."

Zack forged ahead through the water, ignoring the icy temperature stabbing his legs. He grabbed a flailing woman's arm, righted her, and held her tight as he led her out of the water to Amelia by the medical tent. "Here you go, Lieutenant."

Eddie shoved a broken beam aside and hefted a woman into his arms. Blood matted her hair. "If you can swim, head to shore."

"I'll grab the others over here." Zack pointed to his left, upstream.

Eddie nodded. "I'll take the two up there."

Zack glided his feet along the rocks and worked his way upstream, careful not to take big steps and risk slipping. He pushed several wooden boards out of the way and tossed a few onto the embankment.

Zack cupped his hands over his mouth. "Fire Department. We're here to help."

"My foot is stuck under the debris." An older man waved his

arms in the air from his crouched position on a rock. A woman bent low next to him, her business suit sopping wet and plastered to her frame. She worked on freeing him and now fought to yank on something below the water's surface.

"Here, let me help." Zack came up beside the woman and extended his hand.

She turned to face him, and her dark brown eyes bored into his. Zack's mind rushed him back to another time and place. Between her black hair, held back in a wet and matted ponytail, and her melanin-rich skin, there was no mistaking who stood beside him.

"Naya." Her name came out in a whisper, and Zack cleared his throat.

"Zack." She glanced down at his soaked uniform and pulled her hand from his grasp. "This man needs help."

Zack turned his attention to the guy. "What's your name, sir?"

"Jay. I was just trying to support a good cause." The man groaned, his face pinched. "Now look what happened." He waved his hand, but his balance teetered. Zack grabbed the man's upper arm to stop him from falling back from his crouch.

"We're going to get you out of here, Jay." Zack studied the water below, which was murky, given all the debris, but still clear enough to see what trapped the man.

Naya pointed. "This rock rolled over, and it's pinning his foot down."

"Can you spot him so he doesn't fall, and I'll try to move it?" Zack shifted to Jay's right.

Naya nodded, her eyes dark. She blinked and lifted her lips in a polite smile for the man. "How long have you been with this group?"

Zack tuned out their conversation and crouched, feeling around the boulder. No time to go back to the truck for tools, but rolling it would hurt the man for a moment. "Hold your breath on three. Ready?"

Jay nodded.

Zack got the rock over, using the current of the water to send it downstream. Jay let out a groan. "Thank you."

"Stephens!" Bryce stood by the embankment. "You got it under control over there?"

The comment shouldn't bother Zack, but the underlying accusation swelled over him faster than the current he stood in.

Bryce would never say it to his face, but the lieutenant didn't think Zack could hold his own and not cause more problems along the way. Just last week he'd been vacuuming, and the motor had overheated and almost started a fire thanks to the dust bag not having been emptied. He'd wanted to help, and it had backfired.

Zack was determined to prove Bryce wrong and show the whole rescue crew they needed him on their team. They were supposed to be his family, but he still floundered like a fish out of water.

"Never better, Lieutenant." Zack plastered on a smile and swung Jay's right arm over his shoulder. He gripped the man's torso. "Can you stand up fully for me?"

Naya had positioned herself on Jay's other side. Jay let out a groan and stood to full height. A frown filled Naya's face.

"Good?"

She nodded.

"Okay, on the count of three, we're going to move to that path over there." Zack pointed to the smooth dirt area about five yards away that led up to the grass where Bryce waited.

"One, two, three."

"Keep your weight on us," Naya added.

Zack began to trudge toward the water's edge. Naya was really helping him? He was surprised she hadn't turned her back and gone to find someone else to assist, given he'd been the one to leave her all those years ago. Disappearing from her life with no explanation. He wouldn't blame her for reciprocating the gesture, except she didn't know the truth of what had actually happened.

The shuffle of their feet kicked up dirt and clouded the water. There was no way to tell the extent of the injury to the man's foot, but the sooner they got him to Trace and Kianna, the better.

"We're almost there." Zack pushed forward, taking on most of the man's weight.

Bryce maneuvered his way down the path to the edge of the water. "I've got him now." The lieutenant took hold of the man's arm.

"I can take him to the ambo." Zack stepped up onto the grass, still holding Jay's other arm.

"I've got it." Bryce's eyes narrowed. "Go do what you were ordered."

Zack's jaw tightened. He'd done what was asked of him and done it well. Why couldn't Bryce recognize that? "Yes, sir." Zack let go of the man's arm, and Bryce took the lead.

"Thanks for your help." He turned to Naya. "Hey."

She had walked right back into the water, her arms outstretched to maintain her balance. Blood caked her forearm, but it didn't appear to be bleeding anymore.

"Naya." He jogged to her. "You're hurt."

"I'll be fine. I need to find my notepad."

"Paper or a tablet?" Zack stayed close to her side. "Because paper is going to be wet and illegible by now."

"Just give me one second to—" Naya started to fall to the side, and her arms flailed.

Zack grabbed her arm and shoulder to steady her while his own heart pounded. "Easy. These rocks are slippery, and you should really get that arm looked at." He pointed to the bloody area.

Her gaze trailed down to his wrist and the red corded bracelet he wore.

Once *her* red bracelet.

She stepped out of his grasp, her body shivering.

Was she really so surprised? "Naya—"

"Fine. No notepad. Let's go." She trudged through the water, each step spraying droplets around Zack. He followed behind her until they were on dry ground. "I'll see myself out from here." She headed toward the medic area.

Eddie clapped him on the shoulder. "Focus up, man. There're more people to save."

Zack turned away from the past and got back to work.

Three hours later, back at the firehouse, Zack was all done filling out the reporting form from the callout. He leaned back in the chair and raised his arms above his head, stretching out his shoulders.

Eddie walked by, holding a burrito. "Bro, lunch has been ready a while."

Zack stood.

"Also, the lieutenant asked to see you in his office."

So much for food. Zack wandered down the hall and rapped on the lieutenant's door.

"It's open."

Zack took a seat across from Bryce's desk and offered a grin. "We got the job done today. No fish left floundering in the water." Maybe if Zack started off with what had gone well, Bryce would forget anything that he didn't approve of.

"We needed all hands-on deck. It certainly wasn't a joking matter." Bryce raised his brow. "But you're right. We got the job done."

"Of course. I agree." He remained rigid in his chair, unsure where Bryce was going with the conversation.

"I reviewed your application and see you want to get your hazmat certification."

Zack made eye contact with Bryce but couldn't figure out how his boss felt about the request. "I want to follow in my father's footsteps. He was a chemist."

"You like that stuff?" Bryce studied him. "I was worried this was about joining the bomb squad."

"I'm not crazy." Zack shrugged. "But I like reading his journals and figuring out what he was working on. It's like a puzzle. I started the coursework four weeks ago to get ahead." Assuming Bryce would give him the green light for pursuing the certification.

Bryce slid a manila folder across his desk. "As part of your ops training, I want you to take a look at this file. Work through the report and see what you can find on the chemicals used and the protocol taken in the investigation. See if you find anything overlooked. It's a cold case now, but fresh eyes never hurt."

Another puzzle to solve. More like a test to prove he had what it took for the team. "And if I find anything?" Zack took the folder.

"Write it up so we can add it to the police report. I want it back on my desk in a week."

"Yes, sir." He hopped up out of the chair.

"How far are you into completing the forty hours?" Bryce steepled his fingers.

"Halfway sir."

"Good. Once your finish the hours and if you pass the certification exam, we'll talk more. This could be a good opportunity for you. We need more guys on hazmat."

The underlying implication was still there. *If* he passed. Zack wouldn't make it optional. He would succeed.

He headed to the kitchen and poured himself a bowl of cereal to hold him over until dinner, then slid into a chair and opened the file.

He'd bring his A game.

His eyes perused the front-page details and froze at the names of the victims listed. *Douglas and Callie Nelson.*

His hand dropped to the table and hit the edge of the cereal bowl, tipping it over. Milk and soggy grains splashed across the surface, running in every direction.

Zack yanked the papers into the air.

This wasn't just any cold case he'd been given to solve. He'd wanted to learn hazmat so he could feel closer to his father and prove to the squad that he belonged. Not reopen the incident that killed his parents.

THREE

NAYA'S ARM THROBBED AS SHE WALKED THROUGH the automatic sliding doors of the hospital to the parking lot. Just a bandage, not broken.

The medics had whisked her away at the site of the bridge collapse to inspect her injuries. When she couldn't straighten her arm, they thought it best she have it x-rayed. She insisted on driving herself to the hospital. No need for an ambulance. At least she'd been able to help Zack support the injured man with her good arm.

Zack.

A car buzzed past her. Naya jerked back from the curb.

She'd spent the last two and half hours sitting in the ER waiting for results and thinking about a boy who'd grown into a man.

His teenage baby face had disappeared since she'd seen him last. Now he sported dark turbulent eyes, facial hair, and sturdy biceps. The uniform of a firefighter—which suited him more than she'd have thought.

A man who'd once been part of her story. But he'd stayed in the past, there one moment and gone the next. All these years they'd lived in the same town, and they had to run into each other today?

No point resurrecting old memories. If he'd wanted to be part of her life, Zack would have made an effort to reconnect. Instead, he'd chosen to be a hero and have no contact with her.

She needed to focus on the story that Drew had assigned, or she would lose her shot at the job she wanted.

Naya hit the unlock button on her key fob, and the vehicle chirped from its spot a few feet away.

She slid into the seat and shut the door. Pain shot through her arm from pulling on the handle.

Naya blinked back tears and reached for her phone to call Ingram, the closest friend she had here in town.

"Hey, Nay."

Naya leaned her head against the seat and smiled. "Hey, Grams."

"That nickname makes me sound like I'm your eighty-year-old grandma who's about to turn in for the night." Ingram chuckled.

"It's stuck this long, there's no use changing it now." Naya laughed.

"Good thing it hasn't become public knowledge. Will keeps trying to come up with a nickname himself, says he wants something more original than *babe,* but at least he hasn't thought of that one yet."

"I can give your boyfriend some pointers," Naya teased. "Are you still at the office?"

"Yeah. It's been a long day, and the Green Warriors are still picketing outside the main lobby."

"Want me to pick up a to-go order from Backdraft, and we can eat an early dinner? Or we can get Bebe's Indian food like the good ole days." Ingram had befriended Naya on the first day of school in fifth grade, twenty years ago, not knowing the quiet girl in class was in foster care and afraid of getting too close to anyone. Yet her friend's persistence and kindness had pulled Naya out of her shell. She'd had dinner at the Chackos' home weekly, before youth group, and learned all about Ingram's Indian heritage over chicken curry. Eventually, Naya had grown comfortable enough to talk about her own home country, Haiti.

"Pass up the offer to get takeout? No way. Let's do Backdraft. We need to drum up as much good business for them as we can. Count me in." Ingram rattled off her order, and Naya jotted it down.

Backdraft Bar and Grill had gone through a rough patch when one of their employees had been caught sabotaging food to enact revenge on one of the counselors in town. That had been Terry's last article before she'd retired. It had been a crazy story, but the truth had been exposed. It always surprised Naya what extreme measures people were willing to take to achieve their selfish goals.

"Great. I need to talk with the group at Ethos anyway, and I can run some questions by you too. Be there in thirty."

Ingram said, "See you soon."

After picking up their order, Naya parked in the visitor lot at Ethos, where Ingram worked. She made her way to the main entrance, food bag in hand.

The ten-story glass building was a prominent city-like structure in Last Chance County's simple town of three-story brick-and-mortar establishments. Sure enough, a group of protesters huddled by the fountain. No workers were going to enter or exit the building without crossing paths with the group first—or an officer who made sure the group didn't turn hostile. Their signs and chants even made Naya want to avert her eyes and duck into the building without a confrontation. Instead, she put on a smile and walked over to the crew.

It surprised her that people hadn't disbanded for the day, given the events that had taken place at the park with some of their members. Surely they'd want to make sure none of their own were severely injured.

"Excuse me. Have you heard any updates on those who were at the river earlier today?" Naya approached one of the women.

She swung her sign around and kept walking. "Last I heard everyone had minimal injuries."

Naya strode after her. "I'm glad. Has anyone gone to check on them?"

"We can't lose momentum now. I'm sure someone tampered with the bridge to distract us. But we're not going to be intimidated. There's too much at stake." The woman propped her sign between her legs and took a swig of water.

Ironic. Naya couldn't imagine higher stakes than people's lives. Considering people's health was part of the initial problem that had prompted these protests. Naya pointed to the building. "Has the CEO or anyone commented on what's going on?"

"What's with all the questions? Are you a worker here?" The woman narrowed her gaze.

"No, ma'am. I'm an investigative reporter for the Tribune. I want to find the truth and make sure that story gets told." Naya showed the woman her press badge. She pushed her shoulders back, then regretted the movement as pain coursed down her arm.

"Well, in that case, why don't you join us?" The woman stretched out her hand. "I'm Tracy." She glanced behind her, then said, "The higher-ups in there haven't said a word. 'No comment' is all we've received. But"—Tracy waved her hand, and Naya leaned forward—"their products are still on the market, and one of our own saw them hauling their hazardous waste away in an unmarked vehicle. Something fishy is happening behind those closed doors."

Naya leaned back and pulled out her phone to jot everything down. She braced the bag of food on her forearm while she typed. She should really get inside soon before the food got cold.

"We're going to be back out here tomorrow if you want to join us." Tracy smiled. "The more people out here taking a stand to save our land, the better."

"I'll be back for sure." Naya tucked her phone in her pocket.

Right now, there were a lot of conspiracies surrounding the

chemical manufacturer and distribution plant, and her gut told her there was more to this story than met the eye. Possibly even with the environmental group being on the up and up.

"Can't let this food spoil though." Naya held up the bag, then headed for the front door.

The high ceilings and granite pillars inside made the building appear prestigious. Even the orange-vanilla fragrance that emitted from the area spelled *high-end*.

The plastic bag in Naya's hand crinkled and echoed through the empty entryway.

"Can I help you?" A young woman with clear glasses and blonde hair sat behind the reception desk.

"I'm here to meet with Ingram Chacko on floor five."

The woman typed something into her computer. "I just need you to sign in here." She slid a clipboard toward Naya.

Naya filled out her information, then walked down the hall to the elevator to ride to Ingram's floor.

The door dinged and slid open, and Naya stepped out onto the plush carpet that lined the fifth-floor hallway. Voices filtered down the hall, and Naya headed to Ingram's office. The cheesy sauce aroma of the meatball subs wafted from the bag, and Naya's stomach grumbled.

"I think we should reconsider. There's a lot of people upset, and it would give them peace of mind." Ingram's voice carried from somewhere near the copiers.

Naya stopped in her tracks, not wanting to interrupt an important conversation if her friend was still finishing up work. She waited where she was, leaning against the wall.

"We have nothing to prove to them, and it will disrupt our production line and delay distribution times. We've got firehouses and stores waiting to buy our products." The voice sounded like Will, Ingram's boyfriend, but Naya couldn't be certain. Whoever it was, they kept their tone low and gruff. "You should really consider how to be a better asset for the company you work for. Not find ways to tear it down."

"Wow." Ingram inhaled. "This company should take into consideration the people it serves. After all, our products are meant to provide safety for the everyday citizen. Given the amount of complaints and news we're receiving, I see no harm in getting extra tests done to ensure we are following best practices. And if I'm the one to bring it up in our meeting with Hudson, so be it. At least someone will have."

"You're going to show me up like that? Not a smart move," he snapped. "I will not use my position in this company to advocate for something that's not worth our time."

Naya sucked in a breath and took a step back.

Now she was in the awkward predicament of eavesdropping. It didn't matter how she made her entrance, they'd know she'd been listening in the shadows.

She couldn't use any of this conversation in her story. Not when she hadn't been forthright about her presence or getting consent from them. No way would she do that to Ingram. Not even for the job. If Will was part of this conversation, it would further solidify her dislike toward the man. She'd never been a big fan of Ingram's boyfriend.

She uttered a silent prayer this didn't get more confrontational. She would do what she could to relieve it.

"Food's here." Naya walked around the corner and held up the bag.

Ingram moved away from the counter by the copier and walked past Will. "We can finish this conversation later. I'm starving." Ingram turned to Naya, and her tense features softened. *Thank you.*

"See you later." Naya nodded to Will, who replied with a grunt.

"Let's go out back." Ingram led Naya downstairs and found a table outside at the back of the building. The brick patio-like area provided the best view of the rolling mountains and tree line a few miles away.

Don't bring it up. Let her mention it.

"We should take a hike again soon. Catch up on life." Naya unwrapped her sub, trying to act like everything was fine.

"How're you doing?" Ingram pointed to Naya's bandage.

"Grateful it wasn't worse." Naya pulled in a breath. "How're you?" She clasped her hands on the table.

"You overheard, didn't you?" Ingram propped her elbows on the table.

"Yeah." Naya winced.

"Well, your girl needs to eat some calories first before thinking about burning them off. Although, getting away for a day sounds like a great idea."

Naya smiled. "Fair enough."

Ingram blessed the food, and they dug in.

In between bites, Naya said, "I take it tensions are high?"

"Mm-hmm." Ingram chewed and said nothing else.

"The company thinks the problems will simply disappear?" Naya grabbed a napkin and dabbed at the sauce on her lips.

"Bingo. But when you're a manufacturer and distributor of products that include fire extinguishers and firefighting foam for residential and commercial properties, you'd think safety and the customer would be—" Ingram paused.

"What?"

Her eyes followed something behind Naya. She leaned in and whispered, "Don't look now, but your *favorite* person is headed this way."

"Fancy seeing you here." Tucker's voice filled Naya's eardrums with an unwelcome cacophony, and she tensed.

"I could say the same of you." Naya leaned back in her chair and lifted her chin.

"I have a source who asked to meet me here in ten." He smirked down at her from the lofty heights of his own self-assurance. "So don't let me interrupt your girl time. Unless you're hoping to acquire details for your story from her. We wouldn't want to add bias into what we write, now, would we?"

"Actually, I logged a story today." Naya stood up.

He flinched. "You're done?"

Naya gave him a grin of her own. "Firsthand account of the bridge collapse and the valiant actions of the fire department that saved lives."

He glared at her.

"If I were you, I'd get moving with your leads. Don't want to fall too far behind now."

Naya wouldn't let his intimidation tactics scare her. She might have a rival for this story, but that wasn't going to stop her from showing up and finding the truth.

FOUR

PIZZA'S HERE! COME AND GET IT WHILE IT'S HOT."

Zack jerked his head and stumbled out of his chair, which crashed to the floor. He turned around right when Izan walked into the firehouse kitchen with a pile of pizza boxes.

"You good, man?" Izan raised an eyebrow.

Zack blinked and righted the chair. "You bet. Just testing your reflex skills. You might want to work on those." He slapped Izan on the shoulder, then checked his watch. Time to go.

"You better save some of the mushroom toppings for me." Amelia strode in, Eddie and Bryce right behind her.

Zack grabbed two slices of pepperoni pizza and chowed down. The lack of regular meals today had him starving. Never mind it was still too early to be considered dinnertime.

"That's all yours." Eddie wrinkled his nose and grabbed a plate. "Give me all the meat."

Zack laughed. "There's enough here to feed the whole town." He grabbed a napkin next to the six pizza boxes piled high on the counter. He wiped the grease off his fingers, then tossed his plate in the trash. "I'm clocking out. See y'all later." He brushed past the crew, but Eddie gave him a side-eye. The guy never missed a beat.

Zack tossed his duffel bag on the passenger car seat and opened up the report file again that Bryce had given him.

All the memories flooded back, disorienting Zack like being in a smoke house without the proper training gear.

The fire had snuffed out Zack's former existence and taken all traces of the life he'd once known with it.

Screams berated his mind, and the flashes of first-responder cars filled his vision.

They turned into the development and drew closer to Zack's house and where several emergency vehicles were parked.

"Grandma, what's going on?" He smashed his face against the cool glass. "Those are flames in our house."

The commotion that greeted him upon arrival at his house became his worst nightmare.

"It's all your fault. What were you thinking?" The fire chief's shouts pelted the air. Tears gathered in Zack's eyes, and his lips quivered. "You did this." The man bent down to Zack's height and pointed at the ashen house.

"Zack?" Eddie rapped on the window.

Zack's hand jerked, and he snatched at the file to keep the papers from falling. He opened up the door and braced one foot on the floorboard.

Eddie leaned a hand against the car. "You're quite jumpy tonight."

Zack's stomach twisted, and he swallowed. Eating that pizza so fast had been a bad idea. "Bryce gave me a case to investigate for hazmat training."

"That's awesome, dude."

He sighed. "Except it's my parents' case." Policy stated if a conflict of interest arose, it should be handed off to someone else. Each case required astuteness and a clear mind. Emotions could not get in the way of doing one's job.

"He wouldn't put you in that kind of predicament."

"He doesn't know my parents had a different last name than me." Theirs was Nelson. His was Stephens.

"How'd you manage that?" Eddie raised an eyebrow.

"After they died, it hurt to be known as the Nelsons' kid. The one who didn't have parents anymore. So my grandma suggested I use Stephens. My mom's maiden name." It still tied him to his family, but soon people had stopped realizing whose kid he was, and the looks of pity had faded.

"You gonna tell him?"

"I don't know. Technically it's not an active case." Zack flipped through the papers, and his eyes landed on the name of a witness.

Ricky Powells. Former fire chief on the other side of town, and one of his dad's best friends. The man's phone number was listed on the line below.

Zack had been on his way home with his grandma after staying late at school to finish homework he'd missed and not turned in on time. He had been desperate not to fail third grade and get held back, especially when he'd miss the chance to be with all his friends.

"Hurry up, kiddo. I need to get you home before my bingo game night." His grandma ushered him into the back seat.

"Can I come?" Zack sat up. He wanted to win a prize.

"Not tonight, buddy. This is for the old folks. You'll be bored."

She drove down the street with a lead foot. "Your dad should have picked you up. Now I'm gonna be late." She'd mumbled the complaint, but Zack still heard it.

"If I turn in the file to Bryce, he might think I'm incapable of completing the task." All Zack wanted to do was show his team he was dependable and not a liability. That he wouldn't cause trouble but was an asset they couldn't stand to lose.

"Nah, man. He'd see it as a sign of respect. Might even give you another case option."

"I'll figure out what to do." Zack leaned over and put the file on top of his duffel on the other seat. "I've got some other things to take care of right now."

He gave Eddie a wave, then shut the door. Zack rolled down the window to let the evening spring air filter into the stuffy space.

He would do what Bryce had asked of him without giving the team a reason to question whether he could do his job without stirring up more issues.

He'd worry about the file later.

First, he needed to complete some practice training for the hazmat unit he was studying. It would be a welcome distraction to keep his mind from wandering to the people and places he didn't want to dwell on.

Pulling out of the firehouse, Zack headed toward the creek.

Fifteen minutes later, he took long strides down to the water's edge. Zack pulled out his test kit and scanned the area. A crew of workers in orange reflector jumpsuits and tall rain boots waded in and out of the water with fishing nets. The back of their attire read *County Fishing & Boating Committee.*

Zack headed down the embankment to his left and knelt by the water's edge. He put his vials together, mindful to reread all the instructions to make sure he assembled everything in the correct order. Dipping the first vial in the water, he swirled it around before capping it and placing it in the bag holder.

His grip tightened on the second vial. How he wished his dad were here now. To see his son following in his footsteps. To tell him, "Well done."

Except that wasn't his reality. Between his parents' deaths and his past with Naya, Zack had already made enough mistakes in life. He couldn't create more trouble at the station. He'd earn his way into the fold with the other crew members and show everyone at Eastside Firehouse he should be there. Should be part of their team.

"We got seventy-five down here so far." One of the workers held up their net.

Zack couldn't make out what was in the net, but it took two men to haul it over onto a truck bed.

Must be some kind of cleanup from the bridge collapse.

Zack took the next container and followed the instructions. When he swished the water, the cloudiness dispersed and a fish lay belly-side up against a rock.

Zack grimaced.

No wonder an outside agency was getting involved.

"I said we have no comment," net guy said. "We're just a cleanup crew."

Zack glanced over at the commotion. One of the workers waved his hand like he was shooing off a pest.

A woman with long black hair held back in a ponytail shook her head. A note pad and recorder were visible in her hand.

Naya.

And he'd been doing so well not thinking about her.

"People's lives are on the line. Lives that are more important than these fish."

"Excuse me?" the man's voice bellowed, and he dropped his net, taking a step toward Naya.

Zack gathered his belongings and made his way over to the two of them. Best to keep the scene civil before it had an opportunity to go south.

"Can I help you?" Zack shifted his gaze between the worker and Naya.

The guy glanced down at the firehouse emblem on Zack's shirt. "I need to get back to my job. I don't have time to answer questions. The last thing I need is to have my name muddled in with this mess."

"Who can I talk to then?" Naya stepped forward, her pen poised. "Someone has to be responsible."

"You can deal with our agency. Twenty minutes out of town." Before giving anyone a chance to respond, he clobbered away in his boots with a dismissive hand wave.

"One failed lead, another to follow," Naya mumbled under her breath. Still, her eyes glistened, and she tapped her finger against her bottom lip. Despite that guy being bigger than her, and grumpy, she hadn't backed down.

Zack grinned. "More determined now, huh?"

Naya lifted her gaze and connected with his. "I suppose so."

"You did the same thing with your finger when we were younger. Anytime you were passionate about something." It had been cute then. Now she was a beautiful woman, who hadn't lost the zeal for life she'd always possessed.

Zack could still picture them sitting on the floor in his grandma's living room together, dreaming about the future. An idea would spark in Naya's eyes, and they'd end up talking a mile a minute, solving life's problems, until they were lying on the ground doubled over in laughter. His grandma would shush them from the other room, saying she couldn't hear the game show on the TV, and if they didn't quiet down, Naya would have to go back to her house.

"Right. I remember." Naya's tone dropped and she pursed her lips. "I'd like to say it was nice to see you again." She left it at that and stepped back.

Zack might as well have been sprayed with toxic chemicals. "What is that supposed to mean? We were friends, weren't we?"

"Were." She crossed her arms. "Until you left and added more pain to my life."

Her response ripped open the reminder of a past he'd worked hard to erase. In her eyes, he was still a troublemaking kid. The kid who got called into the principal's office on the regular because he'd had some goofy, grand idea that backfired or because he'd gotten into a fight to protect a kid who was being bullied.

He wanted to explain himself. Tell her that the way they'd left things wasn't how he'd meant for it to turn out. He'd never intended to hurt her. But he hadn't had a say in it. The damage had been done. Now he'd have to work to earn her trust again. That was, if she even wanted him around. Zack rubbed his jaw.

Why did their paths have to cross again now? On top of being handed his parents' case? It was a double whammy of the way his troublemaking streak had inflicted pain on others.

Who was he kidding? They weren't friends anymore. They each had a life they'd built.

Separately.

Yet he wanted to hear how she was doing. How had life turned out for her since his disappearance?

Zack pointed at her shoulder. "How's your arm doing?" The words tumbled out before he could stop them. Regardless of her view of him, she was still his sister in Christ. That was, if she'd kept her childhood faith.

"Better." She moved her arm, but Zack caught her grimace.

"What were you testing with those?" Naya asked. Her deflection hurt, but at least she hadn't hightailed it away from him.

"Water samples. Part of my hazmat training." Zack lifted the litmus paper and frowned. "Interesting. It's red."

"What does that mean?" Naya flipped through pages in her notebook and clicked her pen.

"The water is acidic. I was going to compare it to the numbers the city released for the public." Zack folded the strip and tucked it in his pocket.

"I'll have to look up those stats." Naya closed her pad then pointed behind her. "I need to get going. Time's ticking on these leads."

"Of course. Let me walk you to your car." Zack fell in step next to Naya, who shrugged but didn't protest further.

She dug out her keys, and the lights on her car blinked. A compact Impreza, a few parking spots down on the right side of the street.

"Oh no." Naya groaned and hurried to the front windshield. She pushed her purse higher on her shoulder to keep it from falling and snatched the paper tucked under her wipers. "I can't have a ticket right now."

Zack stepped over to the meter and bent to check the time. "You still have thirty minutes according to this. So you can waive the charge." Zack pulled out his phone and snapped a picture.

Silence greeted him. Naya's fingers shook, and the piece of paper flitted in her grasp.

"You okay?" Zack put his hand on her shoulder.

Naya's wide eyes stared up at him. "It's a warning."

"That's okay, then. At least you don't have to pay anything." She had nothing to worry about, but his response didn't seem to help ease her concerns.

Naya shook her head and handed him the piece of paper.

He scanned the note and clenched his teeth.

Quit investigating this story or your name will end up in the paper for a different reason.

This wasn't a warning. It was a threat.

"Naya, what's going on?"

FIVE

NAYA WASN'T GOING TO LET ANYONE INTIMIDATE her into backing down from this story. If she had her guess, Tucker was the culprit behind this threat. Not some malicious outsider.

If she had learned anything during her time dating him, it was that his words were empty. He said one thing and did another.

So she *definitely* wasn't going to be rattled by this.

Zack was waiting for an answer to his question.

"It's just a stupid work thing. Nothing to worry about."

Cars whizzed down the street and someone honked. Naya shielded her eyes from the setting sun and scanned the road, but thankfully, the driver's impatience hadn't been directed at her.

Naya sighed and turned back to Zack.

"I'll be speaking with my boss about this tomorrow." Naya took the paper from Zack. "Thanks for walking me to my car."

"I could send it to my buddy at the station and have it run for fingerprints." Zack frowned. "Or I *could* have, but we both touched it."

She shook her head. "Don't bother. It was probably Tucker."

"Tucker who?" Zack scrunched his brow.

"My coworker who's up for the same promotion. Our boss is

going to decide who deserves the position after we finish our next story." She lifted the letter once more to read it before folding it and placing the paper in her pocket. "Plus, the handwriting is sloppy. Indicative of a guy."

"How can you be certain?" His eyes widened like he was a little offended by that.

"I've seen some of Tucker's notes before. His writing looks like this."

Naya shifted her stance and averted her eyes to the sidewalk. Zack didn't have any right to know her history. It's not like they were friends anymore. Still, an urge to explain herself swirled in her stomach.

She sighed. "We dated for a time, and although things didn't end well, he did write me letters. So I'm familiar with his handwriting."

"I see." Zack cleared his throat like this conversation was uncomfortable for him too. "Do you still have a letter? We could compare the two."

Naya appreciated Zack's willingness to help, but this nuisance wasn't worth either of their time. She'd talk to her boss in the morning and address the situation. Drew wouldn't allow a fellow employee to harass one of their own.

"I got rid of those notes a long time ago. I'll file a complaint with my boss, and it'll all be taken care of." Naya waved her hand.

Her phone vibrated in her bag.

"I need to get going." Naya fished her phone out of her purse. "I forgot my friend Ingram is coming over to help me with something." The words rushed out.

Naya offered a wave before climbing in her car then answered her phone.

"Sorry I missed your call." Naya glanced at the dash clock. "I'll probably be late. I saw Zack, then got distracted. What's up?" Naya buckled her seatbelt and turned the ignition.

"No worries," Ingram said. "I'm so sorry, but I'm going to have to cancel for our painting party tonight. Something came up at work I have to take care of."

"Is everything okay?"

"They called a mandatory staff meeting. Apparently, we need training on how to handle the protestors. What we can and can't say."

"Sounds riveting." Naya kept the car in park.

"I know. Did you get anywhere with your lead?"

"Nope." Naya sighed. For every one person willing to talk, there were five more that proved to be dead ends. Each time, it only made her want to investigate further until she uncovered the treasure chest of information that would make the story. She just had to hang on long enough to hit the jackpot. "But I have a few more sources on my list to touch base with. Although, someone doesn't want me writing this story."

"What do you mean?"

"Someone left a note of warning on my car. Told me to stop or else."

"Nay, did you report it to the police?"

"Why would I? They have much more pressing matters to worry about."

"Your safety is important."

"I think it was Tucker." Naya ran through their conversation. He hadn't been happy then. "There's no one else who would know what my car looks like or that I'm writing this story. Plus, I'm going to address it with my boss tomorrow."

"Just be careful, okay? You have a hunger for finding the truth for your stories, and sometimes people don't want that exposed."

Of course Ingram would allude to the one time a story had gone south. When she'd investigated the attacks on one of the dance instructors in town. The culprit's father had begun stalking Naya to stop her from writing the story. He'd claimed his family had enough heartache to handle without a story being released with the details.

Sure, the situation had been scary, but Naya couldn't stop working because one person wasn't happy. If she didn't find the truth, no one might. Just like her brother and the people sick in the hospital now. They would end up without the justice they deserved.

"Maybe you need a bodyguard. Someone to watch your back. I could put a bug in Zack's ear."

Naya glanced out the window. Zack still stood several feet away. He glanced up from his phone like he could sense her staring. "No need. I've got your number on speed dial if need be. He's got his own life."

"Well, back in the day, you two were tight." Ingram chuckled.

Naya remembered all too well.

They'd both been in foster care and were next-door neighbors for five years. Zack had been in kinship foster care and lived with his grandma. She'd lived with the Tomlinsons, a nice enough family. During that time, Zack had been her big brother. Protector. Confidant.

But he'd hurt her once, just like every other guy she'd opened her heart to. Naya couldn't risk adding more damage to her battered heart. If she did, it might just break her the next time.

The Lord would have to work a miracle to change her mind, and right now, He'd given her the gift of singleness. She didn't have plans to change her status anytime soon. Even if Zack had grown up to be a handsome man. A hero.

She didn't need a hero. She needed a lead.

"Are we still on for our hike tomorrow after work?"

"For sure. It'll be nice to clear my head. I have to go. See ya tomorrow."

A knock reverberated against her window, and Naya's hand flew to her chest.

Zack peered in, his brow creased.

She rolled down the window.

"Everything okay?" He scanned the interior of the car. "Are you having car trouble?"

Naya couldn't figure this man out. He was a good guy, and yet he'd abandoned her once. He leaned his forearm on the windowsill. And he sported her red, corded bracelet. None of it made sense.

"My friend was supposed to come to my house to help me paint one of the rooms. But something came up last minute."

"I'm off the clock tonight if you still want company." He shrugged.

Naya opened her mouth, ready to say no. *You're running away.* He had helped her today. And if he was offering assistance, it would make the project go a lot faster.

"Sure." She nodded.

"I'll follow you." Zack jogged back to his car.

Once back at her house, Naya led Zack to the garage where all the paint supplies were stored.

Naya grabbed some of the paint and trays while Zack picked up the rest, and the two headed inside. She'd dreamt of redoing the workroom in her house one day, and when Ingram had initially offered her assistance, Naya jumped at the opportunity. That and the freshness of the spring season had inspired the action, but now that work had piled up, she couldn't decide if this was a complication she didn't need or a reprieve from the stress.

Naya set the supplies down in the room, then crossed her arms. "It's about time this room got a new look."

"You don't say." Zack scanned the expanse.

"That bad, huh?" Naya raised an eyebrow.

"I'm kidding. Although, a new color always adds a fresh look."

The overhead lights cast shadows from the curtains and darkened some areas of the lilac walls. It had probably been a girl's room at some point before Naya bought the place. But at least the existing color was light enough it wouldn't be hard to paint over with the cream paint she'd selected this go-around.

"Shall we?" Zack laid down the tarp.

There were a few more art pieces on the wall Naya had to take down. She took the frame off the wall, then grabbed a hammer and pulled out the nail.

The last picture was of her and her brother, playing with bubbles in their backyard.

"Who's that?" Zack's breath tickled the back of her neck.

"My brother." Naya put the picture with the rest of the frames and cleared her throat.

Zack shoved his hands into his back pockets. "Do you ever wonder what life would be like if they were still here?"

"Before my mom ran off with another guy and my dad planned to move to the States?" Naya's throat constricted and she swallowed. "Sometimes. But it feels like a lifetime ago, and it won't bring them back." She'd never shared the details of what happened to her brother with Zack. It was one thing to think about it and another to vocalize it, because then reality set in all over again. Naya popped open the first can and poured the paint into the tray.

"Loss is hard." Zack picked up a brush.

"It's one thing to grieve a loss. The betrayal of abandonment is another beast. But it fuels why I write. So the past doesn't replay itself." She'd made it her duty now as a reporter to track down the stories that needed to be told so others would be educated and empowered to create change. Because no one's story should be silenced, forgotten the way her brother had been. She was the only one who remembered Dom, and Naya wasn't going to let that happen to anyone else.

Zack's gaze dropped. "I get it. It's a way to save someone else from the same heartache you endured."

"Exactly."

"Have you found anything from your leads yet?" He slid the roller up the wall.

"Everything and nothing." Naya wiped her brush back and forth on the wall. "Tensions are high for everyone, especially with the Green Warriors protests. Ethos, isn't a fan of the publicity that's being created either. I don't understand why they won't pull the fire extinguishers and foam sprays off the shelf. It would resolve the whole situation a lot quicker because everyone would realize those products are not what's making people sick."

"Maybe they'll have to soon," Zack said. "It would be a start, at least."

"Let's hope so." The sooner Naya could find all the plausible leads and write this story, the quicker people could return to everyday life. And eventually all the turmoil surrounding the situation would die down because there'd be another story to tell, and people would shift their attention.

Naya turned to Zack. "Hey, watch the—" She lunged for the tray on the floor and slid it over just in time to capture the dripping paint from Zack's brush.

"We've got the tarp for that." Zack chuckled. "Makes any incidents easier to clean up." Zack bent and dipped his brush in the paint. A gleam shone in his eye, and he flicked his wrist. "Like this one." Paint splattered on Naya's pant leg.

She squealed. "You didn't."

"We've got to have some fun at a painting party."

"Oh really?" She stuck out her roller and caught Zack on the arm. "Guess it takes two to have a good time." Naya laughed.

By the time they'd finished with the first coat of paint, the sun had set, and Naya let out a yawn.

They sealed the paint cans, then Naya headed to the entryway with Zack.

"Thanks for tackling this project with me."

"You bet." He flashed a smile, but it disappeared as fast as it'd come. Along with...hope? Naya couldn't tell. She'd admit having Zack's company had been nice. But a kind gesture was a far cry from establishing any kind of relationship.

She intended to keep her heart at arm's length. For her own safety.

Naya opened the door and stepped onto the porch with Zack, who paused on the step.

"I know you said that note was nothing to be worried about, but please be careful."

For his sake, Naya nodded. "I will." A light breeze swept by. A shiver slid across her skin, and Naya folded her arms.

Zack walked to his car, then pulled out of the driveway. The single light bulb on the porch shone like a spotlight on her. Giving anyone with the cover of night full visibility of her whereabouts.

Naya shook her head. She was being paranoid now. The note on her car didn't mean she had a stalker again. Nor would Tucker be staking out near her house right now. The idea sounded absurd.

She squinted and scanned the street. Shadows played off the trees and houses nearby.

Be careful. Zack's reminder coursed through her mind.

She had nothing to fear. The Lord was faithful to watch over her. But even as she filled her mind with Scripture, she couldn't shake the tickling of her sixth sense.

Naya pulled in a breath and scurried back inside, then turned the deadbolt. After a quick wiggle of the knob to be certain it was secured, she flicked the switch to turn off the outside lights.

If someone had their eye on her, where were they hiding and why?

SIX

ZACK'S MIND STILL REELED WITH THE REMINDER that someone had their sights set on Naya and they weren't playing nice. Of course Naya didn't need him to stand up to anyone on her behalf, but it didn't change the way he'd kept an eye on the window last night while they'd painted. Just in case anyone decided to make an unwelcome appearance.

Zack stuck his fingers in his mouth and let out a whistle. The shrill pitch bounced off the concrete walls in the empty bay area of the firehouse. "You've got thirty seconds to get into that gear." He gave the orders to the three teen boys who began to suit up. All three had come to him asking for help to get into a summer camp in Montana that taught older teens how to fight wildfires. A lot of them went on to be hotshots and smokejumpers, but Zack planned to convince them to stick around and be local firefighters.

Protect the place where they'd grown up.

And the people who'd raised them.

"Hurry up, slow poke."

"I'm gonna smoke the rest of you." The kids bantered through the drill.

Zack smiled. He wanted to instill in them the importance of

protecting those they cared about. Also, making sure they stayed out of trouble.

Something he'd failed to do well at their age.

Especially with Naya.

Inevitably his thoughts returned to her.

Naya deserved to be treated with respect. And if it was this ex-boyfriend who'd left the note—what was his name?—Tucker, then he'd better not cross paths with Zack anytime soon.

He despised people searching for ways to intimidate others. It had happened too often in his foster care days.

Too often to Naya.

Until...

He shook his head.

"Don't try to cheat now, dude."

"He's not evening watching. Probably thinking 'bout a girl." They snickered.

Zack ignored their comments.

Ever since seeing Naya again, his past haunted him. He needed to share all the details with her, but it wouldn't change the outcome. What had happened couldn't be reversed, and he was to blame.

Yet there was a part of him that hoped she'd forgive him once she understood everything. Zack fingered the red bracelet on his wrist, the cord moving in a circular motion.

Except, Zack wouldn't stir the pot and cause problems unless Naya asked for his help. And the likelihood of that happening was slim. Given he wouldn't even put the two of them in the friend category anymore.

More like acquaintances.

She said she'd talk with her boss. Zack trusted her to do what was best. He could follow up later to make sure everything had been resolved.

Until then, he had other matters to focus on. Like showing Karson and the other boys the ins and outs of being a firefighter.

Every other week, Zack spent a few hours with some of the boys that his friends the Kirbys were fostering. He took the teens out to lunch, where they chatted about life, then he brought them back to the firehouse to get firsthand experience as a firefighter. Depending on Zack's schedule, he or Sam Kirby would give the boys a ride back to their house when they were finished for the day.

The opportunity to invite these guys to the firehouse had become a great way for Zack to mentor the teens and show them Jesus while instilling in them the importance of serving the community.

"All set, Captain." Karson slipped on the helmet and gave a thumbs-up.

Zack folded his arms. "I'm not a captain, kid."

His stopwatch beeped, and the other two boys had just grabbed their helmets.

"Nice work, guys." Zack clapped. "You're making good time with the practice."

"When are we going to put out a real fire training scenario?" Andrew removed his helmet and frowned.

"As soon as I think you're ready." Zack gave him a slap on the shoulder. "Which might be next time you're here."

"All right." The boys clapped in unison and fist-bumped each other. "We're totally gonna qualify for the summer wildlands firefighting camp."

"Don't forget the groundwork is important, though. You have to know your stuff and work as a team." Zack grinned. He appreciated their enthusiasm, which would make this next exercise entertaining.

"Who's on cleaning duty today?" Carlos chimed in while he unzipped his turnout gear and stepped out of his boots.

"All of you. I want it scrubbed, cleaned, and restocked."

"Yes, sir." Karson nodded. "We'll have it shiny red for the festival in a few days."

"That's what I like to hear." The boys would join Zack for the New Blooms Spring Festival and get to ride in the truck along the parade route. An event they were already bragging about to their friends at school, according to Andrew.

The boys hung up the gear on the wall hooks and rolled out the hose to the truck in the parking lot. Zack had added a few extra stains to the exterior paint and removed some of the supply quantity inside the truck. He wanted the guys to work together and help each other remember what needed to be done.

The door to the firehouse opened, and Eddie walked into the engine bay. "You making them do your job again?" He winked.

"When I can encourage hard work and train these men up right? Absolutely." Zack crossed his arms and grinned.

"What you're doing with these kids is good, man." Eddie's face softened. "I heard Karson's dad got into a brawl again at the pub Friday night."

"These kids need a mentor. Someone who will believe in them." Zack pulled over a chair, and the metal screeched along the floor. He sat down by the locker cubbies beside the open garage door. The outside air warmed the bay area. Zack understood the harsh realities of fending for yourself and not knowing who to trust, thanks to his upbringing in foster care after his parents' death—first, in kinship foster care with his grandma, then in the system with a family he barely knew after his grandma's move to a nursing home. "I don't want any at-risk teens getting caught up in trouble. Not when they can be shown how to start out on the right path."

"I get it." Eddie shook his head. "Living in foster care is challenging. The road you've walked is all the more reason why you're great with these kids."

"Thanks, man." Zack fist-bumped Eddie. The two had hit it off when he'd come to the firehouse. Partly because Eddie had been in foster care himself. Having another guy who could resonate with that life had deepened their friendship. "You don't think it bothers the lieutenant?" Zack tapped his foot against the ground, his leg bouncing.

"Why would it?" Eddie raised an eyebrow.

"We are on shift right now. I already get the sense he thinks some of my choices are questionable." Zack valued this team, and the thought of them seeing him as less than because of something he did or didn't do gripped his chest. Like being in a room starved of oxygen with a faulty breathing apparatus.

"Bryce wouldn't have said yes to you having these kids here if he didn't respect you. You wouldn't even be on the team." Eddie shifted and stuck his hands in his pockets. "You don't have to *do* anything to earn his approval, man."

"Sure, but I don't wanna do something that could jeopardize things, either." Zack leaned forward in the chair and propped his hands on his knees.

"This doesn't have anything to do with the hazmat training, does it?"

"Let's just say it's proving to be more complex than I anticipated."

"You have to take it head-on, man. Don't shrink back."

Zack still needed to finalize some details for the festival so the boys knew what to do. He pulled out his phone and made a reminder to jot down his notes later. Okay, maybe he *was* avoiding the report. Finding ways to do anything else but face the details of his parents' deaths.

"Those kids," Eddie said as he pointed at the boys cleaning the truck, "they've had a tough life. But you're teaching them how to work as a team. To face the pain and conquer. You've got it in you, man." Eddie jabbed a finger against Zack's chest. "You're not alone, either. Even if it takes longer than anticipated or you run into a few hiccups along the way, it doesn't mean it was the wrong move."

Zack appreciated Eddie's input, but all it did was solidify that even with the right intentions, a choice could end up being a very, *very* wrong move.

Naya's demeanor around him yesterday was proof of that. Even when he'd tried to do the right thing for her all those years ago and save the one thing that mattered most to her.

That red corded bracelet.

Zack had wanted to give her hope and hold up the promise he'd made. Instead, everything had gone haywire, and it'd not only cost him a friendship but brought the unwanted, hurtful opinions of others.

And just like these boys he was helping now, Zack had spent years of his life attempting to show people he had something valuable to offer and wasn't just a troublemaker. That he wouldn't just cause more problems for people.

The boys finished cleaning the truck, and after they left, he grabbed a granola bar from the kitchen and took his parents' file from his bag. Zack sat on the couch, and this time, he flipped through the pages to read the findings in detail.

Kerosene accelerant located on site and around perimeter of house.

Outside doors barred shut.

Burn pattern and fire indicative of arson.

Zack inhaled and held his breath. This couldn't be right. He ran his pen along each word again until it hovered over the last sentence.

Arson.

He circled the word. The red ink could have burned a hole through the page.

His parents hadn't been the victims of a tragic accident.

Zack's fingers tightened around the pen until his hand cramped.

They'd been murdered.

He closed his eyes, willing the images to stay at bay, but instead they engulfed every inch of territory, leaving no room for escape.

Powells's red face and loud voice filled his mind. The fire chief back then had made one thing clear. Zack was to blame for the fire that burned his home down. If only he'd done his homework the first time and not needed to stay after school. If only he'd gotten home sooner.

If only.

His grandma had told him it was an accident, but it'd done nothing to save him from the night terrors that had woken him up whenever he'd tried to sleep. Ones that still knocked on his subconscious on occasion.

Arson.

R, son.

Just remember the most important word in your vocabulary. So important I had to tell other people about it. R, son.

Zack's throat tightened and he blinked. A few tears trailed down his cheek.

Zack pulled in a shaky breath thanks to the memory. His dad had been the most patient teacher, assuring his son he wouldn't have a speech impediment forever. That Zack would eventually be able to say his *r*'s properly.

R, son. It's important. There's a lot of sentences you can make with r-words. Like this one: rats only go empty'n rivers.

Zack would wrinkle his nose and giggle at his dad. Tell him it was the silliest thing ever.

Wats don't go to the bathwoom in wivers, Daddy.

Even though the sentence never made sense, his dad's goofiness regarding the matter had helped Zack master his *r*'s.

Zack just wished his dad had been around to witness it.

He had helped Zack in countless ways in the few short years they'd had together. And now, Zack would do everything he could to help his dad get the justice he deserved. Both of his parents deserved it.

The alarm blared through the intercom system, and the dispatcher stated the details. "Rescue 5, Truck 14. Vehicle entrapment. Gasoline leak." Zack bolted from the couch and dropped the file in his bag and threw the bag in the bunk room before racing to the truck.

"Let's go, people," Bryce hollered, and the door slammed shut behind him.

Eddie jogged over and hopped into the back of the engine. Ridge hit the gas and they peeled out. He tossed Zack a water bottle. "I have a feeling this is going to be a long one."

Actually, it was going to be a long couple of days. Because Zack didn't see how he could rest until he solved his parents' case.

Lord, why did this happen? I don't understand. Zack cracked his fingers. God had seen fit to bring challenges of many sorts into his life. And he didn't have all the answers. But who was he to question God?

Zack sighed.

It was his job to trust the Lord to work—even when it didn't make sense.

Right now, he needed to stay focused on the call at hand.

Then he would get in touch with his dad's friend, the former fire chief, across town. Find out why Powells had hidden the truth and made Zack the scapegoat.

Part of Zack wanted to ask Naya to do some digging of her own. But could he risk the outcome of Naya getting caught in the crosshairs? She already had enough on her plate.

How could he add one more troubling find to her load?

He couldn't.

Not if his request would stir the coals of a fire that a killer thought they'd snuffed out long ago.

SEVEN

NAYA HADN'T BEEN ABLE TO SHAKE THE FEELING of being watched, and she'd spent the night tossing and turning. A caffeine jolt had become her friend this morning, and now that she'd finished lunch, Naya was already getting the afternoon slump. Good thing she and Ingram were going for a hike.

After a quick change into more comfortable athletic wear, Naya gathered her belongings and closed her office door, then headed out to the parking lot. No one else loitered in the lot as she made her way to her car, keys in hand.

She'd considered calling Officer Tazwell to do a drive by her place, but Naya didn't have any evidence that someone was indeed tracking her whereabouts. The last thing Naya wanted was to take advantage of the contacts she had at the station. Tazwell and the other officers had better things to do than worry about her and chase dead ends.

If Tucker had written the note, what did he hope to accomplish? It didn't matter. She wouldn't let it distract her from the story at hand.

Naya headed to Pine Crest Pinnacle. She spotted Ingram

stretching by the curb at the entrance to the park and jogged over to meet her.

"How'd the meeting with Drew go this morning?"

Naya stuck her keys in her pocket and fell in step with Ingram. "He's going to talk to Tucker. Said harassment of any sort was unacceptable."

"As it should be. I still can't believe that guy has the nerve to assert himself like that. Who does he think he is?" Ingram huffed.

"Whatever his motive, it's not going to deter me from writing this story."

Ingram smiled. "Attagirl. To help you in that quest, I've got news for you." She pointed at Naya and chuckled.

"About the story?" Naya quickened her pace.

The first part to the pinnacle was a nice walk along a dirt trail, but the second half always proved to remind Naya she needed to stay in shape to climb the steep incline among boulders and other rocks and sticks.

Climbing the hill was like going after everything she wanted, step by step. And it gave her the chance to think through the investigation. Sometimes the exertion combined with a mental break gave her a great idea.

"Bingo. The entire staff got an email today from Mr. CEO himself. A follow-up to our meeting yesterday." Ingram whistled. "He told us the company is preparing legal action against the Green Warriors for harassment and invasion of private property. They have three days, until Friday, to pack up their things and find another place to picket."

"Wow. They really don't want to deal with the accusations or remediate any of the claims." Naya walked faster, pumping her arms. They entered the forest brush, and her mind spiraled with an array of questions. "Why don't they make a statement? Or even let a taskforce come in to check their products?"

"Beats me." Ingram shrugged. "You'd think that would be the logical step to take."

This new development proved the validity of Naya's original thought. The one that nagged her like those incessant reporters in other people's business. They wouldn't relent until they had their answers.

Oh, wait.

Someone might say she was that person. Although, she hoped not, because Naya tried to be respectful of people's boundaries.

"Logic might have nothing to do with it." Naya snapped her fingers. "Unless they have something to hide, in which case they'd have every reason to silence the probing."

"For the sake of my job, I hope you're wrong." Ingram groaned.

"I hope I'm wrong too, Grams. But I've got to figure out how the water contamination got to the river in the first place."

"And this is why you're good at your job," Ingram said. "You know how to get to the bottom of something to find the truth."

"It's the only thing that makes sense. We live in a well-developed country with access to top-of-the-line sanitation processes. Something like this doesn't just happen." Bile rose in her throat. She'd read through some of the accounts of those whose health had deteriorated because of the chemicals entering their bloodstream.

How could these preventable situations occur here? Waterborne illnesses were only supposed to be found in third-world countries.

Like when her—

Naya went to step over a rock but missed, and her foot caught on the edge. She stumbled forward and grabbed the top of another boulder to keep herself from slamming into the hard stone.

Oh Lord. Why did you take him?

"You okay?" Ingram extended her hand.

Naya brushed dirt off her leg and straightened. "Life has a funny way of turning out differently than you expect." Naya let out a breath. "Losing Dom. My parents. Even this story." The past should have been washed away in the current that had taken her old life with it, but it always seemed to come back like a tidal wave. "I don't want to forget him."

"Dom?"

Naya climbed over the next boulder.

The picture on her desk of her brother flashed through her mind. "Sometimes I still hear his laughter. Can still smell the mountain air around our village." Naya cleared her throat. "When all we knew was innocence and forever."

"Nay." Ingram stopped walking and embraced Naya, squeezing her shoulders. "It sucks sometimes. It was never meant to be this way."

Naya held on to her friend. "No, it wasn't." She leaned her head back and chuckled. "But who am I to throw darts at God and blame Him? God didn't promise us a grand life."

Ingram offered her a soft smile. "He doesn't expect you to endure the hardships alone, either. Jesus is acquainted with your suffering. He's with you every step. And so am I." Ingram clasped Naya's hand.

One day eternity would come, and the perfect wholeness Naya longed for would be a reality. Until then she'd keep preaching the truth to herself, even when her heart didn't catch up right away.

Naya lifted her gaze to the never-ending array of rocks and trees that littered the final ascent to the overlook. "This last stretch always seems daunting."

"That's what you say until you get to the view." Ingram propped her hands on a rock and hoisted herself up. "One step at a time."

Just like her faith walk. One step at a time. One day her faith would turn to sight.

"Are you sure you're okay?" Ingram stood still, her eyebrows raised.

"I have to be." Naya smiled through clenched teeth. She stepped from one boulder to the next.

"That didn't answer my question." Ingram propped her hands on her hips. "This story and those memories."

Of course Ingram would probe deeper. When all Naya had ever known growing up was rejection by those around her, Ingram had stood by her.

And Zack.

Naya rubbed her wrist, then realized what she was doing. "Seeing Zack again after all these years has added another layer of complication."

Ingram rolled her eyes. "Boys are always complicated." She winked.

Naya smiled. She appreciated her friend's attempt to lighten the mood. "Zack is a part of my past, though." He might have been her second brother. From another mother. But he'd eventually left too, and she couldn't risk the hurt again. Aside from their brief run-ins, and a slip in her judgment to let him help her paint, she planned to stay as far away from him as possible.

"I can't allow myself to go back to that time in life." Or else it would eat her alive. "I need to focus on this story and see it through. For Dom's sake."

Ingram slowed to a stop. "Mm-hmm."

Naya gritted her teeth and dug her heels into the crevices between the rocks. She pushed herself up with her hands and scaled the remainder of the trail. "What happened then is all the more reason to find the truth now. Especially if it will save someone from the same fate I had to endure."

"Well then, you have my support." Ingram smiled. "Whatever happens, I'm here."

Naya braced her arms on her hips to catch her breath. "Thanks."

She pivoted a few feet to admire the overlook. Hundreds of trees dotted the horizon with their green leaves in different hues. The sun cast a golden spotlight on a section to Naya's left, while the other half of the trees were a darker green from the shadows. A subtle visual that spoke volumes to Naya's heart.

A gentle reminder from the Lord.

"Wow, it's stunning." Ingram made a full turn to admire the view.

"You don't say." Naya stared, soaking in every detail.

"Look how far you've come." Ingram smiled.

Naya couldn't help seeing the correlation to her life. She wasn't the same little girl who had prayed for Dom to live.

A buzzing made Naya jump and pulled her from her thoughts.

"Sorry." Ingram bit her lip. She pulled out her phone, then slapped her hand against her forehead. "Good thing I had my reminder set. I almost forgot. Will had plans for us to go see a movie tomorrow night, and he wanted me to order the tickets."

Naya chuckled. "And he couldn't do it because..."

"I'm the rewards member." Ingram rolled her eyes. "Gotta get those points for discounts." She tapped a few buttons before a sigh escaped. "And there's no cell service up here."

"Try around the corner." Naya pointed down the trail to the right.

"I'll be right back." Ingram jogged off.

Naya stepped to the edge of the overlook and pulled out her phone to capture a few pictures of the scenery. A bird soared low over the valley, and she snapped a few more. The angle of the sun added the perfect exposure.

A few minutes later, heavy footsteps came up the trail.

"Did you get those tickets?" Naya laughed and turned, expecting to see Ingram.

Instead, another runner jogged toward her, his head bent low, phone in hand. A man's build, athletic pants and a T-shirt. He sported a black ball cap with a crisscross emblem and wore sunglasses. She couldn't see his face, but if he kept going, he would be in danger of falling over the edge.

"Excuse me." Naya waved to get the guy's attention. Did he realize how close he was to the edge of the cliff? Maybe he had earbuds in and couldn't hear her.

Naya took a step to the side and went to pocket her phone. The runner barreled right into her, and Naya dropped her device. She bent to pick it up.

A hard shove to her back knocked her off-balance.

Naya reached for the person's arm to steady herself, but it was too late. He stepped aside and Naya fell backward. Her foot caught on the edge of the cliff and slipped over the edge.

A scream erupted from her lips.

The air came up to meet her, and she tumbled over the side of the mountain.

EIGHT

ZACK RACED TO THE TRUCK TO GRAB THE BURN blanket in case a fire erupted from the car their victim was being extricated from. Given the gasoline leak, they couldn't risk it. A group of onlookers hovered near the curb, pointing and gasping. Other cars were at a standstill, and Ramble redirected traffic down a side street. An older man talked with another officer nearby.

"Door's removed," Eddie yelled. He handed the rescue tool to Ridge before sliding the driver's-side door out of the way.

"Let's move it. No time to waste." Fire truck lieutenant, Amelia, whistled.

Izan and Zoe, part of the fire engine crew, held the hoses, aimed and at the ready to keep a greater catastrophe from claiming the scene in front of them if the flicker of any flames surfaced.

"I need the spine board, stat," Ridge yelled.

Trace and Kianna, the paramedics on duty, raced over to the patient's side.

"Here." Zack handed Trace the blanket.

"Leak contained so far." Bryce nodded. A bucket captured the liquid before it had a chance to run down the pavement and come in contact with something flammable.

Zack grabbed some biohazard bags and worked with the rest of the crew to secure the scene from any debris and hazardous materials leftover.

"Patient out and being assessed." The update came through Zack's headgear, and he breathed a sigh of relief.

He'd sealed one bag to put in the disposal receptacle when Bryce's radio blared. "Rescue 5. Pine Crest Pinnacle. Victim trapped on boulders. Extent of injuries unknown from fall over edge of mountain."

Zack gritted his teeth. He wished Eddie had been wrong about it being a long day, although they'd been able to stabilize one patient.

He prayed the same for this next call. God had already shown Himself strong in small ways every day since Zack had joined the fire department. He could remain confident that God would show up again.

"Copy. Rescue 5 en route. ETA twelve minutes." Bryce relayed the information through their headsets. "Amelia, you got it from here?"

"Of course she does." Eddie smirked.

Amelia gave Eddie a playful shove. "Yeah, yeah. Get to your job." She turned back to her crew. "I want everything inspected and cleaned up right. No chance for mistakes."

Ridge hopped in the driver's side. Eddie and Bryce climbed in, and the tires of the rescue truck squealed the moment they peeled away from the street. Bryce turned on the sirens, and they headed toward the mountain top. The loud alert sent everyone else on the road parting for them.

Thankfully, a service road had been put in a few years back, a valuable resource for emergency vehicles to get to the summit, where all the trails at Pine Crest met.

Zack scooted forward in his seat, his grip on the door handle.

Ridge gunned it on the incline, and the bumps along the way jostled Zack in his seat.

This terrain wasn't new to Zack anymore. Not when calls came in often for those dehydrated, trapped, or injured one way or another.

"Where's the fuel at?" Eddie groaned, sweat glistening on his forehead.

"In the tank, goofball." Zack nudged his shoulder.

"Hey, watch it. I meant the food." Eddie rolled his eyes, then chugged some water.

Bryce tossed a protein bar to the back seat. "You've got forty seconds to chow down. We need all hands on deck."

"I'm surprised they haven't built a guard rail for the overlook." Zack shook his head. "That would be something for the environmental group to advocate for."

"I second that. It would save us a few preventable calls every year." Ridge turned the wheel to the right into the lot.

The second the truck parked, Zack hopped out of the back and opened the rear compartment that held the gear.

"Grab those rescue ropes and webbing, Stephens." Bryce swiveled on his heel. "Ridge, assess the area. Make sure we don't have any other points of danger."

Zack hefted the rope over his shoulder and handed another to Eddie before heading in the direction of the woman waving her hands. Bryce had let him take the lead. Time to get to work.

Bushes lined the walkway, and Zack's boots crunched over the gravel.

The weight of his gear grew heavier when Zack realized who stood a few feet away. "Ingram!"

She gasped. "Zack! Over here!" Her brows were pinched together, and her messy bun bobbed with her frantic motions. "I can't reach her. I've tried. It's too far down."

He rushed over, followed by Eddie.

Zack tried to speak, but no words came out.

Eddie clapped a hand down on Zack's shoulder and asked, "What happened?"

"She's down there. I didn't see what happened." Ingram covered her face with her hands. "I went to take a call and, and someone screamed and Naya was nowhere in sight."

The words spilled from Ingram's lips so fast it took Zack a few seconds to process what she said.

No. Not Naya. Zack steeled his feet against the ground to keep from swaying. He'd never known her to be clumsy. What had happened?

"Where is she?" Zack set the rope down and followed Ingram to the edge of the cliff.

Ingram sucked in a breath. "Down there." She peered over the edge, and tears streamed down her face. "Naya! Help's here."

"I'm here," Naya cried. She stared up at them, standing on a landing of rock no more than five feet wide. "Get me out of here. I can't..." She lifted her arm halfway before she dropped it back to her side and cupped her elbow with her other hand. "Don't leave," Naya hiccupped, "me here."

Zack surveyed the terrain while his heart pounded in his chest.

At least fifteen feet from the top of the mountainside.

A straight drop down, which meant this rescue fell under high angle. But the right ropes could handle the situation. A few pointy rocks would provide a decent foothold to grab onto if necessary. His stomach flipped and a lump rose in his throat, but he ignored them and turned to Bryce. "Let me go down, Lieutenant."

Bryce nodded. "Grab the line rope and hook up. You and Ridge are going down."

Zack attached the gear and rope to his equipment. Then he tugged on the knots. *Don't let me mess this up, God.*

Bryce inspected Zack's work and did a quick test to make sure the clips were secure. "All good." The lieutenant slapped him on the shoulder. "Let's get to it!"

Eddie manned the truck and had the rope set up to unravel every few seconds for Zack's descent. The line ropes would give Zack and Ridge the ability to pull Naya back up.

Ridge went first, then Zack sat back in his harness and let the pulley drop him down the side of the cliff.

"Good so far," Ridge yelled.

"Keep going," Zack echoed.

He used his feet to scale the rocks and guide his weight down. Ten more feet and they'd be able to assess Naya's condition.

His rope jerked to a stop.

Zack braced his foot against a rock, but the unstable stone cracked under his weight. It broke away from the cliff with a groan and tumbled down the side, echoing across the open expanse. His foot skidded across the terrain, grasping for another landing point.

Ridge dodged the falling rocks. He went to stop, but his foot missed a landing, and he swung into the side of the mountain. His head knocked against the boulders. "Ow," he mumbled.

Zack peered over his shoulder. "Sorry."

"It's all good, man." Ridge rubbed his forehead and waved his hand, but blood dripped off his fingers.

Zack grimaced. He went to keep moving, but his rope didn't follow suit. "Why'd the pulley stop?" He spoke into the radio.

"We've got a predicament up here." Eddie's voice crackled in his ear. "There's a brush fire. Lieutenant wants me working with him to contain it. I need to drop you guys down faster."

"Copy." Zack wrapped one hand around the rope and scaled the wall faster next to Ridge. One hand over the other. "Naya!"

"Zack? I'm gonna fall." She leaned against the wall of rock, as far away from the edge as possible.

He gauged the distance between them. "I won't let that happen."

The rocks were uneven, and Ridge stood a few feet away, higher up on the other side of Naya. Zack shielded his eyes from the sun with one hand and studied the ground, calculating each step. He refused to let a blind spot take him by surprise.

Although, he recognized the area. If it was the same strip of the pinnacle he'd explored a few months ago on a day off, there was a cave nearby that overlooked the river.

He climbed up a few rocks on all fours, then eased onto the ledge and grabbed his radio. "Hold."

"Copy. How's the patient?"

Zack crouched. "Assessing now."

He did a quick perusal for physical signs of injury. Naya's cheeks were damp with drying tears, while blood stained the middle of her right arm. "Where does it hurt?" He took note of her left foot, slightly swollen.

Ridge came down next to them, then unzipped his medical bag. "Did you hurt your ankle?" His eyebrow was caked with blood from the wound on his forehead.

"I slammed my arm against the rocks when I fell. I kept sliding until I finally caught myself." A few tears slid down Naya's cheek, but she lifted her chin.

"We'll get your ankle in a splint and bandage the wound." Zack bent down to inspect Naya's ankle. "It's bruised." He pulled a few supplies from the bag while Ridge bandaged her arm.

"What's your status?" Bryce's voice came through the earpiece.

"We'll be ready in four," Zack replied. This cramped space wasn't the most ideal place to help a patient, and it was taking him longer than he wanted.

Ridge dabbed at his forehead. He pulled away the cloth, now covered in red, and grunted.

"Make it two." Bryce's command echoed loud and clear. "We've got smoke up here from the brush fire. There's no telling how fast it's going to spread."

Zack turned to Ridge and furrowed his brow. His partner's face had turned a shade paler. More blood trickled down the edge of his face.

"That should hold your ankle for now." Zack stood up and returned the supplies to the bag.

"Thanks." Naya swallowed and offered a small smile.

"You ready to hoist?" Zack wrapped the harness around Naya's abdomen, then secured his arm around her waist and turned to Ridge.

"I'm going to be sick." Ridge turned and heaved over the side of the landing. He let out a cough, then suddenly, his body went limp, the rope holding his weight.

"Firefighter down," Zack yelled into his radio and rushed over to his friend. "He's got a gash to the head, and he's unconscious."

"We can pull him up with Naya," Eddie said.

There was no way Zack could hold Ridge's weight and make sure they didn't crash into the side of the mountain on the way up.

"I'm going to need to take two trips." Zack couldn't risk anyone's safety.

"Bring the patient up, stat. This fire is growing, and I don't like it," Bryce said. "There's no way we can lower down a basket."

"Here." Zack handed Naya another clip that would connect her to his rope.

She shook her head and folded the clip back in his hand. Naya's hand trembled and her eyes darted between the two men. "Take him up first. He needs help. Just don't leave me behind again." Naya's eyes widened, shining with unshed tears. "Please."

For a split second, Zack witnessed the terror in Naya's gaze. It hit like a knife to his heart and served as a reminder of the trouble he'd caused that forced him to leave her behind once before. But he wouldn't let it happen again.

"I won't leave you." After the words left his mouth, Zack bit his tongue. He didn't like the choices in front of him, but there was no time to delay. He hoisted his hands under Ridge's legs and yanked on the rope. The pulley tugged them back up, and Zack used his feet to guide them so they wouldn't sway into anything.

"Take him." Zack hefted Ridge up to Bryce, who pulled him over the edge. Smoke wafted through the air, and Zack let out a cough. A quick glance revealed the flames skirting the edge of the path not far from the truck.

More sirens pierced the air from what Zack hoped was the other truck en route.

"I'm going back for Naya," Zack yelled.

Eddie held the rope and nodded.

Zack rappelled down the side of the mountain.

His feet touched the ground.

"I came back." Zack stepped over to Naya and handed her the clip once more.

Naya closed her eyes for a brief second, and more tears peaked at the corners. She blinked quickly. "Thank you."

He pulled her against him and held on for a second. "Anytime." He wiped a mix of dirt and blood from her forehead.

She stared up at him, her brown eyes a well of relief.

In this moment, the past didn't stand between them. She'd leaned into his embrace and let him hold her. He was there for her. Her friend. Her protector.

What was he thinking? She was the patient, and he was supposed to be saving her right now.

Zack cleared his throat and helped her hook onto his harness. Then he pulled on the rope once more to signal they were ready to climb.

"We can't pull you guys up." Bryce's confession in his ear sent Zack's heart into a faster rhythm.

"What do you mean?" Zack gritted his teeth to refrain from shouting.

"The fire is too close. If the wind picks up and catches on the rope, you're toast." Bryce paused. "We can't risk it."

Zack turned to face the edge of the landing and studied the area to place where they were in comparison to the rest of the trails.

If they couldn't go up, Zack needed to find another escape route pronto.

NINE

"WHAT'S GOING ON?" NAYA CLUNG TO THE ROPE, favoring her right leg. They weren't moving, and the ashen color on Zack's face indicated something was wrong.

Naya's nerves still tingled, and she had to tell herself to breathe. In and out. Her ankle throbbed, and her pulse tapped a steady rhythm against the inside of her foot.

She hadn't been able to deny Zack's partner had needed help first. But when the distance had grown and taken Zack farther away to safety, Naya couldn't help the tremors that wracked her body. What if he didn't come back for her, and she stayed trapped on this mountain?

But he had come back.

She'd almost shouted for joy when he'd come into view on his descent.

And the way he'd wrapped her in his embrace. So gentle yet firm when he'd rubbed his thumb across her face. In that moment she'd frozen. Unable to do anything but stare. If she were honest, she liked being held by him. The reality of safety in that moment. But it was a fleeting desire. A vapor that would prove futile to cling to. There one moment, gone the next.

Naya shifted her gaze to peer over the edge. That was a mistake. The drop to the ravine floor covered with trees and rocks sent her head spinning. If her shirt hadn't snagged on a rock, giving her time to grab on to the edge, she would be dead.

A shiver worked its way down her spine, and her teeth chattered.

Sure, if she hadn't stopped her fall, there would have been joy waiting on the other side, meeting her Savior face-to-face. But that hadn't stopped her body's survival skills kicking into full gear with the fight or flight response.

"There's a brush fire." Zack grimaced. "My team's all hands on deck. When they can, they'll bring us up. But for now, we're safe here."

Naya tried not to conjure an image of the fire overtaking the area. Zack and his team were trained. If he was confident, then she should be. Still, she didn't like being a sitting duck here. "Maybe we should find another way out." Naya shielded her eyes with her hand and turned to the left. She kept her back flush against the wall of rock.

"Naya." Zack swallowed. "I'm not going to let you down again."

They both knew what he was referring to. Clearly, he still carried the pain of what had happened when they were teens. It was a weight she still bore too. If she let down her guard, there was no telling the outcome.

"We've all failed people. Lost those we cared about, Zack. It's life." Naya couldn't hold on to a promise he made. Not when it could turn out to be empty. She'd be doing herself a favor, saving herself future heartache.

"I know." Zack waved his hand. "I failed to protect my best friend—my little sis—once, but I'm not going to let that happen again."

A tear slid down Naya's cheek, and she swiped at it with the back of her hand. The quick movement sent pain coursing through her injured arm.

Again?

Of course he thought of her as his sister. But how could she hold out hope once more?

They'd been teens when Zack disappeared from her life. A time when she'd worked up the courage to trust someone again. And when her confidence in him backfired, she'd blamed him for the hurt he'd caused. His broken promise to always have her back had sent her teenage self into another spiral of distrust. He'd said those bracelets were a symbol of a never-ending friendship between them. Until she'd lost hers. Instead of finding it like he'd said he would, he'd up and left for good.

The one person she'd come to depend on.

Gone.

After so much loss of her own, how could she know who would stick around?

But now wasn't the time to rehash the past. They needed to get to safety.

She pulled in a breath and offered a smile. "If you help me, we can find a way out."

Zack's eyes narrowed. He leaned into his shoulder and spoke. "What's the status on containing this fire? I've still got a patient down here."

Naya's stomach flopped at the frown on Zack's face. She wanted to rely on him to get them out of this situation. But she had a feeling she'd need to resort to her own capabilities. It was nothing new. She'd be strong for herself again.

Zack shook his head and turned to her. "The crew is working to put it out, but it's bigger than they realized. The engine just showed up—that's our other crew."

"So we're stuck here until they give the go-ahead?" Naya rubbed her arm, careful not to press too hard and aggravate the injury.

Zack held up a finger before pressing it to his ear.

She didn't want to jump to conclusions and think about the

worst-case scenario. So often people showed her they didn't have *her* best interests at heart; they had their own and no one else's. Growing up in foster care had taught her it was easier to rely on herself than others. And she'd only found that more true after she'd aged out of the system and started navigating life on her own.

Except she couldn't *do* anything right now.

"They want to call in a rescue copter, but based on the altitude and how low they need to get, it's only going to fan the flames of the fire. But I have an idea." Zack bent down and stuck his head over the edge.

"Please don't fall." Naya grabbed the middle of his rope in an effort to keep him from tumbling.

Zack stood up and brushed his hands. "There's another ledge below this one that leads into a cave that brings you out at the other side of the mountain."

"And you know this how?" Naya squinted.

"My buddy showed me one time when we were hiking. I had a feeling we were near the area, I just needed to orient myself to the surroundings." He tugged on his rope. "There's enough extra line here that we can climb over the edge and drop down onto the landing."

Naya gulped. Their options were limited, and she really didn't like being stuck on the mountain.

Could she trust Zack though? He hadn't left her alone. That had to count for something.

What other choice did she have?

"You're the expert." She shook her head. She wasn't sure she could fully trust Zack. But she did trust the Lord. He would never abandon her. And He'd brought Zack and the crew here. With no other escape routes at the moment, she'd follow his lead.

His face sobered. "I'll go first. Make sure it's safe. Then I'll help you down."

"We've found an alternate escape route through a cave, Lieutenant. Permission to go?" Zack radioed in.

"I gave you my orders, Stephens."

Zack turned to Naya, then held down on the radio button. "Our patient needs medical attention, and we're sitting ducks. The cave is three feet below us. We can rappel down. Our job is to rescue people."

"What are you trying to prove, Stephens?"

Zack steeled his jaw, and his neck muscle twitched. "That we help the people we've sworn to protect." Zack tugged on his harness, then disappeared over the edge.

Naya held her breath. Every second ticked by with the unknown. Was the cave there? Or was it a dead end?

A few minutes later Zack called out, "It's here! We're going to make it out. Attach your clip to the rope." Zack gave her instructions to harness herself in.

Let this work, Lord. Keep us safe. Naya tugged on the rope, then averted her gaze from the vast openness around her and focused on Zack's hand.

He reached out to her.

In that moment, it seemed like everything she'd been looking for.

She grabbed hold, then swung her leg over the edge. When she went to move her injured foot, it slipped on loose pebbles and dangled in the air.

Naya let out a yelp, her heart skipping a beat.

"I've got you!" Zack shouted. "Let yourself drop down."

Naya pinched her eyes shut to keep from making a snarky comment about the last time she'd fallen.

Soon her feet were on solid ground again, and she let out the breath she was holding.

"It's just through here." Zack pointed to the dark opening in front of them. The tunnel was small and damp. Each step they took echoed off the walls followed by an irregular trickle of water dripping.

Naya followed Zack, who guided the way with his flashlight. What if they were wrong and this wasn't a way out? They'd been moving for a while, and all the walking was making the pressure on her ankle unbearable. She slowed her pace to favor her good leg and put extra weight on the heel of her foot.

"You need help?" Zack shone the light at the ground. "I can give you a piggyback ride."

Naya laughed. "The last time I agreed to one, I remember tumbling off your shoulders." She'd been twelve at the time, and the two of them had been off on an adventure. "We were pretending to take flight like a plane. Except we didn't make it very far down our imaginary runway in the backyard of my foster home." Instead, they'd been all giggles, growing weak from laughter.

Zack grinned. "You're not wrong. But I am taller and buffer now." He placed his hands on his hips.

"I'll be fine." Naya smiled and continued walking. It might have only been half true that she would be okay, but she wasn't about to resurrect more memories, no matter how good that one might have been. If she did, she would want to rely on him more. Spend more time with him.

She needed Zack the firefighter.

The boy she had loved, who'd grown into a man, would be a distraction she didn't need.

They emerged in the clearing that opened up at the trail head. Zack radioed in their location. A few minutes later, flashing lights and medical personnel greeted them.

Ingram rushed to Naya and enveloped her in a hug. "Ow. Watch the arm," Naya hissed.

"Sorry." Ingram stepped back. "I'm just glad you're okay."

"We're going to take it from here," a woman with short blonde hair in a medic jacket said. The embroidery on her pocket read *Kianna.*

Naya scanned the area for Zack. Their eyes connected. *Thank you*, she mouthed. Then the ambulance doors shut.

After being at the hospital for an hour, Naya still sat on a cot in the ER. She'd already been stuck and prodded. Now it was a matter of waiting on the X-ray results for her arm and ankle. Her mind ran through the events of the last few hours. A reel stuck on replay with a broken pause button.

She couldn't shake the interaction with the other jogger that instigated this whole event. The way he'd barreled right into her. Like he'd intended to push her.

Naya's palms grew clammy. She'd told Kianna what happened when she'd asked on the ride over to the hospital. But she hadn't yet been able to inform the police. Would they even believe her suspicions?

At first, Naya had wanted to give the person the benefit of the doubt. Maybe he hadn't seen or heard her. Although, had it actually been a male? She'd never gotten a good look at the person's face. The strength of their push on her shoulders had sure seemed like a guy. What had started as a mere run-in had turned into an intentional attack. Naya had no time to even defend herself. One moment she'd been bending over, and the next she'd been falling through the air.

"I've got some good news."

Naya jerked at the voice and gripped the scratchy bed sheets.

Dr. Welch walked in with a laptop propped in one arm. His gray hair was slicked back with gel, and he wore a white lab coat over a button-down shirt. "Your ankle is bruised but not broken. Keep it elevated. Ice it until the swelling and pain decrease." He typed some notes with one hand. "Any questions on that?"

"Not that I can think of," Naya said.

"Great. Now the bad news. Your elbow is severely sprained.

We'll put it in a sling until the swelling goes down. The goal is to prevent surgery. So keep it elevated and don't do any strenuous activity that could aggravate the muscles."

Naya cradled her arm against her front. She wished today had a redo. But when had wishing done her any good? She dealt in facts, like this doctor.

At least it wasn't her writing hand. She could do voice to text on her computer. And given the whole incident, her injuries could have been much worse. There was always a way it could've been worse. Indeed, the Lord had spared her life.

One of the nurses, Charlotte, came in and gave Naya her purse, which was sealed in a plastic hospital bag. Then she set Naya's arm in a sling, and an hour later, Naya was handed her discharge papers.

She walked back out to the ER waiting room. Several first responders sat along the wall, still in full turnout gear.

The other firefighter. Naya's breath hitched. Was he okay?

She spotted Zack and walked over. "Any word on Ridge?" Naya's voice rang in the quiet space.

Zack clenched his hand. "They got the bleeding to stop and stabilized him. We took the truck back to the firehouse, and the reserve crew came in to cover us, since Ridge is out. They said they'd let us know when he's settled in a room."

"Oh good." She sighed. "Can I talk to you?" Naya motioned with her eyes to the exit doors. She had to tell someone about what happened, and with their history, Zack had to be the right person. They'd been closer today than she had been with anyone in years—even her ex-boyfriend.

Zack cocked his head but still followed her outside to a bench by the entrance of the hospital. The pain meds they'd given her helped ease the tightness in her foot, but she propped it up on the arm rest.

"Thank you for today." Naya peered up at Zack, who stood against the brick wall. Part of her wanted him to sit next to her. To continue the lighthearted comradery from earlier, like they were friends. But his distance was for the best. It reminded her heart to do the same. No more wishful thinking.

"I'm glad you're okay."

"About that." She could barely get the words out. "I think someone intentionally pushed me off the mountain today."

Zack's voice rose a notch. "What do you mean you *think*?"

Naya grimaced. "I thought the person jogging just didn't see me. They had their head to the ground, phone in hand. But when they brushed me, my phone fell. I—" The images came back, and Naya frowned. "I went to pick up my phone and they shoved me."

"You were pushed?"

She opened her eyes. "I didn't know who to tell."

"This is serious, Nay. First the note. Now this." Zack rubbed a hand over the back of his head. "You need to tell the police, not me."

Naya shrugged. "I don't know. It's not like I have any evidence it was malicious. It's like the note. Just a nuisance."

Zack stepped away from the wall and closed the gap between them. "I meant what I said earlier. You're my little sis."

Right. It was a good thing she planned to keep her heart protected. Closed off.

Saying it like that drew a line between them.

One she wasn't invited to step over.

A flicker of an expression crossed his face, but it disappeared before Naya could figure it out. "Call the police, Naya." Zack pushed off the wall and went inside.

TEN

BEFORE NAYA COULD ENTANGLE HERSELF IN Zack's life any more, she limped to the parking lot. She needed time alone to decompress from the day, and a yawn escaped from her lips. The last rays of the setting sun dipped behind the cloudy sky. The streetlights were her only guide.

Why had she shared her suspicions about the attack on the mountain with Zack? She had the story from her boss to focus on, and it was proving to bring more trouble with it than she'd bargained for.

She didn't need to add any tension with Zack. He'd made it clear what he thought of her.

His little sister.

But how could she even be that to him after the way he responded? He'd basically shut her out, telling her to go to the police. Like he didn't want to take on the role of big brother. She'd act cordial and professional around him, but that was the extent of their relationship. Especially when there was a greater issue at play.

A lack of trust.

When had it all gone wrong? How had their days of promises to one another turned into a series of qualms?

Right now, it didn't matter. Naya had something else to focus on.

Working hard.

Just like her dad used to say. *Hard work will pay off in the end if you keep at it, sweet pea. One foot in front of the other.*

Except the life he'd fought to build for their family hadn't panned out the way any of them had hoped.

Naya blinked several times to clear the haziness and scanned the parking lot. Where was her car?

She rummaged in her purse for her phone and came up empty-handed. It must still be on the trail.

With no way to contact Ingram to pick her up, she headed back to the hospital entrance. There had to be a pay phone or someone's cell she could borrow. The last thing she wanted to do was bother Zack when he should be waiting for news on his partner.

The doors to the emergency room whooshed open, and another family rushed inside. "Excuse me. Sorry." The dad held his young daughter in his arms. The mom refused to let go of the little girl's hand.

Naya ducked to the side and made eye contact with Zack.

"Is something wrong?" Zack's gaze darted between her and the rest of the crew.

She waved her hand and stepped toward the foyer. "I need to call for a ride."

Zack's radio buzzed. *Fire at 270 Cobblestone Court. Victim trapped.*

Naya froze. "That's the address from my research." None of the crew moved from their seats. "That's the CEO's house. For Ethos."

Zack ran his fingers through his hair. "And you want to go investigate it." He scrunched his brow.

"I can call Ingram." Naya scanned the foyer for a pay phone.

"Lieutenant." Zack walked over to his boss. "I'm gonna go take a look. Off the clock."

"Don't forget the team, Stephens. I better see you back here soon."

A muscle twitched in Zack's jaw, but Naya refrained from asking what Bryce meant.

"Come on." He extended his arm to let her through the sliding doors first.

Naya raised her brow. Now Zack wanted to help her? After he'd been adamant about her going to the police instead. If she wanted to get to the scene of the fire, there was no time to argue.

Naya slid into the passenger seat of Zack's car.

Buildings and trees blurred past them, and Naya tapped her foot against the floorboard. "This could be a big lead." The spark needed to write this story. And she was about to be the first on the scene.

"You think this was intentional?" Zack sped through a green light.

"Something warranted the start of the blaze. I want to know what."

They pulled up to the scene, and fire trucks and police cars blocked the several hundred feet surrounding the house. An orange ball lit up the front porch while gray billows spewed into the air. No one was getting in or out of the front door.

Naya closed her door, then followed Zack to the curb. The house was tucked on its own piece of property, but two other four-car garage houses sat back in the distance with enough space to provide privacy for each owner.

Naya and Zack approached the front entrance and walked around the blue police barriers. The flames crackled and snapped. Even from forty feet away, the heat warmed Naya's face. The gated cobblestone driveway provided limited space for entering, and Ramble stood at the gate, arms crossed, keeping onlookers at bay.

"I'm here to help the crews." Zack nodded to Ramble.

Naya flashed her press badge.

"Let the guys do their work." Ramble ushered them through. "This is an ugly one."

Dark, thick clouds of smoke enveloped the area, and the breeze carried them through the air. Gushing water pounded against the roof, combating the flames.

Naya let out a cough. "Zack. Wait." One wrong move and someone could get seriously hurt. Naya gulped. The reality of the situation sat like the thick smoke on her chest.

Firefighters in full turnout gear whizzed past her. Zack spun around. He had one foot on the grass, the other still on the driveway. He turned to the commotion behind him.

"Let's get the ladders ready!" one of the firefighters yelled while the crew raced around. He must be of higher rank given the different uniform he wore. "I don't want this becoming a three-alarm call."

"Be careful. Please." She stepped forward and took a breath to steady herself.

Zack focused back on Naya. "I'll be fine. I just want to see if they need help."

This was what Zack did every day. Put his life on the line.

Naya bit her lip and nodded. "I just don't want you to get hurt." There'd been a time when they had promised to always stand by each other. But the hope of that happening had caught fire and burned a long time ago. So why was her heart yearning for it again?

"I'll be back in a few." His eyes widened. "Watch your back too."

Naya gave him a thumbs-up. Hazards came with the territory of her job. Every reporter understood the risks. But it didn't mean Naya had an excuse to shrink away.

She hobbled over to a clearing where a lone tree grew in front of the sidewalk. A quick glance over her shoulder showed Zack was talking to an officer.

Focus.

Tall oak trees dotted the property. If any of those caught fire, she didn't want to imagine the aftermath.

She needed to figure out who to talk to.

A pungent smell swirled through the air and gripped Naya's nostrils. She let out another cough and held her fingers to her nose. "Why does this fire smell like spoiled fish? Is that normal?"

In the midst of the chaos, a host of voices rose in volume. She needed to get closer. While Zack was occupied with his hero duties, she set off toward the sound of people chanting.

Naya walked around the trucks, back toward the front gate. "Sorry." She ducked around a firefighter. "Excuse me." She brushed past a few onlookers.

On the other corner of the house, a group of people stood with signs, hoisting them in the air, yelling, "You can't hide. Give it up. Save our land."

More police officers planted themselves around the perimeter, fingers hooked around their belt loops.

Sylvia stood on the outskirts of the group, and Naya waved to get her attention.

The woman stepped away from the crowd and crossed her arms. "It's you again."

So much for a hello. "Do you know anything about what happened?"

"There've been rumors floating around. That one of our own had something to do with it."

Naya's jaw dropped and she stared at Sylvia. "What?" The protestors believed there was someone in their group that had started a fire at this man's home? That was a serious escalation from peacefully making a noise on the street out front.

The woman's face remained stone cold. Okay, so she wasn't joking.

Naya said, "What makes you say that?"

"Good ole barrel of fish and oil sent this place up in flames."

Naya's fingers shook. So that's where the smell had come from. She couldn't believe someone could have caused so much damage. Ideology was one thing, but this took it to a misdemeanor. Maybe even a felony.

This group might have crossed the threshold into ecoterrorism if they were really behind this attack. "Why retaliate in this way?" Naya focused on keeping her expression neutral. If their agenda was truly to save the planet, this message counteracted their goals. That's what Naya wanted to tell Sylvia. But given the woman's nonchalant attitude, that may not go over well.

"It might finally get the point across," Sylvia huffed.

"Do you think this will change Ethos's response? If they believe their employees are reachable at their own homes, they won't feel so superior. This could incite real change." Naya's voice cracked, but she cleared her throat. Did Sylvia realize her speculation warranted Naya's need to report the incident? Although, the woman could also open up and say more if she thought Naya was sympathetic. "So you think it will move the needle to real change?"

"It better, that's what I say. We're fed up with Roger's playing dumb." She rolled her eyes. "They are killing off our ecosystem and people are sick."

"How much further is your organization prepared to go to get results? Are you fighting back with legal action? Or getting a petition signed?" Naya hadn't heard anything new from Ingram on that front. As far as she was aware, the environmental group still had until Friday before Ethos proceeded with legal action. Naya said, "It won't be long before they're making trouble for you in response."

"We're not going to let them do that, hon." Sylvia lifted her chin. "And if I were you, I'd watch your back and who you talk to." Sylvia pointed at Naya's arm. "You don't need any more injuries."

Sylvia sauntered off.

Naya's eyes darted to her left and right. The hues of flashing lights played off the shadows of the darkening sky and made her head spin. A cold weight squeezed her chest as if the array of people on scene were pinning her down.

There was no way Sylvia could know the cause of her injury.

Right?

No way she could know her sprained elbow was related to all this.

She was just being paranoid, reading something into what Sylvia had said. This was just the outcome of a life where she'd been hurt one too many times. Pain had left marks like tattoos she hadn't consented to on her heart. That, and a host of memories even time hadn't been able to fade.

Naya turned to see the status of the fire, but it was all just chaos to her. Where was Zack? He could explain where they were at with it.

"Help!" A scream curdled the air and drowned out the noises around her.

A gray-haired woman in a robe dangled from a piece of wood off the side balcony. Flames licked inches below her bare feet. A firefighter perched on the ladder that extended up to the window, but it was just out of reach.

"That's my wife." A man with gray-peppered hair and who still wore a business suit shoved past Naya and ran to a firefighter staring at the scene from the ground. "What are you doing?" he barked. "Don't just stand there. She's going to fall!"

Naya weaved her way through people running about and followed the same route he'd gone. She approached the man and touched his arm. "Mr. Callahan?"

Sure enough, Roger turned around at his name. If she could distract him long enough to let the rescue crew do their job, maybe he wouldn't panic and get in the way.

It was worth a try, at least.

"Naya Michél." She extended her hand, except he stared at her without reciprocating the gesture. "This crew will work hard to get your wife out safely, but they need you to hang back so they can get their job done. It's what they're trained for."

"Trained to stand around and watch while one guy lets my wife burn alive. Same with the cops. Doing nothing while those protestors cause havoc on my street." His face reddened. "They're the reason this is happening."

"Sir—"

"If it wasn't for those protestors, my wife wouldn't be in danger." He huffed, not even watching the firefighter lift his wife to safety. "My house wouldn't be in ruins."

"These people are well within their rights to stage a peaceful protest on public property." Naya stood her ground despite Roger closing the gap between them. His close proximity might make her appear smaller, but she wouldn't take the bait. "You have quite the power, Mr. Callahan, to make a difference. How do you plan to remediate this situation and these people's concerns regarding the products your company puts on the market?"

Callahan took a step toward her and lowered his stature until he was at eye level. "With legal action," he sneered.

He thought she would back down?

He hadn't met her.

"Why not simply take your products off the market until they're tested? Give everyone peace of mind." Naya kept her voice steady. "Surely that would defuse this volatile situation."

"You listen here, little lady." Callahan jabbed a finger in her face.

Okay, now she was getting mad. "Mr. Callahan—" She clenched her teeth.

"We have our best practices, and regulators monitor everything we do. I don't need to answer any of your questions. Now, if you'll excuse me." He took long strides to the edge of the grassy area.

Naya shook her head. Zack stood at the base of the fire truck, spotting the firefighter who had Mrs. Callahan nearly to the bottom of the ladder.

"You firefighters aren't doing your job. Hurry up." A few expletives spewed from his mouth. "Get her over here. Now!"

Two officers raced to his side and blocked his way.

"Let me get to my wife." He shoved at them.

Naya headed in Zack's direction. Her eyes blurred, and she blinked.

"You seem to have a keen sense for following trouble."

Naya spun around at Tucker's voice. Of course he'd find her amidst the crowd. She took a step to the side to keep from falling over. That wouldn't be a good look in front of her work nemesis.

"And it seems to like you too." He dipped his chin at her arm sling. "What happened?"

"You should know better than to think some malicious force targets people. And you should know I don't believe that either." Her mission wasn't to spread gossip or uncover secrets only to splay them on the page for the whole world to gawk at. Of all people, Tucker should know her.

He blinked. "Right. The God thing. How could I forget?"

Naya might not have picked up on it initially when they'd been together, but the telltale signs were there now. His pride wouldn't let it go any other way than to see her crash and burn.

To get her riled up so she spun out.

And abandoned her goal.

Giving him the joy of victory without a fair fight.

"If you'll excuse me." Naya stepped up onto the sidewalk to get out of the way, but someone brushed against her back, and she stumbled forward. Her ankle twisted, and she winced.

A hand grabbed her arm, and Naya let out a cry.

She was done. Today had been *too* much.

She spun, ready to push away whoever it was.

"Whoa. It's just me." Zack stood in front of her, holding her. "I thought I told you to watch your back?" His brow creased. "You don't need another injury."

"I was doing my job." She shifted to favor her good leg and rose to her full height. Was he going to reprimand her, thinking she couldn't hold her own, just like the other men she knew? "I'll be fine."

"But you'll put yourself in jeopardy to do it?"

He thought she was doing that on purpose? "If I recall, you stepped into the crosshairs tonight too."

"I'm just looking out for you." Zack's jaw twitched.

Naya stayed quiet for a moment. Was that really his motive? She didn't know whether to believe him or not. Regardless, she wasn't going to let him deter her from doing her job. "Actually, the information I gathered could keep others from being put in harm's way." Of course, he wouldn't understand her full reasoning. She'd never told him the whole story of why she did what she did.

"Good. Then you're done?" He rubbed his forehead and closed his eyes for a brief second.

There wasn't any use explaining her why at the moment. "Yes, I'm done."

All that mattered was that she'd uncovered valuable insight from Sylvia and Callahan.

Now she needed to figure out who was behind this attack tonight and what exactly Callahan's best practices were. She'd just skimmed the film off the top of a murky lake, and Naya intended to dive deeper to discover what lay beneath.

"Great. Let's go." Zack turned, and his firm hand on her back escorted her to the car. He opened her door and stood there, as if to help her in.

Naya stared back at the fire a second before getting in the car.

He closed the door and rounded to the driver's side. Given her throbbing arm and the flames still licking the house in the distance, how many more people would suffer before she got to the bottom of the truth?

ELEVEN

FLAMES ROARED IN ZACK'S EARS, AND THE SMOKE shrouded him, threatening to take him to an early grave.

Can't breathe.

He raced to the window in his room and yanked on the lever, but it wouldn't budge. His parents stood on the grass below.

His mom dropped to her knees while his dad whipped his hands in the air. One glance behind him at the smoke funneling through the cracks in the door told Zack he was trapped.

Mom! Dad!

An alarm buzzed and Zack shot up in bed. The sheets cascaded to the floor, and the cool air in his room enveloped his sweaty body.

Dreaming. Or rather, a nightmare.

Zack sucked in a ragged breath before leaning back against the headboard.

The buzzing continued, and Zack groped for his phone in the dark and shut off the alarm.

He was safe. In his apartment.

Just to be sure, he flicked on his lamp and sniffed.

Nothing out of the ordinary set off his senses.

Zack rubbed the nape of his neck, then stumbled his way into the kitchen and poured himself a glass of ice water.

The rescue yesterday had impacted him more than he'd realized.

After overexerting himself on the side of a deadly hill, he'd followed it up with going to another call. Even if it was only so Naya could see it.

I just don't want you to get hurt. Their conversation remained etched in his mind. Zack wanted to restore their friendship. Show Naya how much she meant to him. He'd assumed she wanted nothing to do with him. Even more so after how he responded at the hospital. Telling her to talk to the police then leaving.

But her words told a different story.

His heart echoed the same sentiment. He wanted her to take every precaution to avoid getting hurt. If her words were sincere, then he didn't want to lose his chance.

A chance to be part of her life again.

The possibility made him want to take fewer risks on the job if it meant he'd be around longer for Naya. The fire yesterday had been a stark reminder of what his line of work entailed.

Even after he'd driven her home, they hadn't said much to each other, but he hadn't wanted to leave without knowing he'd see her again.

All the events had exhausted him enough for memories of the past to resurface. Memories of his own house fire. The one Zack had blamed on himself for years. Thanks to his dad's friend, the former fire chief, who'd made sure Zack understood whose fault it was.

Now, with the new information from the case, he knew it wasn't true. Zack had been a kid. His parents' deaths hadn't been his fault. But nothing could alter the outcome.

Zack slid the file over on the counter and flipped through the pages.

He wanted to find his parents' killer.

Yet what good would it do? The truth wouldn't bring his parents back.

He closed the file, then turned on the microwave light and pulled out a pan to fry up some eggs.

His phone dinged with a calendar reminder. He and Naya planned to meet up at Bridgewater Café to discuss the details she'd gathered for her story.

Zack might not be able to bring his parents back, but he sure could protect Naya from a similar fate.

He had time before he needed to leave, given it was only six in the morning. So much for sleeping in on his day off. It would give him a chance to be productive though.

He added salt and pepper to his scramble, then sat down and pulled out his Bible. He needed to refocus his mind and prepare for the day ahead. When the sea billows rolled, like the old hymn said, he needed the anchor that would hold him fast.

Zack opened to Isaiah 43.

Do not fear, for I have redeemed you; I have summoned you by name; you are mine. When you pass through the waters, I will be with you; and when you pass through the rivers, they will not sweep over you. When you walk through the fire, you will not be burned; the flames will not set you ablaze.

Zack breathed in.

You are mine.

He was the Lord's. He'd been rescued, and he didn't walk this road alone. How could he take this truth to heart and not let it be head knowledge?

When you walk through...

Zack grimaced. Of course. Experience brought the truth to light. Given the last few days, he needed the Lord's strength for the fiery journey in front of him.

Three hours later, after he'd finished a workout and some hazmat training online, Zack gathered his things and headed for his car.

Zack

Omw to Bridgewater. Do you need a ride?

He shot off the text to Naya. He wasn't sure if she'd gotten around to picking up her car from the trail after the string of events yesterday.

Naya

I'll meet you there. Ingram got my car and my phone for me.

He sent her a thumbs-up and pulled out of his drive.

The café was already packed by the time he arrived, and he stood in the entryway, scanning the tables for Naya.

"Mom, see, see!" A young boy jumped up and pointed to the New Blooms Spring Festival flier stapled to the community bulletin board inside the doorway. "We're gonna get front row seats, right? I wanna see the fire truck. *Beep. Wee-oo.*" The boy mimicked the sound.

Zack smiled. The kid's enthusiasm was what would make the event worthwhile. He couldn't wait to finish planning the truck run with the boys that the Kirbys were fostering.

Zack spotted Amelia first, who sat in a corner booth, and he headed her way. "How's Ridge this morning?" The doctor had kept Ridge overnight for observation.

"How should I know?" She blinked. "Last I heard he was fine and discharged." She shoved a few napkins in her bag, and the motion sent some of her drink spilling over onto her hand.

He was glad his partner was on the mend. Mickey's death a couple of years ago had been devastating. A lump lodged in his throat at the possibility of losing another friend. "Thanks for the update. Enjoy your day off."

"I've got plenty of work to do today." She wiped the liquid off her wrist and made a beeline for the exit.

Odd.

Zack wouldn't bother trying to understand what just happened. Sometimes women had their own secret code that he was better off not deciphering.

Instead, he scanned the menu, then stepped up to the cashier. "I'll take a large dark roast with a pump of caramel."

Zack snapped a lid on his cup, then turned and spotted Naya sitting hunched over in a booth, writing. She flipped the page of her notebook, and her pen continued to fly across the blank space.

He cleared his throat so as not to alarm her. "I hope I'm not interrupting your work." He slid into the seat across from her.

Naya lifted her gaze and shook her head. "Not at all. I was writing out my Scripture memory verse I've been working on." She replaced the blue notebook with a black-and-white marble one from her purse. "But you're not here to talk about that."

Zack smiled. Actually, he was interested in what she was learning. Her brown eyes sparkled, and Zack couldn't help the excitement that built in him. "What part of the Bible were you reading?" He propped his elbows on the table. The other stuff could wait.

"First Peter chapter one. It's been a good reminder that the trials we face are testing our faith." She scrunched her forehead. "Although I don't always like walking through them."

"You and me both." Zack laughed. "Just when I think I've learned to trust God in one area, He has a way of showing me my need for Him all over again." The nightmare reemerged in Zack's mind. He sighed. "Like with my parents."

"I'm sorry. I didn't mean to dredge up any memories."

"Don't be. It's a good reminder I needed today." He traced the cup sleeve with his thumb. "My boss gave me a cold case to investigate as part of my hazmat training."

Naya popped the cap on the highlighter but didn't say anything.

"It's my parents' case. Their deaths weren't an accident." Zack gripped his cup, and his thumb made an indent in the side. "They were murdered."

Naya's eyes widened. "Zack," she whispered.

Tears pooled in her eyes, and Zack broke eye contact. He couldn't go to that place right now.

"Someone trapped my parents inside their own house and set accelerant around the perimeter to make sure the fire did its job. They had no way out, so they died of smoke inhalation before the fire burned them." Zack took a sip of his coffee, but the caramel didn't leave a sweet taste anymore. More like a clump of clay that took every effort to swallow. His hand shook, but he managed to set the cup down without spilling.

How could someone kill another human intentionally? The facts of this case spelled *premeditated*, given the way the doors and windows had been secured shut. It was murder.

And yet no one had ever found the person who'd killed them.

"Did your parents ever show distress over something? Signs that someone wasn't happy with them?" Naya tapped her pen on the table and chewed her bottom lip.

She might seem distant to some, asking questions, but it comforted him to think it through logically rather than absorb the weight of her empathy.

Zack admired Naya's grit. Her ability to give her all to any situation. Like on the side of that mountain yesterday. She hadn't wanted to give up, even when there had been no way out.

He hated seeing her hurt. And yet, none of it had shaken her faith in God, which seemed as strong as it had been back then.

She was beautiful inside and out.

Zack leaned back in his seat. His heart told him to pay attention. But his mind sent off flares, warning him to keep his distance.

What would she say if he told her how he felt?

No, he couldn't open up. He needed to keep her away from trouble. Safety over romance. That was the answer. Otherwise, he might open his heart and have her ripped from his life all over again.

Better to focus on the real reason for their meeting now and not travel down a path he had no right to venture on.

"If they did, I was naïve to it. As an eight-year-old, you don't know everything that's going on behind the scenes."

How many times had adults told him that to explain away the fact they had no answers?

When his parents came home from work, they would drop their briefcases in the mud room like a weight of bricks. "Each night they were happy to see me. Like I was the reason they did everything they did."

"Your dad was a chemist, right?" Naya took a bite of her muffin.

"He worked for a company that created and sold products for firehouses and residential properties. That much I do know. He'd tell me how his work would help save peoples' lives."

"That's why you were always so good at explaining my science homework to me." Naya focused on the table and picked up a few crumbs with the pad of her finger before placing them on the napkin. A slight smile played on her lips.

Was she remembering the good times they'd had together before everything went south? They'd practically been inseparable.

"You'd always end up with the right answer though." Zack grinned. "Even without my help." Although, he wanted to be her helpmate.

Where had that thought come from?

Naya cleared her throat. "What was the name of the company your dad worked for?"

Right, business. This wasn't a friendship hangout, even if he wanted that. "ProEco Plant. Although," Zack tapped his fingers on the table, "he mentioned having a new boss and a new office at one point so there was some kind of transition."

"I can do some research and see what comes up. Can I also have the list of witnesses? I'll see what I can find there." She shrugged.

"Who knows? Maybe I can come up with an answer no one else saw."

And he could show Bryce he'd done the work he'd been asked to do.

Zack grabbed his own pen and starred the names before sliding the paper over to Naya to copy. Would any of these people even remember what happened? If it kept her out of trouble, maybe it was worth allowing her to do some legwork.

"Fancy seeing one of our town's heroes out and about."

Zack stiffened at the greeting and slowly shifted in his seat.

The man who stood at the end of the table had once been Zack's nemesis in grade school, and it had gotten Zack into a couple of detentions when the fists had come out.

"Can't think so highly of myself that I forget to associate with common folk." Zack chuckled, hoping Hudson left the joke at that and didn't provoke the situation more.

Hudson sported a pressed suit and slicked-back hair with enough gel to keep a breeze from disturbing a single strand. "Saw in the paper this morning the crew still has you on the ground. Once a troublemaker, always one. I suppose they can't trust you with bigger tasks."

Zack clenched his hand. "I moved from truck to rescue squad. In case you didn't know, that's a pretty big deal."

A kick hit his shin under the table, and he turned to Naya, whose eyes gave him that don't-give-him-the-upper-hand look.

She was right, he needed to have patience with the guy. He was just trying to rile Zack up. But Hudson's attitude irked him. "I'm just glad it wasn't your place in flames last night. You work at Ethos, don't you?" Zack hadn't kept up on much with the guy who'd made middle school a nightmare. "If you'll excuse us, we need to get back to work." Zack turned his attention back to Naya.

Hudson's footsteps faded. When the overhead bell chimed above the door, signaling his exit, Zack's shoulders relaxed.

Naya rolled her eyes. "I'll never understand his attitude."

She had been the one to take care of a few bruises and cuts he'd gotten from those altercations with preteen Hudson. Eventually he'd learned the arguments weren't making Hudson back down, so he'd stopped paying attention to the kid and turned to praying for him instead. It'd been the right thing to do, but it had still proved challenging.

"Thanks for being here with me."

She smiled at him.

"Speaking of bullies, how is your arm?" Zack pointed at her sling.

Her smile fell flat. "I just don't get why someone would try that stunt. Why try to kill me? And was that the point?"

"You don't think it's Tucker?" Zack had to make sure.

She'd alluded to difficulties with the guy, and if he'd hurt her in any way, Zack would have a harder time restraining himself than he had with Hudson.

Her eyes widened. "No. That's not like him. He's a cocky guy. Rude, like Hudson—and Mr. Callahan. But Tucker would never push things that far. At least, he never hurt me physically in our relationship."

Zack's next sip of coffee went down easier. Her answer gave him some assurance, but he still didn't like the fact that someone had taken such an extreme measure.

Zack flipped his phone over on the table. "Did you file a report with the police?"

She nodded.

"I can ask Lieutenant Basuto to check on Tucker's whereabouts yesterday afternoon, then. They can make sure he has an airtight alibi." He sent the officer a short text.

"But if it's not Tucker, who could it be?" She lifted her good hand and turned her palm up.

"Someone who doesn't want you uncovering information for

your story would be my guess." He shrugged one shoulder, hoping she would listen to counsel. "If there's someone out there who wants their secrets to remain hidden."

"Well, they've messed with the wrong person, then." Naya narrowed her eyes.

"You're determined to pursue the story anyway?" The words left a sour taste in his mouth.

Naya's brows rose. "For the chance to beat out Tucker and get a promotion? What do you think?"

Zack finished off his coffee and set the empty cup on the table with a clunk. He'd have her back whenever possible, which meant doing an investigation when he wasn't on shift.

Like today.

"I just don't know where to begin," she said.

Zack figured the place where her attacker had been would be a good place to start. "Come on. Let's go back up the mountain."

TWELVE

NAYA'S STOMACH SAT IN KNOTS WHEN ZACK parked the car. Had she really agreed to come back up here? Each mile brought them closer to the pinnacle, and her breathing grew shallow. She could ask him to turn back.

"I didn't realize this road came up so far." Naya stared out the window.

"It saves on walking time. How's your ankle?"

"Manageable."

"And the rest of you?"

Okay, she was doing a bad job of hiding how she really felt. She turned in her seat to face him. "I'll be okay."

Zack gave her a raised eyebrow.

Well, she could hope it would be true.

The sun glistened off the trees, a few of which already had their pink blossoms. Birds chirped and flew around, gathering twigs and other objects to build their nests. It was a perfect, serene day.

Just like the previous one, where she'd nearly died.

The blue skies and vibrant scenery painted a picture that didn't share the whole story.

Lord, I need Your peace. I'm tempted to let anxiety take over. I know You've been with me before. And you promise You're near me now.

Naya walked up the short hill and froze halfway. She stood close enough to the pinnacle that she had a full view of the shrubs and brush to her right and the overlook on her left.

Her breath came in short pants, and when she tried to suck in air, her ribcage tightened, refusing to let oxygen into her lungs. Sometimes, revisiting a traumatic situation was good for processing emotions and moving on from the experience. There was no use letting fear hold her captive. But Naya's body protested her decision to come back up here.

"You okay?" Zack stopped in front of her, blocking her view up ahead.

She wanted to scream. Of course she wasn't okay. How could she be after someone had tried to kill her? Naya wished she could shake the memories off and forget anything had ever happened.

Or realize she was reliving someone else's story and the details had become too vivid in her own mind. Better yet, she wished it was a nightmare that someone needed to wake her up from.

"I'm going to be sick." Naya brushed past Zack and walked as fast as her sore ankle would allow and made it to the edge of the burnt grass. A second later she threw up.

She stayed hunched over, her stomach cramping. With her good hand propped on her knee, Naya let the tears come.

There was so much hardship in life, and her job was to seek it out and write about it. But when it came to her own life, she'd rather hide from the story.

In her thirty years, Naya had witnessed more trials than anyone should have to endure. Was it going to end?

Every time, it begged the same question. Where was the hope?

Fix your gaze on Me. I'm your living hope.

The reminder from her time memorizing 1 Peter 1 filled her soul, and a sense of peace came with it.

The Lord was her hope. She didn't have to despair or lose sight of that truth. Yet it didn't change the current situation, did it? It never did, but it was still as real as anything she could see or feel.

"Here." Zack's frame came into view, and he handed her a white cloth.

She lifted her teary gaze to his and wiped her mouth. "Thanks."

"There's a bench over there you can sit on. I can take care of investigating."

"I'll be fine." Naya didn't want to be left alone. Not like last time. Because there might be someone hiding. Waiting. Her eyes scanned the perimeter, searching. "Can you stay with me for now?"

Zack must have understood what she was referring to, because he placed his hand over top of hers and stretched out his other arm.

Beckoning her into his embrace. Like he knew how much asking him not to go had cost her.

Naya wrapped her arm around him and leaned her head against his chest.

He didn't say a word. Simply held her close.

She'd forgotten what it meant to be safe with someone. Not having a family growing up, and needing to protect herself, it almost felt wrong to find solace here with Zack.

Almost.

Zack might be a safe haven for her. A familiar place that was comfortable. But no matter how good it seemed, Naya couldn't risk her heart.

There was too much at stake to put aside logic and let feelings take over. He needed to earn her trust again. And even then, he would only be a big brother to her. After all, he didn't seem interested in anything else.

Naya pulled back from Zack's embrace and created enough physical distance to tell her mind to do the same.

No matter how much her heart whispered otherwise.

"You don't have to write this story if it puts you in harm's way."

Zack's husky tone made Naya inch away more so she wouldn't send mixed signals—even if it was only for her sake.

"I don't have a choice, Zack. I need to."

"You don't have to put that much pressure on yourself." His features softened.

"I need to follow through on it." Naya wrapped her arms together. "Otherwise, everything I've worked for slips out of reach, and Tucker wins."

"Why are you writing it?" He lowered his voice. Like he wasn't trying to argue, but rather he wanted to help her think through her decision. "Who are you writing it for? If it's for that Tucker guy, you don't need to prove anything to him." Zack slipped his hands in his hoodie pocket and his jaw flexed.

It was interesting to see his demeanor change. Naya had half expected him to be jealous, but he hadn't reacted that way. She couldn't quite put her finger on what he was actually feeling.

Given the way she'd unraveled in front of him, she understood his concern. Which meant she needed to come clean about what drove her to write stories. Stories that exposed the truth.

"It's not that." Naya swallowed. "I write for Dominic."

Zack scrunched his forehead. "Who?"

"My brother." Ingram was the only other person she'd shared this story with. Time had a way of dimming circumstances until they were hazy, like a figment of her imagination that only showed up in dreams.

She cleared her throat. "He died when I was nine."

Speaking the words aloud knocked the breath from her lungs. Reality tackled her faster and harder than the person who'd pushed her over the cliff.

"Naya. I—" Zack grimaced. "I knew your dad left and your mom was out of the picture, but I didn't realize you'd lost your brother."

"You wouldn't have known, because I never told you." Naya winced at how harsh those words sounded. Choosing to refrain from sharing the story about Dominic hadn't had anything to do with Zack, but it had been a way to protect her young heart all those years ago.

She stared at the town, spread out below them. "Our drinking water in Haiti wasn't the best. Sanitation processes were basically a joke. Dominic got cholera. His little body couldn't fight it, and without access to meds, he didn't make it." Naya sucked in her cheeks to ward off the tears that threatened to overtake her once more. She whispered, "He was only seven."

"I can't imagine." Zack stood there with his arms tucked by his side, like he wanted to do something, anything, but couldn't.

Nothing anyone could do would bring her brother back.

Just like Zack's parents. Even solving their case wouldn't give him peace.

Zack stared at the expanse in front of them.

Naya sniffed. "After that, my dad brought me to the U.S. with the promise of a better life. But his work hours got later and later. One day, he never showed to pick me up from school. I sat there in the school office until CPS came, and I was eventually placed in a foster home." Naya stared off into the distance. She'd hugged her dad that morning. One hand wrapped in his black curly hair. "He promised we'd go for ice cream that night. Except he never came back." Naya shivered. The life she'd known with her family had disappeared, and she'd landed in foster care. Right here in Last Chance County.

Now here she was, standing outside, baring her heart years later. The raw honesty left her as exposed as the day she'd sat in the principal's office.

Waiting to be found.

Like the truth of every story she wrote.

She'd been unwanted then. Her dad hadn't seen his daughter as valuable.

Which was exactly why she needed to write this story.

Everyone deserved to be seen. Each life was valuable.

And everyone deserved clean water.

"I'm doing this for Dom." Naya lifted her chin. "For those who don't have a voice. Who've been tossed aside. To show others their story matters. To show people what I can do." She patted a hand on her chest.

Zack smiled. "You have something to give people that extends far beyond the words you write."

"I do?"

"Empathy. The Lord has given you a gift to care for others in their distress. It's why you tell their stories, and that's why what you do is so impactful. Because it *means* something to people."

Naya couldn't help the wide smile that spread across her face. "Thanks."

The words he spoke were a balm to her heart like she hadn't experienced since her father used to pull her and her brother onto his lap and read to them.

"I get it." Zack studied her with a soft expression. "I know why you do what you do."

Could she say the same about him?

Zack snapped on a pair of gloves. He gave her a glove for her good hand, then extended his hand to the open land in front of them. "Shall we?"

Naya took his hand and stood.

They spent the next hour combing the landscape in search of anything that would tip them off as to who had been at the site when Naya was attacked.

They'd covered at least a quarter of a mile. Naya waded deeper into the shrubs, where several of the leaves were now brown. Branches fell to the ground with a gentle brush of her hand thanks to the fire that had swept across the area. Officials were still trying to figure out how the fire had started.

She wasn't exactly sure what she was looking for right now.

She focused on what was around her but never strayed far from Zack. Still, she didn't want to completely lean on the comfort of his presence.

It wasn't like it would turn into a relationship when every single one she'd had turned bad.

"Check this out." Zack waved his hand, bent down and pointed to a brown rectangular bag similar to burlap.

"What is it?"

"A sandbag."

"Don't you use those for stopping a fire from spreading?" Naya recalled something about the tactic from a TV show. "Or protecting against flood water."

"Yeah, but not this kind." Zack hefted the bag in the air. "It doesn't have the same feel as sand. Much lighter."

"Interesting." Naya snapped a few shots of the bag.

Something glinted in the reflection from her phone screen. "What's this?"

She picked up the silver circle and turned it over in her hand. The front was shaped like a globe of the earth with a heart in the corner.

"Looks like someone's keychain." She held it in the air for Zack.

"That's quite the design." Zack squinted.

"I feel like I should recognize this, but I don't know why."

"Do you think someone from the Green Warriors group has one?" Zack lifted his brow. "Maybe the heart and the earth are an eco thing."

"I think you're on to something. But would they set fire to this area when it could harm the wildlife and destroy the trees?" Naya shook her head. "It doesn't make sense."

"They certainly have motive to keep you from writing the story," Zack said. "Especially if there's something else happening behind the scenes with this group. Maybe they aren't who they say they are."

She'd be doing more research when she got to her computer.

They bagged the keychain as evidence they'd be able to show the police, even if it wasn't an official search—or an official case. That wouldn't stop her from writing up her findings later and publishing the story one day.

Zack carried the weighted brown bag back to the car. "I'll drop you back at Bridgewater, then swing by the station to hand in our findings."

"Sounds good." Naya rolled down the car window to let the fresh air in and leaned her head back.

Zack weaved his way down the service road.

A strange smell wafted past Naya. It grew stronger with each second that passed on the drive down the mountain.

"Is that gas?" She stuck her head out the window and sniffed.

"I smell something too. Hang on." Zack put the car in Park and walked around to the back of the vehicle.

In the side mirror's reflection, Zack ducked behind the right rear tire.

A second later he called out, "Something's leaking."

Naya got out of the car, walked over to the fuel tank, and popped open the compartment. "What's that?" She stared at a metal pipe with a cap on each end.

"It's a bomb." He backed up a step and grabbed her hand, tugging her away from the vehicle.

His pull sent her stumbling into him.

"We've got to move," he gasped. "It's going to explode."

Naya wrapped her arm around his and ran. Her breath caught in her throat, but she followed Zack's lead down the gravel path. An explosion rocked the air in the same moment the force reverberated in her chest.

A boom resounded in her ears.

A wave of heat propelled her forward and sent her tumbling to the ground. Shrapnel rained down around her and several nails bounced off the ground.

And all she knew was Zack, holding her, shielding her with his body.

THIRTEEN

ZACK STUCK OUT HIS FOOT TO HALT THE MO-mentum that kept them rolling. He tugged Naya closer to himself. His leg skidded across the gravel until they came to a stop. Specks of dirt burned his eyes, and he blinked.

An explosive?

The fuse poking out from the capped end of the pipe had alerted him to the danger.

Someone had tried to kill them.

The heat from the blast was so intense that the back of his shirt stuck to him with sweat, and Zack breathed hard. Naya's body trembled next to him, and he eased up on his grip to give her room.

"Are you hurt?" Zack slid back so she could sit up. His shoulder throbbed, and pain radiated down his arm. Blood and small pebbles caked his forearm where the skin had broken.

"I think I'm okay."

He pushed aside the pounding of his own injuries. As long as she was okay, that's what mattered.

A few minor cuts covered her face, and some leaves were caught in her hair. He reached out his hand and plucked the leaves and let them fall to the ground. Then he used the pad of his thumb to wipe away dirt on her forehead.

"I hope I didn't injure your arm more." He scanned her face, waiting for an accusation or indication that she was hurt more than she let on.

"I'd rather be hurt than dead. You saved me." She offered him a faint smile.

Zack gulped. He stared at her, and his thoughts drifted.

Either of them could have died just now.

Were both of them the intended target in this attack?

She had enough trauma to handle from the attack the other day, and the news about her brother cut through his heart. He'd made it his duty to be her big brother when they'd first met in foster care.

Two broken kids finding solace.

"Zack." Naya waved her hands in front of him. "Did you black out?" Then she shrieked. "That fire is getting close to the trees."

He whipped his head around, and a wave of lightheadedness clouded his vision.

Wrong move.

He put his hand to his cheek to massage the corner of his eye. But when he pulled away, his palm was stained red. He'd have to assess the extent of the injury later. Right now, they needed to stop a wildfire before it started.

Flames engulfed the vehicle and licked at the grass along the gravel road. Smoke rose in the air. Tall oak trees stood a few feet off the path. It was only a matter of time before the leaves succumbed to fueling the blaze.

"Call 9-1-1. Tell them we need the fire department and police here, stat." He tossed her his phone and stood up. "I'm going to find something to contain the flames before they get worse. I won't go far." The gravel road could work in their favor, keeping the fire in a contained area, but they'd have to work fast.

They were close to the main road, which meant the stream that ran through the mountain trail should be nearby. But was there enough time to get the water up here?

Naya called dispatch while he searched for anything that could hold liquid, or a way to smother the fire with dirt.

Footsteps descended behind him, and a twig snapped. Was her attacker back?

He spun, prepared to defend himself with his fists.

"It's just me." Naya held up her good hand. "I'm going to help you put out the fire."

"Sorry." Zack grimaced.

He found a few pieces of wood that had broken apart in a U-shape. Thick enough to hold dirt. It would be slow going, but at least it was a way to starve the fire of oxygen.

Zack handed Naya one of the pieces. "Shovel some dirt into here. We can throw it on the fire."

Naya followed his lead. They threw dirt on the edges of the grass, which smothered some flames.

"It's working. Keep at it." Zack shoveled more dirt into his makeshift basin.

A few minutes later, sirens pierced the air.

Zack raced back to the road but kept his distance from the car. He braced his hands on his thighs to catch his breath.

Engine 14 screeched to a stop, blocking the width of the road. Amelia hopped out, decked in her black-and-yellow reflective gear. The other crew members, Izan, Zoe, and Della, followed behind. "Let's get the hoses started. I want a trench around here. Don't let the flames touch any kindling."

Izan pulled out the hose and ran it toward the blaze while Della cranked the wheel to start the water.

Zoe grabbed a pickaxe and began to rip out the grass to make a barrier.

They'd come.

Zack knew what to do to put the fire out. But with the rest of the squad and their equipment here, he wouldn't have to face the blaze alone.

Two police cruisers whipped around the corner and parked behind the engine followed by an ambulance. A few seconds later, Basuto climbed from one while Ramble and Wilcox stepped out of the other.

"You two okay?" Basuto looked between Zack and Naya.

"I think so." Zack turned to Naya, who nodded.

Basuto raised a brow like he didn't quite believe them.

Trace stepped up next to Basuto. "I'll be the judge of that." He frowned.

"Whoever did this needs to be stopped." Naya piped up. "Before someone gets killed."

"What happened?" Ramble pulled out a pen and paper.

They all walked over to the ambo so Trace could evaluate Zack and Naya.

"Someone put a pipe bomb on my car." Zack pinched his lips.

How had anyone known they were going to be up here? He hadn't paid attention for a tail, but he also hadn't thought there'd been a need to. Surely he would have noticed someone behind them. The service road wasn't that wide.

Wilcox stood with her arms crossed, looking every bit the detective she was. "And why would someone place an explosive in your gas tank, Stephens?"

Zack shifted his stance. He tried not to glance at the burning car that his colleagues were working to put out. He'd brought them all into this mess, and yet they hadn't responded to the situation any differently than if this were a callout for someone else.

Zack didn't know whether to be grateful or annoyed.

"Someone wants to silence me." Naya spoke up before Zack had a chance to explain the situation with his parents. "I filed a report yesterday when someone attacked and pushed me over the edge of the overlook." Naya talked with her hand, but her fingers shook.

Zack wanted to take her hand in his and still the tremors. Now wasn't the time to provide solace. He'd certainly get a few stares from the officers if it looked like he and Naya were more than friends.

Besides, it would be a lie.

"Yes. I remember. Walk me through it again, please," Wilcox said.

Naya explained the situation with the story she'd been tasked to write. The note. The attack. This. She recounted it all.

Lieutenant Basuto folded his arms. "We've got a lot of conflicting opinions with both of the groups involved in this mess. With the protests and the fire at Callahan's, it doesn't surprise me someone wants the truth to remain hidden."

"We found evidence," Zack added. "Although it's burned to a crisp now. There was a key chain shaped like a globe and some type of burlap bag. Similar to a sandbag." He pointed to Della, who carried one from the truck to spread on the fire. "Like that. But not quite."

"Are you able to ID your attacker? Or did you notice anyone today?" Wilcox wrote down a few notes.

"I wish. But no." Naya sighed. "I'm pretty sure it was a guy who pushed me, though. He had a ball cap on and kept his head low, but his stature was indicative of a male. And he was strong."

Zack wanted to tug her to his side. "The incident today might not have been the same person." He needed to give them details about his parents. Otherwise they might miss a lead that could point them to the attacker. "My parents were killed when I was a child. Arson. I started looking into their file again to try to find who's responsible for their deaths."

"What are their names?" Basuto's radio squawked with intel on another incident, and he turned down the volume.

"Douglas and Callie Nelson. It's a cold case from twenty-three years ago." Zack's throat and eyes burned at the mention of his parents, although maybe it was from the smoke in the air. "The bomb was planted on *my* car. What if it was done by someone who doesn't want me uncovering decades-old secrets?"

Wilcox scrunched up her nose but still wrote the information down. "It's a long shot, but right now any theory is a good theory. No one is willing to risk either of your lives on an assumption."

"You're both cleared." Trace closed up his bag. "But you should take it easy."

Zack nodded. "I'll make sure of it."

"You guys need a ride back to town?" Ramble closed his pad.

Zack turned to the fire crew. He couldn't just leave them here to finish putting out the blaze without checking in.

He jogged over to Amelia. "Do you need any help?"

She took a sip of water before putting back on her helmet. "No way. We got it under control. You should go home and take it easy."

Zack stared at the blackened metal that lay in a mangled heap. Smoke continued to rise from the ground, but no flames surfaced.

"Go, Stephens." She shooed him away.

Zack turned to see Naya sliding into the backseat of Wilcox's car. He ran back over and slid in after her.

Wilcox pulled out. "You said your car is at the café in town?"

"That's right." Naya's voice sounded small.

They were both dusty, and the backseat of this car would smell like smoke for a while after they got out.

While the detective drove through town, Zack's mind raced with different ways this day could have ended and all the possibilities of what this attack could mean. He needed to write it out in order to work through the threads. Yet his body screamed at him to rest.

Now that the adrenaline had started to wear off, his muscles hurt with the slightest movement. Like getting out of Wilcox's car and into Naya's.

His cheek burned, and Zack rubbed the bandaged area.

"Do you need a new Band-Aid? I have a first aid kit." Naya smiled despite the hint of dirt still on her cheek. She leaned over to the glove compartment and pulled out a white box.

"Nah. It's just tender. But at this point, you're a pro at being my nurse." For a split second, Zack wasn't sitting in Naya's car but on the bathroom floor so many years ago.

"Sit still so I can clean your face." Naya playfully hit his shoulder. "Hold this to your eye too." She handed him a cold paper towel to help with the bruising that was sure to draw attention at school tomorrow.

He couldn't even remember what that fight had been about now.

All he remembered was Naya.

Zack squinted at the bright light that streamed in through her car window.

"You did good today. With Hudson." Naya closed the glove box and shifted back in her seat.

"Thanks." Zack rested his arm on the center console next to hers.

He swallowed, trying not to think of how close they were in this enclosed space. It was one thing to have let Naya take care of him when they were kids. Back then girls had cooties, and she'd only been a friend. Now she was a grown woman who carried herself with poise and grace. The whole package added another dynamic that left his heart wanting to explore more.

Zack trailed his finger down her hand, then took hers in his. His pulse throbbed in his thumb.

Could she feel it too? They were both still breathing. Still alive.

What if this was his chance to make things right between them? Show Naya that she could trust him. That he wouldn't leave her side again—the promise he'd broken once when they were teens.

Naya squeezed his hand and leaned forward. "Thanks for getting us out of that car," she whispered.

Zack brushed his hand against her cheek to remove the dirt

still there, then drew her to himself. He wanted to hold her and never let go. But would she let him in again?

Naya rested her head against his shoulder. The smell of smoke in her hair wafted into his nostrils but he didn't care. He wanted to be her safe place.

"I'd do anything for you, Nay." He kissed her cheek, ready to leave a trail of them along the side of her face.

Naya sucked in a breath and pulled away. "Zack, I can't." Her eyelids dropped. "Not now." She tucked her hands in her lap.

It didn't take long to imagine how the cold would seep into the space between them. Zack gritted his teeth. He'd failed her once, so why did he think she'd be willing to give it another go?

"I never meant to hurt you." Zack fisted his hand and covered his mouth.

Lord, I care about Naya. A lot. Show me how I can pursue her and earn her trust.

She had told him *not now*. A very different response from *never*. He wasn't going to let this deter him. Not from keeping her safe. And not from showing her that he could be the man who treated her right.

"It's in the past." She sighed.

Zack didn't believe her. The way he'd left without a word, never reaching out to hear how she was doing, had wedged a barrier between them. Zack didn't want to consider the possibility of the past being unmovable.

So he'd keep praying he could show her that she could trust him. Before it was too late.

Whether that person had intended for Naya to be with him today or not didn't change the fact that she could have been hurt far worse.

Zack wished his dad were here to tell him what to do. To help him make sense of it all.

But he wasn't, because someone had committed arson.

R, son.

Just remember the most important word in your vocabulary. It was so important I had to tell other people about it. R, son.

No, he didn't want to relive that moment right now.

"I want to believe you. I just need time." Naya's words sliced through the silence.

"I want to give that to you." He'd wait until she was ready. "You know, my dad was the most patient person ever."

"You want to talk about it?"

Did he? Not really. But saying it aloud might help keep it from occupying his thoughts. "It's silly. My dad would play the 'R game' with me when I was little. To help me practice pronunciation. Said it was the most important word in my vocabulary."

Naya stared at him. Eyes attentive.

Zack sat up straighter to imitate his dad. "R, son. It's important. So important I had to tell other people about it. There's a lot of sentences you can make with r-words. Like this one: rats only go empty'n rivers."

Naya's eyes creased with a smile.

"He helped me with so much." Zack needed to visit their graves again. It had been too long.

"He sounds like a great dad. I would have loved to meet him."

His parents might not be here anymore, but he could honor them by finding out what had happened that fatal day. Even more than that, Zack could aspire to be half the man his dad had been. A man of patience and integrity.

"No matter what happens, Naya, I promise I'm not leaving."

Because after today, one thing was clear. Someone had ramped up their threats. But why? And who was the intended target?

FOURTEEN

"I'M TRYING NOT TO FREAK OUT HERE." NAYA spoke to Ingram on the phone. She opened her closet in search of a professional yet comfy outfit. "He kissed me on the cheek yesterday, then told me no matter what happened, he wasn't going to leave." Naya pulled a patterned blue-and-yellow blouse from a hanger and tossed it on her bed with a pair of dark-wash jeans.

Ingram squealed. "Girl, he likes you."

"Yeah, well, he broke my heart once. The thought of it happening again is terrifying."

"I don't want to negate your feelings, but do you know that for a fact?" Ingram asked.

After several long minutes, thanks to the sling, Naya finished changing and sighed. "We were best friends one day, and the next he was gone. No goodbye. Even his grandma's house went up for sale." Naya plopped down on the edge of her bed. The clock reminded her she only had forty-five minutes until she'd told Zack she would pick him up. She'd crashed and slept for ten hours thanks to the events of yesterday.

"Has he done anything to make you question his character?"

Naya slid her hand through her hair. "Nothing that I can think of." Zack had protected her yesterday. "He didn't leave me in the car. Or on the mountain either. If that's not enough," Naya laughed, "he's even reminded me of the truth of God's word." A smile parted her lips. "He's not only shown interest in what matters to me; he cares about what Jesus is doing in me."

"Girl, he's a keeper. I wish Will reminded me more of the truth."

"Zack seems to always have a desire to do what is right." The ways Zack had matured from a boy into a man reeled her heart in faster than the tips that came in on a reporter's hotline. "I just don't know what to do." Naya stood up and grabbed a ponytail from her dresser and attempted to secure her hair in an updo with one hand. It was messy but it would do.

"I think you know what to do, but your mind is telling you a different story."

Naya propped her hands on the dresser and stared at her reflection in the mirror. "It's just a far cry from what I've experienced with other guys. Including Tucker."

"Ask Zack what happened when you were teens. When he left. It'll give your heart closure. It might even help you both move on in the right direction. Together."

Together.

"The thought of partnering on anything with anyone makes my stomach hurt. I *know* Zack is different, but it doesn't fit with the reality I've known for years, of others looking out for themselves, leaving me in the dust." Hurt and alone.

Before Naya could come up with another excuse, Ingram said, "I'll be praying the Lord gives you courage to have that conversation. Sooner rather than later."

Naya chuckled. She could picture her friend, head cocked, eyebrows raised. "Thanks, Grams."

Her phone pinged with another message.

"Looks like someone else is seeking a heart change." Naya scrolled through the words. "Tucker texted. An apology about how he handled things when we saw him at Ethos and when I saw him at Callahan's."

"Good. That boy needed to be put in his place."

"Except he didn't apologize for writing the note."

"That's some serious downplaying of what happened."

"You don't say." Naya sighed. "Drew told me he followed through and spoke with Tucker about professional etiquette."

"Well, Tucker still has some manning up to do then," Ingram said.

"It's a matter of getting through that big head of his, which might take a while." So were Tucker's words sincere? It seemed more plausible that he would continue with his sarcastic comments and prideful attitude. "Words on a screen only hold so much weight. I'll have to talk to him myself. Get a better read on his demeanor." Which reminded her to follow up with Zack about Tucker's whereabouts the other day. "I have to get going." Naya grabbed a pair of flats from her shoe rack and headed to the kitchen. "Zack and I are meeting with one of his dad's former friends."

"Give Zack the benefit of the doubt. The truth may surprise you."

"Maybe." Naya chewed her lip. "It often does surprise me, and usually not in a good way."

Help me see Zack's heart, Lord. Bring the truth into the light.

Naya wanted Zack to be a man she could trust. Dare she say love? But she couldn't get ahead of herself. There was still investigating to do. And unearthing the truth of the past and letting her heart catch up would take time.

All the turmoil and stress made Naya want to curl up and veg out on some *pain patate*, a sweet potato bread pudding dessert her family used to make. She could almost taste the warm, fluffy center. The vanilla and cinnamon wrapping her in a comforting embrace.

Instead, she opted for a protein granola bar. The recent events hadn't allowed for much time in the kitchen.

Fifteen minutes later, Naya pulled up to Zack's house. He jogged down the drive and slid into the passenger seat. "Thanks for not making me call a cab."

Naya feigned a gasp. "That would be cruel of me." After yesterday's events, the lighthearted banter eased the tightness in her shoulders.

As if she had someone else to carry her burdens with her.

Like real friends.

Still, the cuts and bandages on Zack's face reminded her why they were even taking this trip.

Zack provided navigation while they drove, and eventually the houses grew farther apart and traffic waned. They wouldn't have to worry about parallel parking out here. Former fire chief Ricky Powells lived on the other side of town and had agreed to meet with them.

"Thanks for coming along."

"It's the least I can do after all you've done to help me." Naya kept her gaze on the road, one hand on the wheel. A glance at Zack would risk a greater collision than the one in her heart. His car was already totaled. She didn't need to add hers to the tally.

"Powells told us to park around back and use the deck door. Said there's an old gas station parking lot we can pull into."

"I hope this turns out to be worthwhile." Naya glanced in the rearview mirror before making a left-hand turn, to ensure no one was following them.

The gas station was closed down, and the building was falling apart. A few shingles littered the pavement, and a dumpster sat to the side.

Naya took a deep breath. "You ready?" She studied Zack's face. This meeting might be difficult for him. Dredging up memories of the past. Reminders of what no longer existed.

“Ready or not.” Zack shrugged.

Naya didn’t believe this was no big deal to him. She took his hand in hers and squeezed it—a gesture she’d started back when they’d been next-door neighbors. A simple reminder that he wasn’t alone.

This moment was important for Zack. For his own sake, she wanted him to find the truth and get closure. He had to realize that he wasn’t to blame for his parents’ deaths.

“Well, partner, let’s get this show on the road.” Naya opened the door.

Powells’s backyard stood three hundred feet from the gas station. Six other houses lined the area. Each property had enough space to warrant a riding lawn mower.

Arborvitaes lined the perimeter of Powells’s house.

“He seems to like his privacy.” Zack brushed back a few branches and followed the stone path to Powells’s deck.

“It’s quite a nice house for a single guy too. It must be lonely living out here by himself.”

“If that’s how he wants to live, that’s his choice.” Zack surveyed the area around them before stepping up to the back door.

Naya’s shoulders relaxed. They were both on alert. No one had followed them out here, and with the tree covering, it would be easy to spot something—or rather, someone—who shouldn’t be in the backyard.

Zack pressed the doorbell. It sounded deep into the house.

A middle-aged man opened the door a crack. He peered out from the corner. “You Stephens?”

“Yes, sir. Thanks for agreeing to meet with us.” Zack motioned to Naya. “This is my friend, Naya Michél.”

Powells ushered them inside, then locked the door. “Have a seat.” He showed them to the dining room table. The space was void of any personal touches. Minimal light peeked through the closed curtains. A damp, musty smell filtered through the air, and Naya shivered.

The man was sturdy, a guy who'd been built for his job, but his face was hard. Stoic. Gray peppered his brown locks, and he bore wrinkles that showed the toll his work had taken on him over the years. He wore a flannel and whitewashed jeans that were well past their prime.

Zack cleared his throat.

Naya didn't want to overstep boundaries, so she waited for one of the men to speak up. This was Zack's battle. Often the best information came from being silent and observing body language.

Powells's shoulders remained rigid, and his eyes fixated on everything around the house but his guests.

"All these years I believed my parents' deaths were an accident that I was to blame for." Zack scooted closer to the table. "That's what *you* told me. The report tells a different story. Arson. You want to help me understand what that means? Why I was told a different narrative?"

This man had been a friend to Zack's dad and a witness to his parents' deaths. He should have known better than to instill a lie in a child—the lie that Zack was responsible for what had happened to his mom and dad.

She couldn't imagine how hard it had been for him. Losing them. Believing he was at fault. Not knowing the truth told a different story. And now, he was so close to finding out what had happened.

Give him the benefit of the doubt. The truth might surprise you. Ingram's response echoed in her mind. What if the truth of Zack's disappearance was different than what she'd believed all these years? She tucked the thought away for later. Right now, she needed to focus on the situation in front of her.

Lord, is he going to find answers, or will all this be for nothing?

Naya wanted to help him find closure and move on. No matter what it took.

She owed their friendship that, at least.

"There wasn't much. Not much for good reason." Powells swallowed, his Adam's apple bobbing. "I'd have put my life in jeopardy by sharing anything."

"So you kept quiet and made sure I believed it was all my fault." Zack gripped the edge of the table.

The man licked his lips. His eyes blinked fast.

Naya said, "You're still scared?" It had been years since that incident.

Zack just stared at the former fire chief.

"So I'm supposed to tell you what I know, then read about a fire in the paper that took your life?" Powells stared at them. "Same as your parents?"

"That fire was arson. Something my dad used to stay has stuck with me all these years. 'R, son. It's so important I had to tell other people.' I thought it was a way to help me learn to enunciate my *r*'s. But now I'd beg to differ. Did he tell you what's so important about the R?" Zack's gaze never wavered from Powells.

The man blinked and averted his eyes to the ground. If it wasn't for the dimly lit area, Naya guessed she'd see sweat breaking out on the guy's brow.

"You have no idea what you're asking for." Powells swallowed.

"To have a chance to find the truth and not live with misplaced guilt. That's what I'm asking for." Zack steeled his jaw.

Naya wasn't going to let Zack fight this alone. "The truth is beautiful because it sheds light on darkness and exposes it."

Powells's attention bored into her. "The truth gets good people killed."

"I'm not afraid of it." Naya lifted her chin.

"You should be."

Zack laid a hand over hers. "You know what happened to them." He let out a breath. "Tell me what it was that got them killed."

Naya nodded. "Then we can figure out who is behind it, and they can finally get justice."

"You don't give up, do you, girlie?"

No, I don't. Naya just wasn't sure if this was about the truth or the fact that it would help Zack.

Powells leaned back in his chair and sighed. "Douglas—your dad—he was a great guy. No matter what it was, his conscience wouldn't let him rest until he did the right thing." He glanced at Naya. "Like someone else you know."

"Doesn't sound like a bad thing." She shrugged.

He shook his head. "It is when you get killed over it. He paid the price."

"What do you mean?" Zack narrowed his eyes and leaned into the table. "What did he know?"

Naya held her breath. The truth of what had happened to Zack's parents could cost him more than he'd bargained for. What if this was a mistake? What if her quest for truth came with consequences neither of them could reverse?

"Your dad was supposed to sign off on a product to go to distribution that had high toxicity levels and would have a negative, long-lasting impact on the community."

Naya pulled out a pen and scribbled down some notes.

"Your dad came to me and asked for my help. He was convinced it was poison. In the testing stages it was effective. But the cost was the death of all the mice in the lab. Your dad couldn't just let the higher-ups make such a detrimental call." Powells grimaced. "When execs found out that your dad talked to me, they threatened me. Told me I would regret it if I said anything." Powells rubbed his jaw. "I couldn't afford to lose my job so I told Douglas to let it go. He didn't have the power to change anything."

"But he didn't give it up," Zack whispered.

Powells shook his head. "Your dad told me if the product went to the market, my firehouse would be first in line to use it. And suddenly my own ethics were put in the hot seat."

"What was the product?" Naya looked up from her paper.

"Firefighting foam. Basically a commercial grade fire extinguisher."

Naya and Zack both looked at each other. He said, "How was that bad?"

"More fluorine was added to the foam because of its performance-boosting effects. But the chemical also contains high levels of PFAS. Any runoff from the use of one would contaminate the ground and water supply long term."

Naya's breath hitched. "How'd he figure it out?"

"He was in charge of all the safety data sheets. Including what chemicals were used in each product creation." Powells rubbed a hand down his face. "He showed me the list. Did some research. Confirmed the toxicity levels of the fluorine in the products were way too high for human exposure."

"Have you been following the news lately?"

"Why would I?" The man's brow furrowed. "There's more than enough for me to worry about for myself without getting entangled in other people's drama. I learned that the hard way with Douglas."

Naya blinked. "So you'd rather save your own skin?"

"I warned you, didn't I?" Powells stood up. "I really hope this doesn't bring more trouble on you, but I can't be part of it."

"Your friend was killed by people determined to bury the truth." Naya stood up, though with her smaller height, it didn't put them on an equal footing. "All you're going to do is hide? People are getting sick from water contamination. More people will lose their lives if you don't say something."

"I've already said more than enough. It's time for the two of you to leave." He ushered them toward the door.

Zack crossed his arms. “I think you need—”

Glass shattered next to them, and the window broke inward, spraying across the room. Something rolled across the floor, spewing out flames.

Naya screamed.

A pop followed. A whoosh filled the space, and the curtains caught fire.

FIFTEEN

ZACK GRABBED NAYA'S SHOULDERS AND PULLED her and Powells away from the flames. "Stay back. Naya, call 9-1-1."

She nodded, already reaching for her phone.

The once dark room was now illuminated by an unwanted orange glow. One that was too close to the kitchen cabinets. Soon, the whole house would be on fire.

"Where's your fire extinguisher?" Zack yelled.

Powells cupped his hands. "Under the sink."

Zack kept his back flush to the wall and skirted past the flames in front of him. The heat stung his face, but he wouldn't let it deter him. Not when someone wanted the place to crumble into a heap of ashes—with them inside it. He wrapped his hand inside his shirt before he pulled on the handle, just in case it was hot.

He grabbed the fire extinguisher from its holder and pulled the pin. Zack couldn't think about the irony of the situation now. Using a product his dad had died for in order to save Naya and Powells from the same fate.

Foam spewed from the canister, and smoke rose from the curtains.

Zack let out a cough and buried his mouth close to his chest.

Powells raced to his side with a bucket and splashed the water along the curtains. The flames hissed before going dark, and more gray smoke billowed up to the ceiling and out of the window.

They needed to get out of here. If the fire didn't get to them, the smoke inhalation would.

"I knew they'd come back. I never should have agreed to this meeting." Powells dropped the pail on the floor with a clank.

"Who? Tell me who did this."

Maybe the former fire chief was right. If it meant more people were at risk of getting hurt, Zack should stop his investigation. Let whoever was behind his parents' deaths live with the guilty conscience.

But what would that solve?

He was more determined than ever to get to the truth now. Before someone else got killed.

Zack set the extinguisher down, and glass crunched under his feet. Giant shards from a bottle littered the ground. He could still make out the partial logo on one piece. Someone had concocted a Molotov cocktail.

His chest burned. Zack wanted answers. He would do what he could to honor his parents' memory and not let the truth die with them. He wouldn't let it be in vain.

He turned from the debris where Powells stood by the doorway. "Where's Naya?"

Zack spun around, but she wasn't in the dining room.

"I thought she followed me to get a bucket of water from the bathroom." Powells turned to the hall.

Zack raced by him, opening each door. "Naya?" Had she passed out somewhere?

Each room was void of anyone. Smoke laced the air, and he couldn't yet hear sirens outside. Where was help?

"We need to get outside now." Zack found Powells staring at his living room, everything covered in black soot.

"Let's go." Zack yanked the man's arm.

Powells laced his fingers through his hair and coughed.

Once he got the chief outside, he'd go back in for Naya. Zack clenched his jaw, the muscles in his neck and shoulders already taut. He wanted to shake the man. Tell him to think harder. Where was she?

He opened the back door and ran onto the deck, Powells next to him. The fresh air burned his throat yet helped him breathe easier. "I'm going back in. You scan the front and back." Zack pointed to the edge of the property.

Through the clearing, a figure moved off in the distance near the dilapidated gas station. It was too far away to make out who, though. Naya?

Zack tore through the grass to close the distance. It was her. "Naya!"

Tires squealed and dust kicked up from the parking lot.

She limped toward the car, but the vehicle sped out of sight.

When Zack caught up to her, Naya was standing on the pavement with her hand on her hip. "I almost had the license plate." She groaned. "If it wasn't for my sore ankle..." Naya bent forward, breathing hard.

"What were you doing?" His question came out in short gasps. Zack kept his focus on the road in case the car decided to circle back around. He couldn't afford to be caught off guard if they came for another try.

Where were the police?

Naya straightened. "Trying to catch the guy who did this. But I wasn't fast enough."

"It's a good thing you weren't. You could have gotten yourself killed." Zack swallowed.

The weight of those words lodged in his throat. Not only would he have lost the girl who'd once been his best friend, but he would have lost his chance to pursue her. The thought of not having Naya in his life sucked the oxygen out from around him.

He wanted Naya to be more than his friend.

"How could I let them get away when we're so close to exposing the truth?" Naya folded her good arm overtop of her injured one.

"Is it worth it if people get hurt?" Zack rubbed the nape of his neck, then let his hands drop to his side.

Naya lowered her voice. "The truth always costs something."

And that's what Zack was afraid of. Her tenacity might be admirable in one regard, but if he let her help, her life would be at risk.

For Naya's safety, he needed her to step aside.

"I don't want you investigating my parents' case anymore. It was a mistake for me to even let you help."

Naya sucked in a breath. "I thought we both wanted the same thing here."

"Not if it means I put your life on the line." He still wanted justice for his parents, but not if she got even more hurt.

Naya closed the gap between them and tapped a finger on his chest. "You want to do what's right."

Zack couldn't believe Powells was saving himself at the expense of the truth. The guy had been doing it for a while, too. Blaming Zack for his parents' deaths.

"And look where that got my dad." Zack's nostrils flared. "You heard Powells. My dad couldn't rest until the truth was told, and it cost him his life."

"Your dad did the right thing." Naya pouted. "And you're not a coward, unlike Powells. He kept the secrets and hid, but what has that done for him?"

Zack groaned. She was right. This was why Naya pushed so hard for answers. For truth. He now understood the need for a story to be told no matter the cost. But how could they reconcile the two things? "I don't know how to find the truth and keep you safe."

"I can hold my own." Naya lifted her chin.

"I have no doubt you have the strength for the task." Zack shook his head. "But even my dad's determination didn't stop the production of the equipment he tried to keep off the market." His dad hadn't known when to stop, and now Naya was headed down the same path. "Sometimes the consequences are far too great."

"So you just want to sit on the sidelines and believe the lie that you were to blame for your parents' deaths when Powells kept silent to save his own skin?" Naya's eyes widened. "That man was your father's friend. And for what? To watch your dad do what was right and get killed for it? Justice for your parents won't happen if the truth remains hidden." She jabbed her finger in the air. "I know the risks of my job."

There. That was the problem. She'd just admitted to it. "This isn't part of your job." Bryce had given Zack a task to complete, and he couldn't do his work if he was worried Naya would be caught in the crossfire. The last thing he needed was Naya injured—or worse, dead—because of him. "You're right. I've lived long enough believing I was the reason for my parents' deaths. But I'm not about to add any more to my conscience." He ground his teeth.

Saving people who couldn't save themselves was Zack's job.

He kept trouble from wreaking havoc on someone else's life.

Naya might not be able to see it now, but he was protecting her in the long run. He just hoped she listened to reason and focused on the story she needed to write, without letting him muddy the waters.

"I'll decide what leads I need to follow as part of my job." Naya waved her hand in the air. "I should have known we'd get to this point." Her gaze traveled down to his wrist.

Zack shoved his hand in his pocket. He should give her the bracelet back. It was a way he'd promised to protect her and look after her. And that's exactly what he was doing now. Except she didn't view his efforts in the same light.

"I'm doing this for your own good." Why couldn't she see that he could be trusted?

Sirens pierced the air.

Zack sighed. "We'll finish this conversation later. We need to go check on Powells. And talk to the police."

"Fine." Naya crossed her arms.

They walked back to the house and around to the front yard. Powells sat on the front step, his hands clasped.

Officer Ramble stood on the sidewalk.

Amelia and the engine crew had a supply line hooked up to the fire hydrant, and they scoured the area.

"Did you fill the police in yet?" Zack turned back to the former chief.

Powells's eyes widened. "And get entangled in this mess even more? No way." He shot up and crossed the yard.

"Part of his house is ruined, and he's just going to let whoever did this get away with it?" Naya shook her head.

"We'll worry about him later." Ramble pulled a pen from his shirt pocket.

"The fire's out. I don't need you here." Powells swung his hand in the air. Izan stood his ground next to the hydrant. "The next thing you know, the news crew will be here. I don't need more attention drawn to the scene."

"I suggest you back up and let us do our job, sir." Amelia stared Powells down.

Zack and Naya gave their statements to Ramble. "Do you need anything else from us?" Zack glanced at his watch.

"Everything's covered." Ramble hooked his thumb over his shoulder. "We'll take care of Powells."

"Good. I need to get to the firehouse. My shift starts soon."

"I'll drop you off," Naya said.

They headed back to her car, and Naya unlocked the door.

"Wait." Zack held out his hand to stop her from touching the handle. "Let me check first. Make sure there aren't any surprises."

Sure enough, a tiny black dot sat right underneath the license plate. An attempt to mimic a backup camera. "I think we're all good now." He held up the tracking device, then set it on the ground and crushed it with his foot.

One more reason to add to the growing list for why Naya needed to heed his warning and step back from helping him with his parents' case.

Forty-five minutes later, Naya pulled into the firehouse. Zack kept a change of clothes in the locker room, which would come in handy so he didn't smell like smoke the entire shift.

His hand hovered over the door handle. "Do you need anything?" he asked. Part of him was afraid to leave Naya alone. There was no telling if or when someone might attack again.

"I'll be fine. I'm going to head into the office to get some work done."

He opened the door and stepped out, then leaned back inside. "Please, be careful. And focus on your *real* job."

Naya kept her hands tucked around the steering wheel. "I'll do my job while you do yours." Her forehead creased.

Once Naya drove away, Zack walked into the firehouse and headed for the locker room. He was prepared to handle his parents' case alone. This was his battle to fight, and he wouldn't put Naya's life on the line while he investigated.

But a sinking feeling rested in his stomach.

Zack might have learned from his mistakes, but the past still had a way of repeating itself.

He could only pray he and Naya lived long enough to rewrite the ending.

SIXTEEN

NAYA PULLED INTO THE TRIBUNE'S PARKING LOT and keyed into the building. Each step on the metal staircase resounded with a clank, and it only made her want to make the noise more prominent. If it weren't for her ankle, she'd stomp.

The conversation with Zack still reeled in her mind.

No one had followed her to the office, which was a good sign. But after the situation at Powells's house, she wanted to get to the bottom of this story even more. Her nerves tingled, and she couldn't get into her cubicle fast enough.

She called Ingram and put her phone between her shoulder and ear, then fired up her computer and opened a new browser.

"I have so much to fill you in on. You're never going to believe this." Naya didn't even say hello. She wanted to cut straight to the point.

"Well, at least one of us doesn't lead a boring life." Ingram chuckled. "What's up?"

"Are you at work right now?"

"Where else would I be on Thursday afternoon, Nay?" Her friend had a playfulness to her tone.

"Just checking. I found something out about Ethos that changes the whole playing field." Naya lowered her voice to a whisper.

She'd called Ingram on her cell phone, so it wasn't like anyone from the company would overhear what she was about to share. But she didn't want to take the risk.

The former chief's confession about the firefighting foam being the cause of the upheaval and the distrust Zack's dad had of the company rubbed her the wrong way. Those chemicals could contaminate water.

Naya picked up the picture of Dominic and herself. *I won't let anyone else's story go untold, Dom. Your life was valuable, and so are these other people's lives.* "It won't be in vain."

"What won't?"

Naya hadn't realized she'd spoken the thought aloud.

"Zack and I just got back from a meeting with the former fire chief on the west side of town. The information he shared brought back memories of Dom."

Douglas Nelson, firefighting foam, ProEco Plant.

Naya typed in the keywords, and several results populated the screen.

"I'm sorry, Nay."

"Don't be. It's fueled why I write." Naya rubbed the back of her neck. "But Zack doesn't see it that way. He wants me to stop searching and let it go." How did he have the audacity to tell her to back down after he'd been the one to let her help with his parents' case? Zack's comment earlier stung. Telling her to focus on her job had been a slap on the face, like she didn't have anything of value to offer him.

"What if he's afraid? All your nosiness, no matter how well-intended, could get you hurt. He's been able to witness that firsthand with this other story you're working on."

Naya opened different articles in separate tabs and perused the information. Pictures were included in one of the posts, and Naya picked out Douglas right away. A mirror image of Zack. Probably close to the age his son was now.

Naya paused for a moment and sighed.

"That's just it. Douglas was too young when he died. Like my dad when he left." Gone too soon.

"What if heeding Zack's advice is a chance to not lose someone else you care about?" Ingram spoke softly.

"When did you get to be so wise?"

"I just care about my friend."

Naya closed her eyes and could still picture her dad's hand in hers. The way he'd cared for her with his gentle tone and hugs that always comforted her. Or when Dominic had gotten sick. She and her dad had stayed by Dom's side. Ready to stay there until he got better so they could go outside and play again. Except he never had gotten better.

Why, God? Why?

"I have to fight for them, Grams. Because if I don't, who will? Zack needs someone to stand by his side too. To show him his parents' deaths haven't been in vain. That he wasn't to blame for their deaths either." Like a treasure hunter, Naya intended to locate the key that would pop the top off.

"I want to help him get the answers he's searching for. I want to do this for Zack."

Ingram said, "You should want to help Zack. The truth always requires risk. But there are many ways you can show Zack you care."

"It's just a matter of knowing which choice to make." Naya propped her elbows on her desk. Was staying silent the best option? She'd seen the ways silence left destruction that could never be reversed in its wake.

Like Zack hiding his wrist when she spotted the red bracelet again. The truth was disguised in his eyes—the full story of what had actually happened that day when he'd disappeared. Yet Zack still hadn't shared all the details with her. To her knowledge, he'd made a promise to her, then broken it by disappearing without any trace or explanation. Leaving her to pick up the pieces of a heart that had just begun to hope again. Proof of the consequences that came with not speaking up.

The hurt, confusion, and mistrust that resulted from unspoken words.

Still, here she was, helping him behind the scenes because she wanted him to find the truth and move on in life. Wanted to be the helper he needed in his life, the one who understood him in a way no one else did.

Could she be that for him?

God, is this what You have for us?

The idea was like the first rays of sun in the morning, a glimpse of what could be. The promise of warmth and light.

Naya opened up the next article and stopped scrolling halfway through. She sucked in a sharp inhale.

Her gut instinct had paid off. "Guess what I just found? Zack's dad did get a new boss and office. Ethos bought out another company almost three decades ago. That company was ProEco Plant. The employer Zack's dad originally worked for before Ethos took over." Naya squirmed in her seat. "And get this—we know now that Ethos was responsible for adding extra fluorine to the foam that can cause long-term harm to people if it gets in the ground water."

Ingram let out a whistle. "That feels too close to home. How did you put that together?"

"Zack's dad was a chemist, and Zack mentioned his dad getting a new boss and office. If the company dissolved and Ethos took over, of course there would be a transition. And when his dad tried to blow the whistle, he died."

Footsteps and voices sounded outside her cubicle.

Naya swiveled in her desk chair. Her heart pounded in her ears.

Soon, whoever had been nearby walked away. She sank back into the chair and loosened her shoulders.

"Nay, this is serious."

"I know, right? This could be the story of the year." Of course, there were still missing pieces that needed a place in the puzzle, but it was a start.

"No. I mean this is serious for you. For both of us. Douglas was killed for what he knew, and you've already been targeted. The car explosion and a fire at the former chief's house? That's serious, Nay." Ingram sighed. "If someone finds out we both have intel, who knows what they'll do?"

"Now you sound like Zack." Naya leaned her head against her hand.

"I get why he told you to stop digging around. He might be on to something there."

"How am I supposed to stay silent when I know details that could keep other people out of harm's way?" Especially when it seemed like his parents' deaths were connected to her story.

She could end up helping him *and* getting what she wanted.

"But do you?" Ingram whispered. "You know information that was true years ago, but facts don't always equal a need for action. There's nothing that can be done about it at this point. What does finding their killer give Zack? It won't bring them back."

Naya didn't want to argue with her friend, but why wasn't anyone seeing her side of the story? "That's exactly why I need to keep digging. Until the answers provide a call to action on the part of whoever is responsible for their deaths. Responsible for hurting people and contaminating the water in Last Chance County." This was her way of caring for the people in her life. Right?

A ding buzzed in Naya's ear, and she put her phone on speaker so she could pull up the notification.

A social media update.

Naya went to exit out of the app, but that's when the picture loaded, along with the notification that she was tagged in the post.

The Green Warriors had posted an update on their protests, and the first image was from the fire with the barrel of fish. Naya was front and center with her pen and paper.

"You still there?" Ingram's voice filtered through the speaker.

"Yeah. Sorry. It looks like I've just made headlines with Green Warriors. Check this out." Naya forwarded Ingram the picture.

"That you have." Ingram paused. "Hey, I know that other girl."

"Which one?"

"The gal sporting the brown shirt."

Naya zoomed in on the picture. "Sylvia?"

"Yeah. She works in one of the departments here at Ethos."

Naya frowned. Apparently, there was more to this photo than met the eye. "What is one of Ethos's workers doing at the protests targeted at the CEO's house?"

"Beats me. But she'll be hounded by management here soon enough."

"That email you all received from Callahan didn't seem to deter her."

"And none of this seems to be doing the same for you either, Naya. At what cost will you stop? You've already been targeted in your car, pushed over a cliff, and almost blown up."

Naya swallowed. Ingram wasn't wrong. "I just want the truth exposed. So those involved are prosecuted and the innocent are informed and able to move on, free from hurt because of other people's choices."

"Nay..." Ingram drew out her name. "I'm saying this because I love you. What is your goal in this? To bring healing to a community or prove a point about what *you* can accomplish? You'll destroy the company I work for whether you have evidence or not, and you won't bring Zack's family back. You just want that promotion."

Naya sucked in a breath. The words stung like ripping a band aid off, exposing the wound underneath. She didn't like what her friend had said, but it didn't make the question any less valid. Because deep down, her own desires waged a war over what to do. She wanted to do her job well *and* bring healing to the community.

"I want both," Naya whispered. Silence lengthened on the other end. Had she just thought her answer or actually verbalized it?

Was she being prideful with her desires? Or were her intentions pure?

God, I want the posture of my heart to please You. Show me how to move forward.

"Tensions are high at the office, and people are growing more combative with each other. Is it really worth stirring up more conflict for the sake of the story?"

"Two people are dead because the company you work for might be hiding a secret. And you don't want conflict between employees?" Naya's cheeks burned. "That's all the more reason to fight for this story."

"You heard my conversation with Will the other day, Naya. People don't like being told what to do. I've been trying to get my concerns on the agenda for a board meeting. But management has a reputation to uphold, and they aren't afraid to make their position in the company known."

Naya leaned back in her chair and took a swig of water.

Too many people were involved in this situation for her to make a selfish move.

Though that didn't give her answers on how she should move forward.

She might solve this case and write the story. But at what cost?

She could lose a friendship with Ingram. If she pressed further, what would that mean for the two of them? Zack had already told her to back down too. Was she willing to give up the chance of exploring a possible future with him?

If neither of her relationships were severed, it could very well cost them their lives. She needed to make a decision, but her future hung in the balance.

SEVENTEEN

ZACK PULLED THE FIREHOUSE GYM WEIGHT UP to his chest, then released the bar and let it bounce on the floor. He picked it up again for another set of reps and blew out a breath. More like steam at this point.

Every muscle in his upper body burned, yet somehow the feeling was therapeutic. There were several tasks still on his to-do list today, including a stop at the Kirbys' house to finalize plans for the New Blooms Spring Festival tomorrow with the boys. Something that had been put on the back burner thanks to all the other events that had him fighting to stay alive. But he needed his head on straight before he completed anything.

Which was why he was listening to worship music through his earbuds. Not exactly the first go-to when working out. But the drumbeat kept the songs moving, and the lyrics motivated him to think on what truly mattered in life.

He'd read through his parents' case again last night and planned to research more about the firefighting foam and extinguishers on the market. Still, the answers he needed seemed hidden behind a fog and left Zack squinting in the haziness to figure out the path forward. It irked him that Powells had information on a culprit but wasn't willing to disclose the name. All of it could end now if the guy spoke up.

Zack put the weights back, then moved to the pull-up bar. He hefted himself up and did a set. The door closed behind him, and Eddie made his way in.

"You're about ready to fly off the wall, man. Practicing to be cast as the next superhero?" Eddie straddled a bench and grinned.

Zack grabbed his water bottle and took a sip, then joined Eddie on the adjacent bench. "You know, I was just thinking that workout might be a good video to add to my application." He laughed.

Although, that was Eddie's area of expertise. His friend had been working toward getting a grant to start up a youth center for underprivileged kids in the community. A place for them to go to stay out of trouble, especially in the wintertime. If the paperwork was approved, Eddie would become those kids' hero like in the movies.

Except, on the big screen, the superheroes didn't really save anyone. There were safety measures already in place, like foam mats and escape routes to make sure no one actually got hurt. And that wasn't the case in real life.

"The hero is supposed to save people from harm, not get them mixed up in more trouble." Zack propped his elbows on his knees.

"Good thing you don't have to be the hero of your own story then." Eddie winked.

Right. He couldn't save himself, or anyone else for that matter. He had the head knowledge of that truth, but the follow-through of living it out proved harder. "I've already been the reason for enough trouble in life. I don't want to let people down."

"How so?" Eddie cocked his head, his eyes focused on Zack.

Zack swallowed. "I've been investigating my parents' cold case." He sighed. "Naya tagged along to help. After the incident at Powells's house, I told her I'd handle it alone."

"She didn't take it too well?" Eddie propped his hands on the bench. "You couldn't have known someone would find out about the investigation and start targeting you. Plus, you can't control someone else's response."

Zack frowned. "I know she can hold her own, but I don't want her getting hurt. Not on my account." Heat rose on the edges of Zack's ears.

"We all want to help each other. Maybe this is her way of showing it."

Zack ran his hand along his jaw. "Naya's back in my life for the first time in years. I finally have a chance to make it right with her. To pursue something more than a friendship. I could even close my parents' case. But risking our lives? I don't know, man."

Please don't let her stubbornness get in the way of wisdom, Lord. And help me know what I should do.

He wanted to show Naya and the team what he had to offer. But he couldn't do that if they got hurt in the process.

"Whatever happens, you aren't in this alone." Eddie propped his hands behind him and leaned back. "You care about people. They know it and care about you too."

Without coming out and saying it, Eddie had still dug under the surface to what Zack was really processing. "You, Naya, the crew. You're all my family." Zack leaned forward, hands on his knees. There, he'd said it. And in the same moment, he wanted to tuck that statement under lock and key where nothing could strip his hope.

He was the goofy guy on the team. The one who got the job done and observed his coworkers from a distance, careful not to share too much of life.

He'd lost his family once.

The reality that something could happen again to those he'd come to love was like a dark storm cloud that hovered over him, threatening to open up at a moment's notice.

Zack shoved his hands in his pockets and stood.

"Exactly. We're all your family, dude. And we stick by each other through thick and thin. You're one of us, and you can't do anything to have it taken away. Isn't that the gospel?"

Eddie's rhetorical question prodded at the lies Zack held on to. Yet there was no condemnation in his friend's demeanor. Only kindness. Trying to help him remember.

"You've been brought into God's family because of His love. And you can't do anything to get kicked out." Eddie smiled. "I can't speak for everyone else, but your true family won't leave you, no matter what happens. And you've got at least one brother right here." Eddie stood and slapped Zack on the shoulder.

A cheesy grin formed on Eddie's face. Zack raised an eyebrow. "What's that look for?"

"Since we're brothers, I also need to state the obvious, dude." Eddie shook his head. "You like Naya, big time."

There was no use hiding the fact. "You say it like it is."

"And you're not denying it," Eddie said.

"I want to be someone she can trust. Someone who reminds her of her worth." Not because of what she did but because of who and whose she was. A daughter of the King.

"Then tell her that." Eddie shrugged.

"Because of our past, it feels complicated." Zack grabbed a roller, then sat on the mat.

"How so?"

"She's already been hurt and let down by men. When I disappeared from her life when we were teens, I basically handed her a loss that settled deep in her veins. I became another statistic on her record." Zack dug the roller into his leg muscles to work out the knots.

"Does she know the whole story?"

"No. But I'm not sure how much it would change. She hasn't verbalized it, but I can see it in her eyes. She half expects me to up and leave again."

"Give her a chance to hear the truth from you. Then she can make a decision."

Zack didn't want to entertain the thought of losing her again. But would telling the truth be worth it?

"Don't be afraid to open up." Eddie jabbed his finger in Zack's chest. "You'll figure out how to care for and protect her best." His friend broke eye contact and stared at the wall, like he was preaching to himself.

In the meantime, Zack would help those who'd become his family. He would show up for them. Because that's what family did. They stuck close by in adversity.

He might not have told Naya all the details about that long-ago day yet, but he'd prove to her he wouldn't leave again.

He'd touch base with her and invite her to the spring festival tomorrow. Not only would it give him peace of mind that she would be nearby, but after the truck run, they could enjoy the festivities together. That was, if she wasn't mad at him after their conversation earlier.

"I'm heading over to the Kirbys' house to run through the plan for tomorrow's parade with the guys." Zack grabbed his duffel bag from the gym cubby.

Eddie waved to him, then started his own workout.

Zack changed and headed out to his rental car. He sent a short message to Naya about tomorrow before pulling out of the firehouse.

When he got to the home, several of the boys, including Karson, Andrew, and Carlos, were outside playing a pickup game of basketball.

Zack hopped out of the driver's seat and waved his hands. "I'm open!"

Karson chest-bumped him the ball. Zack spun and made his way around the perimeter of the court, keeping his hand out to ward off his opponents, and went in for a slam dunk.

Cheers erupted.

"I call dibs on Zack."

"No way, bro. He's on our team." The boys bickered.

"Who's winning right now?" Zack scanned the group.

"We are." Andrew's hand shot in the air, then he pointed to his team members.

"Great. I'll join Karson's team. Level the playing field." Zack winked.

Before they could argue, Zack passed the ball, and the game restarted. When they finished, Zack grabbed his belongings from the car.

"I call for a rematch." Carlos stuck his chin in the air.

"We've got some business to attend to first. If there's time afterwards, we'll hit the court again."

Thankfully, the boys agreed without any objections, and they headed inside. The three boys who were helping Zack with the truck run followed him into the kitchen, and the rest headed in separate directions.

Zack spread out papers on the table. "This is the map for our route tomorrow during the parade. We'll toss out candy along the way for those who are gathered on the sidewalk."

"Will we get to blare the siren?" Karson sat up in his seat.

"There's three blocks, so I think we can arrange for each of you to do it once."

The boys high-fived each other.

"We're going to start at the firehouse. I already spoke with Mr. and Mrs. Kirby about meeting us tomorrow morning. What time do you need to be ready to go?" The Kirbys would make sure the guys arrived on time, but Zack still wanted the kids to realize it was their responsibility to be prepared.

"Eight," Carlos said.

"That's so early," Andrew moaned.

"It's later than when we have to get up for school." Carlos shrugged.

"I know I can count on all of you," Zack said. "Once we finish the route, there will be a tent set up near the city hall where we'll hand out more candy, stickers, and fliers about the firehouse."

"This is awesome. We're going to be famous for a day." Carlos pumped his fist in the air.

Zack smiled. *This* was what made investing in these kids worth it. Showing them they had value. They weren't forgotten or unseen. No matter how trivial the experience appeared to onlookers, this event would be a highlight for the boys.

Looking around at each of these boys, Zack couldn't help but see himself in them. Their enthusiasm and determination in life. How amazing would it be to show these kids they had family surrounding them too? Like Eddie had done for Zack.

A crazy thought crossed his mind. What if Zack adopted some foster boys? The undertaking would be hard to manage by himself. But if he had a wife...

Would Naya ever consider adoption? He didn't know for sure, and he was definitely jumping the gun, but the thought of raising kids alongside Naya prickled his skin with goosebumps. Zack shook his head. He couldn't put stipulations on a relationship that didn't even exist.

Zack cleared his throat. "Any questions on what we just went over?"

"Um..." Karson's eyes darted all over the room. "Do we have to have a tent by the city hall?"

Zack took note of the teen's quiet voice. Something wasn't right. "It's at the end of the route in a central location. Do you have another suggestion?"

"Will I get in trouble for disagreeing?"

"Not at all. Your opinion is valid."

Karson swallowed. "I heard Green Warriors is going to be there.

And some people aren't too happy about that. What if there's a confrontation?"

Zack steeled his jaw. He wanted these kids to have a better life, not get caught up in the wrong crowd or worry about being pegged as part of the wrong crowd.

"You guys focus on our booth, and I'll make sure nothing happens.

Zack wouldn't let the rift between Ethos and Green Warriors affect the teens' contribution tomorrow. Eddie and the rest of the crew would make sure of it too. They were family, and family stuck by each other no matter what would come their way.

EIGHTEEN

NAYA WOULDN'T LET ANYTHING STOP HER FROM getting answers for Zack. She parked her car in the alleyway behind the firehouse, then made her way down the side street toward the New Blooms Spring Festival.

She would pursue this story for Zack's sake. Show him they were on the same team. Any success at work from this story was an added bonus.

Naya opened up the festival map to check the route. She wanted details on why Sylvia had been part of the group that had sabotaged the CEO's house. Which meant she'd arrived early to the festival.

The Green Warriors booth would be right next to the firehouse booth. It made her second stop even easier.

If things went south during her interview with Sylvia, cops were on standby thanks to extra security measures for the day and the crowd this event drew.

Tazwell stood at the entrance to the line of booths along the sidewalk. Ramble had staked his claim by the speakers next to the steps of the city hall.

Zack would be nearby too, although he wouldn't be thrilled if he found out what kind of investigating she was doing. Still, her body flooded with warmth at the thought of being around him.

He'd texted her with information about the festival and suggested they meet up after the truck run was finished. But his message had given no indication as to where he stood after their previous conversation.

There was no use creating imaginary scenarios that would only serve to tie her stomach into a tight knot.

Naya waved to Tazwell, then headed toward the Green Warriors booth. Even from far away, the lime-green tent stood out among the other vendors. Barricades stood in place along the perimeter so pedestrians wouldn't mill around the streets where the trucks would make their entrance.

Music flowed through the air as Naya walked toward the center of the hubbub. It reminded her of the *kanaval* she and her family would attend every spring in Haiti. The music, vendors, and vibrant colors that lined the marketplace always drew locals and tourists. And the best part was the celebration lasting for three months. Each Sunday after church, Naya, Dominic, and their dad would head to the town square to join the festivities.

A fountain stood in the center of the walking path, and Naya squinted against the sun. Was that Ingram? She approached the sitting area, and sure enough, her friend sat on a bench, her long black hair pulled back in a braid.

"What are you doing here?" Naya slid on her sunglasses.

Ingram stood and hugged Naya.

After their conversation yesterday, Naya was almost surprised her friend had come, but it did make sense since Ingram knew Sylvia from work. Ingram had an amazing ability to separate the personal from her professional life, whereas Naya often had few boundaries between her professional and personal lives. When work took her out of the office space, it made it even harder to separate the two.

Naya could probably learn a thing or two from Ingram.

"I couldn't let you do this alone. Not with so much at stake."

"Thanks." Naya hugged Ingram again. "I appreciate it."

"I'd be a terrible friend if I didn't. Someone has to watch your back when you get an idea in that head of yours." Ingram tapped her temple. "I might work for Ethos, but I care more about you than a paycheck."

Naya blinked, then swallowed. The Lord had blessed her with a friend who had her back. Just like she had Ingram's. There was no telling how this interaction with Sylvia would go. Naya just hoped it didn't turn ugly.

The woman unboxed signs at the group table. She sported a hunter-green T-shirt with the *Save Our Land* logo.

It didn't matter whether the recent attacks had been intended for Naya or Zack. Although, after yesterday's findings, her gut said the two were related somehow. Today would be one step closer to finding the answers.

"This is a nice spot for raising awareness." Naya stepped under the canopy.

Sylvia put the empty box under the table, then turned her attention to Naya. "You here to join us? The city council won't miss us today, that's for sure." She crossed her arms. Her lips turned down. "Ingram. You decide to come to the good side too?"

"Just tagging along with a friend." Ingram placed her arm around Naya's shoulders.

"Actually, we had a few questions we were hoping you could answer." Naya smiled.

Sylvia huffed. "She works for Ethos. Why not get details from her?" She pointed to Ingram.

Interesting. Naya raised an eyebrow. She didn't want to reveal Ingram had told her about Sylvia working for Ethos, but the woman must know she couldn't prevent others from finding out that information.

"I like to go to sources who I wouldn't have bias toward. Make sure I get the full story."

Sylvia huffed. "I don't know what I can offer you."

"As an employee of Ethos, I'm sure you have valuable insight."

Sylvia's eyes widened. "I will not—"

Naya interrupted. "I'm curious about your involvement with both groups." Naya needed to change tactics if any answers were to come from this conversation. "It's noble of you to want to preserve the environment. Are you getting information to present reform ideas to the Ethos staff?"

Naya refrained from pulling out her recorder or paper. She needed to build trust with the woman first, not make her think she was being interrogated.

Sylvia's eyes darted left and right, then she leaned over the table. "Something like that. But I can't share anything here." She leaned back and motioned to Ingram. "Can you watch the table while I go talk to your friend?"

Ingram turned to Naya and pursed her lips.

I'll be fine, Naya mouthed.

They were in a highly populated area, so it would be silly for someone to pull a stunt now.

"Let's go chat by those trees." Naya pointed to the shaded area by a fence. It would be out of earshot but still visible.

They made their way over, and Naya kept her back to the fence just in case. There was no point being caught off guard.

She turned to face Sylvia. "What are you hoping to present to Ethos?"

"Proof of malicious intent." Sylvia sneered.

They were jumping right in. Naya swallowed. "That is quite the claim. How so?"

"I have sources that say the environmental group is causing the destruction by dumping chemicals into the water. Then they try to blame it on Ethos!"

"Have you gathered any evidence to support the hearsay?"

"I'm trying!" She huffed. "It takes time to build people's trust. They want to make sure you're one of them first."

"In the meantime, people are getting hurt."

Sylvia set her hands on her hips. "I'm doing the best I can."

"But it's all to benefit Ethos." Naya didn't condone Sylvia's approach, but she understood. "If the environmental group is doing it, how are they going about it without anyone finding out?"

"They have a drop-off point, but I haven't been able to figure out where it is yet. Everyone knows money is at the root of this problem. Government funding is assisting those who are sick. Insurance companies are winning too. The faster this group can make claims against Ethos, the more money the organization gets to 'support the environment.'" Sylvia used air quotes for the last part.

Naya read between the lines. The group was getting monies that would benefit its agenda, even if they didn't say it outright. Although, the insurance company's involvement piqued Naya's interest. How were they winning?

Surely an insurance company would be more likely to conspire with a large company like Ethos over a local environmental group.

She stowed the thought away for later. Right now, it seemed more like quibbling than someone causing the problem in order to cash in.

"How did you know I worked for Ethos?" Sylvia narrowed her eyes. "This is supposed to be an undercover task. Did Ingram rat me out?"

Something about the woman's tone made Naya ready to defend her friend. What might Sylvia say to Ingram when they were back in the office? Her friend had enough to worry about right now without an altercation added to the list.

Naya winced. "You were in a picture Green Warriors posted on social media." She didn't want to lie. Better to get Sylvia to confirm

Naya's hunch rather than throw Ingram under the bus. "How long have you been working for both sides?"

"I guess you didn't get the job as reporter for nothing." Sylvia backed up a step. "I'm gonna find that evidence before you rat me out." She walked off.

Naya headed back to the environmental group's table and gave Ingram a discreet thumbs-up. "I want to go check out Eastside Firehouse's set up."

Ingram eyed her.

"I'll tell you later."

"Fine. That craft tent is calling my name," Ingram said. "I'll meet you at the firehouse spot after."

Sylvia's deflection to Naya's question about her work at Ethos and Green Warriors told her there was more below the surface. Between a supposed drop-off location for waste and the insurance company claims, Naya had enough leads for more searches.

She wanted to ditch the rest of the festival and get back to the office and see what else she could find. But people were more important than work. Even if the two mixed. She wouldn't shut others out or make them think she only needed them when it benefited her.

Several young boys stood at the firehouse table, handing out fliers and candy. Naya recognized some of the fire crew who chatted with each other a few feet behind the teens. They weren't in turnout gear, but they all sported matching navy zip-up jackets. A few had the truck emblem, while others sported the rescue one.

"How did you all get chosen to man the table?" Naya pegged the boys as early high-school age.

"Stephens gave us an in," one boy piped up, his chin lifted. His nametag read *Alex*.

"Here's information on fire safety." Another boy handed her a pamphlet.

She took the flier. "How do you know Zack?"

"Our foster parents are friends with Zack. And now he hangs out with us too."

How had she not known Zack helped out with foster kids? Given the smile on these kids' faces, the interest Zack showed them might have changed their whole outlook on life.

If she'd needed a reason to be impressed by him, this would've been a good one. Too bad she didn't.

An ache grew in her chest.

Alex nudged his friend with his elbow. "Ow. What was that for?"

"She doesn't need to know all that information."

Naya understood too well the stigma that came with being labeled as a foster kid. A somebody nobody wanted. "I was in a foster home at your age too."

"So you get it?" Alex lifted a sad gaze her way.

"I do. I know you might feel alone but it's not true. I had people who supported me while in foster care who are now like family to me. My best friend is right over there." She pointed to Ingram at the booth next to them. "And her parents have become like a second mom and dad to me."

"Whoa. That's cool."

"And I know Zack sees you all as his friends too."

"Oh yeah. He's the best." The curly-haired boy puffed out his chest.

The smiles on their faces gave Naya an idea. This connection would make a beautiful story. One that highlighted the importance of community and raised awareness on the realities of foster care.

She was ready to ask them their names, but a siren broke through the air, grabbing everyone's attention.

Several short beeps blasted afterwards.

"That's them." One of the boys hopped up out of his seat.

Another called to the firefighters, "They're coming!"

Sure enough, the fire engine rolled down the street. The big red truck flashed its lights, sirens going.

Naya moved up to the front of the crowd to get a better view. A couple of other boys waved from the windows and tossed candy.

Naya pulled her phone out to capture the moment.

This story definitely needed to be told. She'd be able to ask Zack for more details in a little bit. The route was almost complete. There was one corner up ahead before the parking spot outside the city council where other floats were already lined up.

Several pops pierced the air.

Screams echoed all around.

A woman wheeled her stroller to the side while a group of teens shoved past an older man.

Naya crouched to the ground by the table for cover, and her pulse pounded in her neck.

Officers raced toward a building where the shots had come from. The engine horn blared. Naya couldn't make out Zack in the chaos, but one thought plagued her mind.

Had the shooter hit anyone?

NINETEEN

SOMEONE WAS SHOOTING AT THE TRUCK.

The dashboard lit up with the low tire pressure warning, and a beep dinged in response.

Glass shattered to Zack's right.

He jerked the steering wheel and ducked.

The truck teetered to the left and Zack yanked the wheel the opposite direction. He couldn't afford to overturn the truck. Not with the teens onboard and pedestrians all around.

A prick hit his cheek, but he didn't have time to worry about what struck him.

The teens screamed.

"Get down," Zack yelled to Karson, Carlos, and Andrew. "Move away from the windows." *Dear God, please don't let any of these boys get hit.*

The front two tires bounced from the loss of air.

Zack focused back on the road and hit the brakes. He turned the vehicle to the left to keep from hitting an older man who dashed across the crosswalk.

Trouble might as well be plastered on Zack's forehead.

There was no way for him to hide from the shooter. Not driving in such an easy target.

A woman raced by, her purse slung over her shoulder.

Zack hit the horn, gripped the big steering wheel, and turned the truck toward the curb to avoid her and a cluster of people.

Lord, don't let anyone die. This should have been a fun ride in the truck. Instead, he might end up killing someone.

The tires jumped up onto the sidewalk. Zack pitched forward, and his seatbelt yanked him back. On the front dash, the radio cord swung to and fro.

Zack's ears rang.

His head pounded.

They weren't moving anymore.

He clicked off his seatbelt and swiveled. "Everyone okay back there?"

All three boys stared back at him with wide eyes and open mouths.

Karson finally broke the silence. "Bro, that was wild. You just saved the day."

Now it was Zack's turn to remain speechless. "What?"

Andrew said, "I wish I got that on camera. I could use it the next time I'm playing those racing video games."

"Any of you hurt?" Zack scanned them but couldn't see any injuries.

The boys glanced at each other and shook their heads.

"All good." Andrew gave a thumbs-up.

Whether the shock was keeping them from processing the extent of what had gone down or not, Zack was thankful they didn't appear injured.

No more gunshots had come their way, but Zack wasn't about to open the door and become an easy target. "Stay put guys. No one gets out until we get the all clear." He peered out the window.

People congregated in the street, pointing. Two kids huddled in the grass, their mom rubbing their backs.

Basuto, Ramble, Trace, and Kianna jogged over to the truck.

Basuto rapped on the door, and Zack stepped out, scanning the area for anything that appeared off. "That's one way to end a parade," Ramble said.

Zack hopped onto the ground. "Is anyone hurt?"

"Negative." Trace moved to the side, and lifted a brow. "Are you? You look like you're gonna hurl."

Zack figured that wasn't far from the truth. He lifted his hand to his cheek and a splotch of blood covered the pad of his finger. "I'm fine. Make sure they're okay first." He pointed to the teens still huddled in the truck.

Ramble helped the teens out, and Trace walked over to the first kid while Kianna unzipped the medic bag.

Zack turned to Lieutenant Basuto. "Did you catch the person?" He wanted to hold his breath, but then he'd pass out.

"There're footprints. But whoever it was had an escape route planned." Basuto steeled his jaw.

Bile rose in Zack's throat. "I can't believe someone opened fire. And with so many civilians around." He'd brought trouble into innocent people's lives by investigating his parents' case. Zack's nerves still buzzed at the realization.

Bryce made his way over to him and Basuto.

"I could have hit someone." Zack met Bryce's gaze. What would his boss think? Zack swallowed.

"You reacted to the situation. Nothing wrong with that." Bryce clapped Zack on the shoulder.

"They're all clear," Trace called out and gave a thumbs-up.

Bryce nodded. "It could have been much worse. But everyone is safe. You had no control over the situation."

The teens' foster parents, the Kirbys, now stood with the boys. Creases etched Alexia's tanned brow, and her husband, Sam, ran his fingers along his beard. "We're going to take them home now." Sam escorted the boys back up the hill.

"Take the rest of the day off, man. We got it from here," Bryce said.

His boss was right. What mattered was that everyone was safe.

He'd been ordered to take the rest of the day off, but Zack would rather stick around and help fix things. The two officers were already in conversation with Bryce, which made his standing there awkward. Much better to clean up the mess like they did after any traffic accident.

Zack grabbed his gloves.

The grass and sidewalk were littered with debris. He picked up some plastic water bottles and threw them in the trash can at the side of the building.

"Excuse me, sir." A man in a hoodie and sneakers stepped up to him. A young girl with blonde pigtails sucked on a lollipop while her other hand was tucked in her dad's. "You saved my kid's life."

"I did?" Zack furrowed his brow.

"Yeah, man. You stopped the truck before it could hit my daughter. You're a hero." The man's face beamed. "Thank you."

Zack stood up straight and smiled. Here he'd thought everyone would be angry, and this dad was thanking him. "Instinct kicked in, and I couldn't let anyone get hurt."

"We're glad to have you on the first responder crew. The team in this town is amazing." The dad extended his hand and Zack shook it.

He'd barely let go of the man's hand before Izan, Eddie, and Ridge showed up.

"Thought you could make a mess and not worry about cleaning it up?" Ridge winked.

"Ha. Let you guys have all the fun without me?" Zack shook his head. "Not a chance."

"That was something else." Izan shook his head and slapped Zack on the shoulder. "I'm glad you're okay."

The way his buddies surrounded him sent a surge of pride through Zack's veins. He'd invited the trouble that could have gotten them hurt. Yet, they didn't see it that way. How had he been blessed with supportive and gracious friends?

Zack scanned the crowd. Naya stood at the edge of the sidewalk. When he made eye contact with her, she hurried over.

Eddie must have taken note of the brief exchange, because he smiled. "Get in here too." He waved her over.

Eddie moved away from Zack, and Naya slid into the empty spot and wrapped her arm around Zack's torso. The gesture sent heat up his neck, and given the guys' faces, none of them missed it.

Her close proximity made him want to gather her in his arms and hold tight. Show her she would be safe with him. That no one would hurt her, and she wouldn't have to worry about looking over her shoulder.

"Your cheek." Naya leaned in and whispered to Zack. The smell of peppermint on her breath tickled his senses, and Zack took her hand in his and squeezed. "It's just a scratch."

"You sure you're okay?" She stared at him.

He smiled. "Shaken? Sure. Hurt? No."

The urge to kiss her built in him like kindling that had just lit a campfire. Sparks rose with the heat that worked its way up his arms. The coziness and security she exuded reeled him in, but one step too close would only get him burned.

Instead, he nuzzled his nose against the side of her face and placed a gentle kiss on her temple.

They needed to have a conversation first. Otherwise, he'd regret letting his emotions take the reins. She deserved respect, and that meant clearing the air after their argument.

Naya must have read his mind. "Can we talk later?"

"Of course." Zack wrapped his arm back around her and looked at his friends. Colleagues. Family.

Just as his team would stand by him, he wouldn't let her do this alone.

Everyone needed a partner. Someone to catch their blind spots and be their champion.

A speaker crackled to life and broke his train of thought. Someone tapped a microphone, then said, "Thank you to all our first responders and their swift action today. Because of their work, everyone is safe. We'd also like to thank you all for coming out to the New Blooms Spring Festival. Let's give it up for our vendors and first responders. We hope you'll join us again next year. On your way out, please stay on the sidewalks and let the cleanup crew do their job."

"All right. Let's get this mess taken care of." Ridge broke away from the circle first.

"I'll take the boxes back to the firehouse with me." Zack pointed to their booth. "Clocking out for the day."

"You sure? We can load it in my truck after we're done here." Ridge snapped on a pair of gloves.

"Nah. I don't mind. I'm going to walk back. Let out some of the nerves from earlier."

"Mind if I join?" Naya asked. "I parked by the firehouse."

"I'd be happy to have the company."

They gathered the bins, then he and Naya walked back down Main Street in silence. A dog barked, and two kids ran past them with cotton candy in hand. "You can't take mine!"

"Wait up, kids." The mom pushed a stroller. "Excuse me." She wheeled past them.

They were half a block from the firehouse when Naya slowed her pace. "I didn't realize you hung out with the boys the Kirbys are fostering." When he looked over, she said, "I met some of them earlier."

"I've taken a few of them under my wing." He shrugged. "Want to show them they're seen. Make sure they don't get caught up in the wrong crowd."

"They really admire you. And after today, it sounds like you're the town hero." She smiled. "I might just have to write a story about it."

Zack laughed, but Naya raised her eyebrows.

"For real?" He shifted the box in his arm.

"Yeah. More people need to know how to help these kids. And you're the perfect model to show them."

"Well, I might need to take a few extra classes on that first." Zack puffed out his chest and began to strut down the sidewalk. With his head held high, he took several strides before pivoting.

Naya laughed and clapped. "Bravo."

He started walking again, but his foot caught on the sidewalk, and he stumbled forward before catching himself.

"You okay?" Naya's eyes widened.

Zack smoothed his shirt and grinned. "Yeah." He liked making her laugh. Actually, he liked a lot more than just hearing her laugh.

He liked her.

He needed to get a grip. She hadn't told him she liked him. But her affirmation about his work was a good sign, right?

Zack cleared his throat. "I'd be happy to sit down anytime with you to share more."

"Great. Speaking of stories, I need to fill you in on some details."

"Let me set this box down, then we can chat." Zack opened the firehouse door for her. "The lounge is right around the corner on your left."

Zack dropped the container off in the storage room, then checked his mailbox. What might have been a tragedy today had ended with only property damage and a fire truck out of service. God had been gracious, and no one had been hurt.

He grabbed a folded letter from his cubby and opened it on his way back to the common room.

The black, boxy letters typed across the center of the page stopped him in his tracks.

If you want to see another day, stop helping that reporter. Or else you'll end up just like your parents.

TWENTY

"ZACK?"

His face paled.

Naya closed the distance between her and Zack and took hold of his trembling hands. "What's wrong?" She stared into his dark eyes. Ones that a few moments ago had glistened with spunk and made her laugh.

That was one of many qualities she appreciated about Zack. His wit had a way of soothing the edges of any situation and reminding her that life was full of joyful moments, no matter how small, even in the midst of difficult circumstances.

She couldn't believe he'd maintained enough control of the truck that he'd been able to keep everyone safe. He'd saved lives today. She could have lost him. For good. They hadn't had a chance yet to make things right between each other.

"What's wrong?" Naya lifted her gaze from his shaking hands. Now, those same eyes held determination and something else she couldn't quite put her finger on. *Protection? For her?*

She wanted them to clear the air. To agree to fight on the same team, not against each other. Life was too short, and today had reminded her of that reality. Their end goal was the same. To have justice and truth exposed.

Could they find a way to see eye to eye?

"Someone has taken these threats too far." Zack's jaw twitched. "A threat against you is a threat against me."

Naya lifted the note out of Zack's grip and read the words.

"This note makes it sound like your story is connected to my parents." Zack scrunched his brow. "But that doesn't make sense."

Naya finished reading and folded the paper again. "Actually—"

A door slammed shut, and baritone voices filled the air. The rest of the crew was back.

That would make it more difficult to share what she'd discovered today with Zack. The information wasn't confidential, but she didn't want speculation and gossip starting over details that weren't confirmed.

Would he want to get coffee?

"Anyone want pizza from Backdraft?" Ridge yelled from somewhere, and a few seconds later he meandered into the common area. "I thought you were heading home to chill, hero." Ridge plopped down on a sofa and pulled out his phone.

"That was the plan. Until I found a note in my mailbox. Did you grab the mail today?" Zack asked.

"Ah, I do remember that handwritten card being in the pile. A love note?" Ridge winked.

"Far from it." Zack's body tensed next to Naya. "You didn't see anyone drop something off?"

"Sorry, man. I just took the mail, then distributed it in our boxes. Security cams might show someone." Ridge tapped a few buttons on his phone. "Do you two want pizza?"

It might be a tad selfish, but Naya didn't want to stick around for dinner. Not when she had details to share with Zack. The two of them debriefing alone was more appealing.

"Would you like to stay here and eat?" Zack turned to Naya.

She bit her lip.

Zack turned to his colleague. "We have some other things to take care of. Later."

Ridge chuckled. "Have a good night, you two."

Naya stepped out into the hall with Zack, and he said, "Do you mind if we check the security footage?"

"Good idea. It might show something."

Naya followed him into a room with three monitors. Several camera angles were displayed in tiny boxes on the screens with real-time footage.

Her stomach growled. "After, we can head back to my place to talk. I can make some dinner." Why was she so nervous? "If you want..."

Zack pulled out a chair and sat down, then swiveled to face her. "It's a date."

Naya swallowed. She couldn't read Zack's expression. Did he mean a date for the two of them, or a work date? *Why am I so bad at this?*

"You can sit down." Zack slid another chair closer. "If you want..."

She caught the tug of amusement on his lips and cleared her throat. "I don't mind standing."

The distance should keep her heart from racing and leaving her breathless. Too bad the closer she was to Zack, the harder it was to focus.

This is about work, remember?

Zack clicked a few buttons and rewound to the beginning of the day. His mouse hovered over orange-marked areas, which indicated when the cameras had picked up on activity.

The first timeframe had the crew coming in and out of the garage, getting ready for the festival.

Zack sped up the playback, and several minutes passed by until someone came into the frame.

"There." Naya pointed at the screen.

Zack slowed the recording while the mailman walked up to the mailbox, grabbed letters from his satchel, and put down the flag.

Two minutes later, another person walked into view of the camera. Their ball cap rested low over their face. After a quick glance to check the surroundings, they pulled the folded letter from inside a jacket and shoved it in the mailbox before hurrying out of view.

Naya touched his shoulder and leaned down. "Can you zoom in?"

"Definitely a guy. His stature and gait give it away."

Naya stared at the grainy image. Something else familiar tickled her brain. "The hat." She gasped.

"What about it?"

"It has the same logo on it as the person who attacked me on the mountain." The crisscross pinstripes etched into the circular emblem mocked her. "It has to be the same person."

Her heart sank. The image on the screen was too blurry, and the man's face was averted. There was no telling who hid under the disguise.

No way to identify the man who'd nearly killed her.

After a few clicks, Zack had an email pulled up. "I'll see if Detective Wilcox can run this for any facial recognition."

Naya wouldn't hold her breath. The chances of an ID coming back were slim on such a grainy photo, but she appreciated him for trying. Maybe Savannah would recognize the man and they'd be able to ID him some other way.

She needed to do something, though.

Naya said, "I'll see what I can find on the hat. Figure out what stores sell that specific logo." Sometimes the minor details held the greatest significance.

Zack clicked out of the replay, then stood up. "Good thinking."

"You're okay with me investigating this thread?" Naya held her breath.

Just the other day Zack had wanted her to stay out of danger. Thanks to Ingram, she understood why he'd view it that way. Trauma impacted each person differently. And after his parents' deaths, of course he wouldn't want to live through other people being hurt.

She would be careful, for his sake. But it wasn't going to change her mind on getting to the bottom of this story.

"I'm not going to let you do this alone." He took her hands in his. "I trust you to know what you're doing. And someone's got to have your back." He wrapped his arms around her and pulled her close.

"Thanks." Naya relaxed in his embrace. His strong arms brought comfort. Safety.

Zack leaned back and settled his hand against her cheek. His eyes searched hers, and she didn't want to look away. There was no need to hide or cower.

She wouldn't have to pick sides—Zack or the story. Which was a good thing because she wanted both.

Zack lowered his head and brushed his lips against hers.

He hovered there.

Waiting.

His breath tickled her skin, and Naya cocked her head and wrapped her hand around his neck.

She sealed her lips on his and he deepened the kiss.

Naya never wanted to leave. She wanted to stay in this moment where they would choose to fight for each other.

She eased back to catch her breath, and a smile captured Zack's face.

"Well, that was one way to clear the air." She swallowed. For the first time in a while, Naya couldn't breathe for all the right reasons.

Zack stepped back and cleared his throat. The space between them left Naya cold and missing his sturdy frame wrapped around hers. "What did you have to tell me?"

"Why don't we head back to my place, and I'll give you the rundown."

Zack followed behind her car in his white rental sedan. Ten minutes later they pulled into her driveway.

Naya unlocked the door, and paint fumes still hung in the air. "Sorry about the smell." She dropped her keys on the entryway table. "Guess I haven't aired it out enough yet."

Zack peeked into the office space they'd worked on the other day. "The new color looks good."

"It should be all finished by next week." The DIY had turned into a fun hobby. Gave her something to do when she wasn't working. Although, except for right now, when wasn't she working?

Naya opened the fridge and wrinkled her nose. The smell of rotten eggs was prominent. She'd just gotten groceries a few days ago. Surely they wouldn't have gone bad already. She'd have to inspect them later.

Naya pulled out a tray of mac and cheese and grabbed two bowls from the cupboard. She heated each one up in the microwave.

"Here you go." She set the bowl down and handed Zack a fork.

"This looks amazing." He took a bite. "And certainly not a box mix."

She chuckled. "Homemade. I make a pan of something on the weekends so I don't have to cook every night after work."

"I could eat this every day." The stringy cheese dangled from his fork. "My mom used to make it from a box, and we'd eat it straight out of the pot." He smiled. "A Friday night tradition before watching a movie."

"Do you ever feel like you're going to forget your parents?" Naya frowned.

Zack set his fork down. "That's why I think about the good moments whenever I can. Helps me remember life with them. Then they'll always be in here." He placed a hand on his chest.

Naya finished chewing. "The festival reminded me of a time like that too."

"How so?"

"We had what's called a *kanaval*—it's Haitian for 'carnival.' My dad would take Dominic and me. We'd dance to the music and marvel at all the crafts people had for sale. We always had to get a beignet too." She laughed. "It's a crepe-like dessert made with bananas. By the time the sugar set in, my dad probably wished he'd had my brother and me split one."

"See, they'll always live on. No matter how much time passes." Zack reached across the table and squeezed her hand.

Naya wanted to make more memories to treasure.

This time with Zack.

She wanted to admit how scared she'd been about losing him today. Naya swallowed. If she did, he might vanish again. No, she couldn't bring herself to do it. She smiled, then pulled her hand away.

"Your parents' story deserves to be told. So you can move on and remember only the good times." She slid her notebook over to Zack. "That's what I was coming to tell you when the truck went out of control." She sighed. "I think your parents' deaths are connected to my water contamination story."

"Why do you say that?" Zack grabbed a napkin from the holder on the table.

"Remember how you said your dad got a new boss and office? Well, ProEco Plant, the company he originally worked for was bought out. By Ethos."

Zack's hand froze. "Interesting."

"I spoke with Sylvia today, the woman from the Green Warriors group. She confirmed that she works for Ethos."

Zack furrowed his brow. "Why would she be part of the environmental group?"

"Hang with me for a second." Naya pushed her empty plate to

the side. "She claims it's undercover work for Ethos. Rumor has it that the Green Warriors are the ones using the river as a dumping ground for waste that is contaminating the water."

"Okay. That sounds more like blame shifting, but go on..." Zack pulled a pen from his pocket and scribbled down notes. "What do they gain from that?"

"Grants from the government. Money from donors who think they're trying to protect the environment. Insurance coverage for those who are sick."

"If that's the case, the environmental group is hurting for funding."

"Exactly. But I haven't come across any information to support that claim—yet."

"If they are behind it, where are they dropping off their waste?"

"That's what Sylvia is trying to find out too."

"The sandbag. On the mountain." Zack stood up and paced the length of the table.

"That's an idea. You did say the burlap bag didn't fit the typical kind used to put out fires."

"The river's not far from the mountain. What if those bags are being used to transport the waste?"

"It still doesn't answer the why. Or how the two cases are connected." Naya tapped her knuckles on the table. "But it's absolutely worth looking into."

"I still think we're missing a big piece to this puzzle." Zack paused and ran his fingers through his hair. "Does it seem like the paint fumes are getting worse?"

She should open a window.

Naya headed for the kitchen. "If the note was only a warning for me to stop writing this story..."

"Then that means the explosion at Powells's house and my car were intended for you."

Naya turned from the window and frowned. There were too many parts to this story that could be interconnected or one-sided. How were they going to put this together?

"Powells's comments suggest the opposite. He seems convinced whoever killed my parents is still out there and doesn't want to be found." Zack opened the fridge and sniffed. "Nothing in here smells bad."

"You sure?" Naya bent her head toward the appliance. All good. But the rotten smell wafted to her nostrils too, different than the paint fumes. "Then where's it coming from?"

"Do you have natural gas?"

She nodded.

Zack slammed the refrigerator door shut and yanked her stove away from the wall. "I think you have a leak."

Naya stepped back and gripped the counter.

Zack opened her cupboards until he found a cup, then filled it with water and soap. "Where's a brush?"

She pointed to the canister of utensils under the microwave.

Zack rubbed the solution on the pipe.

"Open the windows and call the fire department." Zack's tone was sharp.

Naya raced to the windows off the eating area and yanked them open. She rushed back to him, pulling out her phone.

Zack moved to the back of the oven and twisted the pipe's valve. He straightened, then grabbed her hand. "We need to get out until the crew can vent the place." Zack pushed open the back door. "One spark and your house could be seconds away from exploding."

TWENTY-ONE

A DOOR SHUT AND FOOTSTEPS SHUFFLED INTO the firehouse kitchen. Zack set down the bowl of eggs he was mixing and turned to find Naya in the doorway. She wore jeans and a sweatshirt, and she still looked gorgeous. Her black curly hair fell across her shoulders. She might have tried to conceal the bags under her eyes, but he didn't miss them.

After the events of last night, he'd barely slept. He couldn't imagine it had been any better for her.

"Thanks for letting me hang around here today." She pulled out a chair and sat down.

The realization that someone had broken into her house and sabotaged her oven in an effort to create an explosion that could have killed her made Zack livid. Not only that but it'd brought recurrent nightmares to the forefront of his sleep last night.

Except this time, it hadn't been his parents who'd succumbed to the flames—it'd been Naya, and he'd been helpless to stop it.

That was just a dream.

This was real life.

Zack could do something to protect Naya. He'd comb that mountain again for evidence. See if he could find any more makeshift sandbags. Help her with research. Install a security camera at her house. Whatever it took, he'd have her back.

"How'd you sleep?"

"Okay. I suppose it just hit me." She bit her lip and blinked.

"You have every right for it to." Once the police had left Naya's house last night, she'd tried to call Ingram, but her friend hadn't picked up. He hadn't been about to leave her alone, but instead of him staking out on her couch, she'd taken a spare bed in the women's bunk room at the firehouse. He'd hoped it would help her sleep better, knowing she was safe with the crew. But he thought he'd heard her walking around in the wee hours.

"Ingram's going to pop over here for lunch later, if that's okay."

"I don't see a problem with it. If there's a callout, it might be a while until we get back. But the building is always locked and under surveillance."

"Thanks. I'm going to watch the Sunday worship service online and try to relax."

"I was making breakfast. Want any eggs?" Zack wished there were a way to erase Naya's unease.

She was strong, but the events they'd endured would shake anyone. Still, he'd do whatever he could to ease her burden. Especially if that meant being a safe place for her to go.

"When a guy's willing to cook"—the edges of a smile broke on her face—"I'll never turn down the food."

Zack turned on the burner. "I've learned a few tricks thanks to Trace and Charlie." He grabbed the container of oats from the pantry and sprinkled a few into the egg mixture. A secret ingredient that added texture and flavor. "Trace is one of our EMTs. Charlie left last summer to be a hotshot—that's a wildland firefighter—up in Montana."

Once the eggs were cooked, he plated the food and sat down across from Naya. He slid the salt and pepper her way.

"Oats in eggs?" She raised her eyebrow. "Intriguing." She added a dash of salt and took a bite. "I'm pleasantly surprised."

"Good?" He took a bite from his plate.

"Better than good."

Zack could get used to slow mornings with Naya. She'd been the closest person to family he'd had growing up, and the idea of starting their own family together left him wishing for a future that hadn't been written yet.

There was just one thing that could stand in the way of her ever saying yes to him. He still hadn't told her the full story about his disappearance from her life when they were teens in foster care. And once she learned the truth, she'd have every right to tell him to have a nice life.

He set his fork down and rubbed his wrist. The red bracelet spun around. A constant reminder of what his actions had cost him.

But after that kiss, there was hope they could move forward, given she'd reciprocated the gesture. Although, right now wasn't the time to dredge up the past. Not when they both had bigger things to worry about.

Naya set her dirty plate in the dishwasher and pulled out her laptop from her backpack. "Have you touched base with Powells since we met with him the other day?"

Zack moved his chair next to Naya's and straddled it. "Not yet. I'll follow up with him today."

"Great. So we know there haven't been any incidents at your house." Naya rattled off details of her attack, his car, the fire truck, and her oven.

He hadn't had any attacks when he'd been by himself aside from the truck incident at the parade.

"All this makes me think maybe I was wrong and the two cases aren't related," Naya continued.

"It could be."

Naya's sleuthing skills were top notch.

He didn't want to tell her what route to investigate, but the incident at the parade made it all feel confusing. "Although, my boys didn't like that our booth setup would be so close to the Green Warriors. Said they were afraid of getting caught up in the turmoil."

"Hmmm." Naya typed a few notes. She had a gleam in her eye.

"What is it?"

"Nothing." She dismissed the question with a hand wave. "If it *is* the environmental group, why all of a sudden target you?"

"Beats me." Zack cleared his plate and started a sink of soapy water.

"If we can nail down who our mountain man and mysterious letter guy is, we could have something more to go on."

"Find evidence on that hat to nab our guy, and I'll get Basuto to lead the arrest." Zack scrubbed the skillet. The sooner the person behind this mayhem was in jail, the better.

The alarm intercom blared. "Rescue 5. Ambo 21. Entrapment at Ethos Fire Solutions. Number of victims unknown."

Zack tossed the pan on the drying rack. "Will you be okay?" He put a hand on Naya's shoulder, knowing there could be no time to lose. "Truck will still be here."

"Yeah. Go do your thing." Naya placed her hand on top of his. "Be careful, please."

He read between the lines. She was just as curious about the callout to Ethos.

Zack bent down and pressed a kiss to her forehead. A peppermint scent wafted from her hair and provided a comforting feeling, but he couldn't linger right now. "I'll be back." He raced out of the room and down the hall, then grabbed his gear from the cubby.

Zack hopped in next to Eddie, and Bryce took the front seat with Ridge at the wheel. "Rescue 5 is en route. Seven minutes out. What's the status?" Bryce released the radio button.

They took the turn onto the street so hard Zack had to grab the handle at the top of the door. They all swayed, and Eddie bumped his shoulder. "You think Green Warriors has upped their antics?"

"If that's the case, I hope the police catch whoever is responsible." Zack braced one boot against the front seat to keep from being jostled along with the truck.

The dispatcher's information crackled over the radio intercom. "Forklift drove into an office wall. Unknown number of people trapped in the room."

Bryce pulled into the fire lane at the front of the building, and the guys grabbed their equipment.

Trace and Kianna parked the ambulance behind them and followed the crew inside.

A young woman with a pencil skirt and heels waved them through. "I was working at my computer when I heard a crash." She scurried down the hall with them and wiggled a doorknob, but it wouldn't open. "And I came to find this."

Cries echoed from the space. "Get us out!" A man in a suit banged on the window.

"She's bleeding." An older man in a polo pointed to a woman curled up on the ground.

"Please hurry." More cries came from the room.

Zack was surprised to see so many employees here on a Sunday. Didn't they realize taking a day off work never killed anyone?

Eddie stepped up to the door and knocked. "Rescue 5 is here. We're going to get you all out soon."

Dust coated the carpet floor. Zack peered through the window into the room. "The wall on the left is collapsed in."

Bryce turned to Zack and the crew. "Get struts off the truck to shore the building."

The receptionist grimaced and rubbed her forehead. "This headache just isn't going away," she said, smacking a piece of bubble gum.

Zack frowned. "We need to get the gas shut off. Where's the valve?"

The receptionist pointed. "Around the corner and out that door."

"Let's go." Bryce hollered. "I want this place vented stat."

"Copy that." Eddie ran for the truck and Ridge went with him while Zack bolted out the side door.

He scanned the wall for the gas line then let out a groan. The metal pipes and wheel were bent and mangled. "No. No. No." He gripped the wheel and tugged, but the mechanism didn't budge.

"I've got no way to shut off the gas," Zack radioed in. "It's been compromised."

"We need to move." Bryce's voice came through his earpiece. "Circle around the hall and cut into the wall on the other side and stabilize as you go."

"Shores are in place," Eddie replied.

Zack sprinted back into the building. Eddie handed him a pick, and he hefted the axe up and slammed it into the wall. Wood chips and dust flew to the ground.

"We need everyone to stay in the far back corner." Eddie cranked the saw and bored into the wall.

The noise reverberated through Zack's skull.

Zack kicked the wood with his foot and brushed away the plaster. The exertion left him winded, and he paused to let his breath even out.

"We've got a woman down," Trace yelled, and grabbed the receptionist, who'd crumpled in his grasp.

Zack wiped the dust off his goggles. "We're in," he shared into the radio. Zack glanced down at his four-gas meter. The CO levels were climbing. They needed everyone out minutes ago.

He and Eddie ducked into the brightly lit room. Pain pricked at the edges of Zack's brow, and he swiped at his forehead. He couldn't succumb to the odorless gas—not before he got the other civilians out safely.

"If you can walk, go through the hole and down the hall." Zack pointed to the makeshift entrance. Two men and women held on to each other's arms and limped out of the room.

Zack took the hand of an older gentleman and helped him stand up. The man swayed, and Zack grabbed his forearm. "Easy there. Come on." He swung the man's arm over his shoulder and walked him into the hall. "Medic!"

Kianna raced to the man's side and escorted him down the hall.

Zack turned around and held out his hand to another woman. "I've got you. Follow me." He pulled her up, and she let out a cough.

Zack's pulse throbbed in his head. The hole in the wall blurred, and he blinked several times to clear away the haziness.

He ducked through the hole behind the woman but misjudged the opening and slammed his shoulder into the corner. That was going to hurt later. His nerves shot off tingles up his arm.

"I don't feel good." The woman turned to him, and her frame wilted. Zack held on to her and lifted his hand to his radio. "I need backup." Nausea swirled in his stomach.

"Everyone out. Now," Bryce yelled into Zack's earpiece.

"That was the last one." Eddie rounded the corner. "I can—" He dropped face first to the ground.

"Firefighter down," Zack yelled into his mic.

He couldn't leave his buddy, but the room started to spin, and Zack stumbled to the side. He had to get out of here. He'd promised Naya he'd be back. He couldn't repeat the past and fail her again.

Oh Lord. I need Your help.

Zack fell to his knees while stars danced in his vision.

A few seconds later, his world went black.

TWENTY-TWO

THE INTERCOM BUZZED, AND A NEW ALERT blared through the speakers.

Naya jumped to her feet, then spun around to make sure no one had witnessed her moment of panic. She'd been so engrossed in the pastor's sermon she'd lost track of time and her surroundings.

Zack had made sure she had a safe space to stay. More than that, he'd become her safe place. *Lord, there's no use in denying these feelings for this man. But my faith is lacking. Could You really restore our relationship and lead us to pursue something more?*

Even though her nerves were still on edge, the thought of his gesture steadied her racing heart.

"We've got an MCI. Truck 14 needed to assist Rescue 5. Chemical leak and crew incapacitated."

MCI. What did that mean? Naya's pulse beat in her neck. Something had gone wrong.

She raced out into the hall right as Amelia, the truck lieutenant, shoved out the doors into the engine bay. Seconds later, Izan and two women ran after her.

She followed them into the garage, where they suited up in

those heavy pants and big jackets, grabbed their helmets, and hopped in the truck in a matter of seconds.

Zack had promised her he'd come back.

Their kiss yesterday had kept her up last night. All the possibilities of what this could mean for them moving forward ran circles in her head. And the way he'd planted another one on her forehead before he'd left told her there was more to that promise than he'd conveyed with his words. She needed to make sure he was okay, or she would never be able to find out if she was right.

Her mind told her not to forget what happened last time she'd gotten close to him. That there would always be a risk in opening her heart to him.

He'll just leave again.

She shook the thought away. She might not know exactly what had happened when they were teens, but his character now and the way he'd stuck around to have her back told a different narrative. One that made her confident in Zack—the man she knew now. She wanted to believe the best about him. He wasn't the boy he used to be anymore.

What if the Lord had put him in her life to teach her to trust?

Naya raced back to the common area and grabbed her purse. She darted out to the parking lot, mindful to check her surroundings in case anyone lurked nearby. With the click of a button, she opened her car door and slid inside.

Ingram was supposed to have met her for lunch thirty minutes ago, and her friend still hadn't shown. Naya sent her a quick text with an update on where she was headed, in case they missed each other and Ingram came to the firehouse when no one was around but the receptionist.

She peeled out of the parking lot and headed to Ethos.

Gray clouds covered the sun and threatened to sprinkle rain at any moment. The crew might not be thrilled she'd shown up, and

Zack would definitely be concerned for her safety. But technically, she'd be safer around all the people than by herself at the firehouse.

At least, that's the argument she'd make.

Incapacitated.

The thought of Zack being hurt sliced deep in her heart. He was family to her. And if she admitted it, more than that. She liked Zack Stephens as more than a friend she bantered with and had come to count on. He'd become a confidant. And the way he'd talked about the foster boys earlier like they were his own kids stirred the kindling of an already warming fire in her heart.

Did he feel the same way? That maybe there was a chance at them being something more?

Naya pressed down on the gas. The speedometer climbed as she merged onto the highway.

Please, Lord, protect everyone involved in this situation from evil. Give the truck crew wisdom on how to respond and get everyone out safely. Remind Zack that he is safe in Your hands.

When troubles came and Naya couldn't do anything to fix the situation, she'd come to find solace in prayer. A first line of defense she'd discovered would bring peace to her heart each time.

No matter what lay ahead.

Naya pulled into Ethos and was greeted with the commotion of first responders dashing in and out of the building. The ambulance sat by the entrance with its lights flashing, the two trucks in front and back.

Amelia's crew of firefighters donned their masks and went inside while several employees stood outside, a few sitting on the curb or a bench.

She slowed down to study the crowd, searching for Ingram, but didn't see her. Had she been caught in this? There had to be a reason her friend hadn't shown up for lunch, but she didn't want it to be because Ingram was hurt.

Zack had all his firefighter friends to help him get out.

Who did Ingram have?

Naya pulled around and parked at the back of the lot, out of the way. A quick glance at her phone showed no new messages.

She dialed Ingram's number, but it went to straight voicemail.

Naya gripped the door handle. "Hey, Grams, it's Naya. Not sure if you got my message, but I'm at Ethos. I'll have to take a raincheck on lunch. Give me a call when you can."

Naya hung up and an unsettling feeling grew in her stomach.

Ingram had never been one to ghost someone or forget to respond to messages when they had plans.

Naya slid her purse over her head so it rested like a crossbody, then got out of the car. She passed the staff lot and recognized a yellow Jeep.

"Please don't let it be Ingram's," she whispered. Naya peered in the driver's side window and took note of the flower-shaped air freshener and the sticky note attached to the center console. That was Ingram's car for sure.

A few raindrops plopped onto Naya's head, and she quickened her steps to the front entrance, where a crowd of people faced the fire chief, Macon. Did he know if Zack was all right?

Pleas for help came from every direction. "We need to call in another ambulance."

"There's still people inside."

"My coworker isn't out yet."

Naya fought past people and got to the front door of the building.

"I'm sorry, we can't let you inside." Tazwell stuck her hand out.

What could she say? Her friend and...her boyfriend were in there? That she was a reporter?

Naya pulled out her Tribune badge. "I'm with the paper."

"You can cover the story from out here." Tazwell crossed her arms. "You step in there without proper equipment, you'll be on the floor in seconds. It's safer out here."

"What do you mean?" Naya pictured Ingram and Zack lying somewhere in an office or dark corridor. "What happened?"

"There's a chemical leak." Tazwell's radio squawked.

"I know that. I was at the firehouse when the call came in."

"Good for you." She turned her back to Naya.

What if they didn't find them in time and the gasses were deadly?

Guide the crews, Lord. Let them find everyone before it's too late.

Naya paced the sidewalk. She needed to do something. "Excuse me." She walked over to an older man who leaned back against a bench. "What's happening?"

"Some hooligan rammed the forklift into a conference room. Brought a wall down and started some kind of gas leak."

Naya listened to the man but kept her focus on the entrance, where more people were being escorted out. She hoped Ingram and Zack appeared next.

"I always knew having the warehouse connected to the office building was a bad idea. Too many hazardous materials. I'll be writing a complaint to Mr. Callahan the moment I get back to my computer." He huffed. "You'd think working overtime on a weekend would make them treat you better."

That's right. Today was Sunday. Why was Ingram in the office on a Sunday? She never worked weekends.

"Has the legal process begun yet?" Yesterday had been the cut-off. At least, that's what she remembered, given the warning Mr. Callahan had shared when she'd run into him during the fire at his house.

"Everyone got quite the email about it yesterday." He coughed. "Green Warriors is going to be bankrupt by the time Callahan's done with them."

"You should let the EMTs look at you." Naya typed a few notes into her phone. "What did he say?"

"That's beside the point. All I know is it doesn't matter who is responsible for this catastrophe today, it will stir the pot between Ethos and the Green Warriors."

Naya needed to find her friend. She walked away, down the sidewalk. What if her conversation with Sylvia had added fuel to the fire and propelled the environmental group to attack Ethos?

Ingram had gotten caught in the crosshairs. Now Zack was in there too. All the first responders were in danger.

She swiped at the tears that trickled down her cheek. Was this her fault?

The cost of writing this story continued to grow with every move she made. But if she called it quits now, the only person who would win was the perpetrator. Giving up wasn't an option.

Naya scanned the crowd once more, searching for a familiar face. Instead, she was like a buoy in a sea of chaos.

Tucker had spoken with Will that evening Naya had been with Ingram. He wasn't out here working on the story.

There was no time to waste second-guessing what Tucker would think of her call. She dialed his number and listened. Please, pick up.

"This is Long."

"It's Naya. Do you have Will's contact information? He works for Ethos."

"I doooo." He dragged out the word. "Why?"

"There's an emergency at Ethos, and I think my friend might be trapped in there. Will might know where she is."

Thankfully, Tucker didn't protest and gave her Will's number. She hoped Ingram had carpooled with Will somewhere and left her car here. That she was nowhere near this terrifying situation right now. But if she was fine, why wasn't she answering?

Naya's fingers shook. She typed in each number and hit the green call button, her foot tapping.

This is Will. I can't come to the phone right now. Leave a message.

The beep resounded in her ear, and Naya left a brief message.

Sirens broke through the commotion around her. One ambulance pulled out of the lot, and another came in.

"We've got another one."

Naya turned to the entrance and spotted medics carrying a woman toward the back of an ambulance. She caught sight of dark hair and almond skin.

"Ingram!" Naya raced to her friend's side just as they laid her on the gurney.

"Nay?" Ingram's eyes flitted around, unable to focus.

"I'm here." She patted her friend's hand while the EMT took her vitals. "It's going to be okay."

"I..." She scrunched her face. "I was in my office, then..." She paused like she was trying to place what happened.

"Hey, it's fine." Naya smiled. "You don't have to think so hard right now."

The medic put an oxygen mask over Ingram's mouth. "We need to get her to the hospital." The paramedic turned to Naya. "Are you coming with us?"

Naya wanted to be there for Ingram, but what about Zack? She glanced over her shoulder at the entrance. "Do you know if they've found Zack Stephens? He's with Rescue 5."

"They're working to get the crew out now." The medic attempted a smile, but it did nothing to console Naya.

She leaned close to Ingram. "I'll ride over in my car and meet you there. I'll see you soon, Grams."

Naya dragged her feet along the sidewalk to where Bryce stood talking to an officer. Maybe he had intel on Zack.

"That's the last one. Everyone's out." Bryce spotted her and pointed over her shoulder.

Naya whipped her head around. The front doors slid open, and three firefighters walked outside, supporting each other.

Naya raced over to the three guys and barreled into Zack.

She didn't care who witnessed the interaction. Right now, Naya was simply relieved to see him up and walking. Alive. He stumbled back, breaking away from the two other guys, but caught her in his arms. "Oof. Watch the shoulder."

"Sorry." She leaned back. "Please tell me you're okay." Naya choked back tears.

He rubbed his temple, one arm still around her. "I'll be fine, best friend." Zack attempted to wink, except his eyes rolled.

"Take it easy, man." Ridge laughed.

"Not when I missed her like crazy." Zack leaned forward, his head tilted.

Naya lifted a finger to his lips. "I think we better hold off on that. Until you're feeling better."

"It's important," Zack mumbled. His eyes flitted for a brief second, then landed on Naya. "The most important. Your r's are the most important. Don't forget. Rats only go empty'n rivers."

"All right, Stephens, time to get you looked at." Bryce stepped up to the group. "All of you need to get checked out at the hospital." He crossed his arms. "Mandatory, so don't argue. I don't want anyone from my crew having delayed effects from the exposure."

"Don't forget, son."

"Come on." Bryce wrapped an arm around Zack's shoulder and escorted him away. "Don't fall down in front of your girl."

Naya stood there processing what Zack had said.

His boss might think he was going crazy from the chemicals, but Naya couldn't shake the way Zack had stared at her as he'd spoken.

Almost like he'd been trying to communicate something to her. Like that phrase his dad had used to help his son all those years ago actually held a deeper meaning.

But what was he trying to say?

TWENTY-THREE

ZACK OPENED HIS EYES AND MOANED, WHICH prompted a cough. The forced movement thrummed the dull ache that still lingered in his head. Ouch. He turned to his side in the bed and grimaced. His shoulder was definitely bruised.

Where was he?

He blinked a few times to clear the fogginess away. The bright lights overhead and the beep of a machine nearby brought back the memories.

He'd been called out to the entrapment at Ethos and he'd blacked out.

Although, he remembered seeing Naya at some point. Or had that been a dream? Whatever it had been, she'd thrown herself at him, and having her snug in his embrace was where he wanted to stay.

Where was she?

He pushed himself up to a seated position. He needed to touch base with Naya. Make sure she was okay. If she'd heard anything about the situation, she'd be investigating it.

What if...

"You're awake."

Zack jerked his head to the side, having been unaware that anyone else was in the room.

Naya sat in a chair by the wall. She smiled at him and slid to the edge of the seat. Her ebony complexion and dark eyes sparkled, but he took note of the lines that creased her brow.

"You're here?" He swung his legs over the side of the cot, the blankets dangling to the floor. Someone had pulled off his boots, but he was still in his turnout gear—minus the jacket.

"Of course. I couldn't let you experience all the excitement by yourself." She chuckled, then sobered. "How are you feeling?"

Zack rubbed his temple. "My head still hurts. But all things considered, not terrible." Being alert was a better state than the previous one he'd been in. The Lord's grace had been over him. For that, he was grateful.

"What happened in there?" She scooted the chair closer.

Zack took a moment to get his bearings and remember all the details, some of which still seemed fuzzy. "Someone drove a forklift into the office building. It set off a CO leak, and people were trapped in the conference room." He sighed. "We got everyone out of the room before I blacked out." He recalled helping a woman when Eddie went down. "Is the rest of the crew okay?" He leaned forward, and the motion tugged at the IV in his arm. "And the employees?"

"They got everyone out of the building, but I haven't heard any other updates."

"My lieutenant—Bryce—should be close by." Zack glanced at the clock on the wall. It was already the afternoon. He located the red call button on the bed and pressed it. Better get a nurse in here sooner rather than later to speed up the process.

"Zack, was Ingram trapped in the room?" Naya whispered. "They pulled her out with the other victims."

He tried to picture if he'd recognized anyone when they'd first gone in. "No, I don't think so."

"She was there, Zack. In the building. She never works weekends." Naya propped her hands on her knees. "I tried calling her boyfriend, Will, who also works for Ethos, but he never responded. Why was she at work when she was going to meet me for lunch?"

A knock sounded on the door.

"Is everything okay in here?" A nurse peeked her head in. Her brown hair sat in a topknot, and her name badge read Charlotte.

"Yes, ma'am," Zack said. "I'd like to know when I'm going to be discharged."

"The doctor will be in soon." She smiled before ducking out.

Zack reached for his phone on the side table. "So Ingram got out okay?"

"Yeah. She's a few doors down on this floor." Naya sniffled. "I need to hear what happened. Find out why she was in the office." Her eyes widened. "Someone I spoke with outside thought this might be the environmental group's doing."

"Could be, but since it was a forklift, they would have needed access to the warehouse."

"Or it's another employee working both sides." She bit her lip. "Zack, what if it's all my fault? I talked with Sylvia, and she works with Ingram. Now this?"

"Hey." He leaned forward and took hold of her hand. "You couldn't have known Sylvia's intentions."

You couldn't have known either.

Zack shook his head to clear the thought. He needed to come clean and tell her what happened when they were teens. When he'd gone to find her bracelet. A symbol of the promise he'd intended to keep. The promise he'd made to never leave her. Regardless of how she responded, having all the details might ease her anxious heart regarding the current situation.

"There's something I need to tell you." He pulled in a deep breath.

Another knock sounded, and an older man in a white lab coat

stepped into the room. "I'm glad to see you're awake." He pushed down on the sanitizer dispenser and rubbed his hands together. "I'm Doctor Welch. Seems like your crew had quite the run-in today."

The man took Zack's vitals. "Seems like you and a firefighter by the name of Rice caught the brunt of the exposure."

"Eddie?"

"That's the guy. He just woke up, so my colleague is checking him out now."

"In addition to CO exposure, your labs showed the presence of acetaldehyde." He handed Zack a paper. "I'd like to keep you for observation. There's quite a list of symptoms to watch for over the next forty-eight hours. Vitals are good, but anything could change."

Zack scanned the details on the page. He was familiar with these chemicals from his hazmat training and reviewing safety data sheets. They were no joke. No wonder the environmental group was up in arms. The IV pulled on his skin again. The last thing he wanted, though, was to be stuck in here any longer. "With all due respect, Doc, I'd like to be discharged. I know what to look out for." He held up the paper.

Dr. Welch's brow furrowed. "If you stay here, we can monitor any changes and act quickly."

"At the first sign of any symptoms, I'll be back. My job comes with risks, but I also know how to stay safe." He only had a lingering headache, and the bright lights and noises in the room wouldn't help the pain.

"All right." Dr Welch sighed. "I'll need you to sign off that you're leaving against our recommendation."

An hour later, Charlotte walked back into the room. "Here are your discharge papers." Zack signed off, then let the nurse take out his IV. "You're all set," she said.

"Thanks."

He stuck his feet in his boots, and Naya stepped out into the hall in front of him. "Can we stop over to see Ingram before you find your colleagues?"

"You bet." Zack wanted the events of the last few hours from her perspective too. He prayed it would shed light on the situation and who might have been part of the incident.

Naya knocked on the door, then pushed it open. "Hey, Grams?"

Zack followed behind.

A smile lit up Ingram's face when she caught sight of the two of them. "You're here." She held out her arms, and Naya hurried over to the bed to give her friend a hug.

Zack pulled out a chair from the table by the window, then decided against the idea. He wanted to give the two of them space for a minute. "I'm going to grab a water bottle. I'll be right back."

He located the nearest vending machine and inserted a handful of quarters. His head still had a dull ache, which he hoped would go away soon, or he might need to take some pain meds.

"Stephens. Glad to see you're up and moving." Bryce patted him on the back.

"Lieutenant." Zack nodded, then pulled the water from the machine's receptacle.

"How're you doing?"

"Grateful to be alive. How're Eddie and Ridge?"

"They're fine. Eddie's getting discharged now."

"Good." Zack took a swig of water. "This team, they're everything to me, sir. I don't know what I'd do without 'em."

A smile tugged on Bryce's face. "We plan to keep it that way. Ridge and I are taking the trucks back to the firehouse. Everyone will be clocked out from there. Go home and get some rest." Bryce started down the hall, then stopped. "And make sure that girl of yours is taken care of."

Zack stood in the hallway for a minute. The crew had his back. And they cared about his life.

Your girl.

Would Naya ever be his?

Zack needed to gather his thoughts. He and Naya had been through a lot together, and instead of the present circumstances pulling them apart, he found himself yearning to stick close by.

A far cry from where things had stood between them when they'd first crossed paths again a week ago at the bridge.

He wanted to make his intentions clear, but first he needed the chance to explain.

Zack took another sip of water, then he returned to Ingram's room.

Ingram was upright in bed. "I had to pick up papers." She looked up and spotted him in the door.

Naya turned, perched on the edge of the bed. "Gram was just talking about why she was at the office today."

Zack sat down in the chair and set his foot on top of his other leg.

"Will needed to get some papers he'd left in his office. Said he had some extra work to catch up on. Since I was already out running errands, I offered to bring them over to his place."

"It couldn't have waited until Monday?" Naya shook her head.

"Apparently not." Ingram shrugged. "When I found them, they were in a sealed envelope."

"Did you find that odd?" Zack chimed in.

"I wouldn't have if Will hadn't been so adamant about not snooping around. He said the information was confidential for a project, and since it wasn't in my department, I could get in trouble if I leaked any of it." Ingram sighed. "Guess that shows he doesn't trust me if he thinks I'd stick my nose into something that isn't my business, then go and make it public."

"I'm sorry, Grams. He doesn't deserve you if he can't have faith in you." Naya raised her brows even as a sad smile turned up the corners of her mouth.

"I suppose." She sighed. "Once I got the folder, I went to pick up my purse from his desk, then the office door slammed shut." Ingram's shoulders shook. "No one was there, but when I tried to open the door, it was locked."

That didn't make sense to Zack. Most doors locked from the inside to keep people out, not the other way around. Especially in a corporate office setting. "Someone must have barricaded it."

"I tried calling for help, but my phone didn't have any service, and Will's office phone was disconnected. The last thing I remember is feeling lightheaded. Then I was in the ambulance."

Zack planted both feet on the ground and leaned forward in the chair. "You need to tell all this to the police, Ingram. Let them know what happened."

Naya nodded. "He's right."

Someone had deliberately targeted Ingram. "Where's Will's office in relation to the conference rooms?"

"Right around the corner. He has the prime spot for when he needs to meet with different teams."

So the chemical leak would have easily penetrated into his space. "Sounds like someone either set you up, or they thought you were Will." Zack frowned. "Either way, they locked you in there so you wouldn't be able to escape the leak."

Ingram pinched her lips, then exhaled. "What if he's mixed up in something between the two groups? He's been so on edge lately. I thought it was me, but what if it has something to do with the Green Warriors?"

"We need to check on Will." Naya stood up. "If someone wants to hurt him, he needs to know he might be in danger."

"I have a few questions for him myself." Zack crossed his arms.

"Do you want me to give him a call?" Ingram asked.

"No," Zack and Naya said in unison.

"I want the element of surprise." Zack stood and pushed in his chair.

"We'll let you know what we find out." Naya gave Ingram a quick hug.

Zack wanted to tell Naya to stay with Ingram and let him confront the guy, but it would be a pointless argument. At least she wasn't going off on her own again.

They headed for the elevator to take them outside. "His house is ten minutes from here." Naya rattled off the address.

"Just follow my lead when we get there, okay?"

"This is my friend we're talking about. Whose boyfriend has crossed the line."

Zack held up a hand. "I'm not saying you're wrong. And I don't doubt your capabilities. But I like you too much to let you get hurt."

"Oh." Naya stepped out of the elevator and into the parking garage.

Well, that comment had rendered her mute.

They walked in silence to her car, where Naya climbed into the driver's seat. "I guess we have a lot to talk about."

Zack slid on his seatbelt, and they pulled out of the garage. "I'd like to finish the story I was going to tell you earlier after we chat with Will."

"I'd like to hear it."

A few short minutes later, they turned into a suburban development lined with townhomes, and Naya parked two doors down from Will's.

Zack wished he had his weapon on him, but he kept it locked in his glove box when he was at work, and his car was still at the firehouse.

His gut told him to be on guard. The neighborhood was quiet this afternoon, but that didn't mean something sinister wasn't going on behind the scenes. The gray clouds still covered the sun, and a light breeze rustled the leaves.

Zack stepped up onto the front porch first and tapped the door with his knuckles.

No answer.

He knocked harder and the front door swung open. "Will?"

He glanced back at Naya, who shrugged.

She cupped her hands around her mouth. "Will, it's Naya. Ingram's friend. Are you home?"

Still no reply.

Zack stepped into the dimly lit foyer, Naya on his heels.

They cleared the first room and walked down the hall into the kitchen.

Naya let out a scream.

Zack turned, and his gaze locked on a hand sprawled out on the floor. He raced around the counter to where Will lay in a pool of blood.

Zack crouched down and put a finger to the man's neck. "He's dead."

TWENTY-FOUR

NAYA PINCHED HER EYES SHUT. SHE WOULD never be able to unsee Will's body in a heap on the floor—the life of another person taken too soon. Her gaze seemed unable to focus on anything else in the room.

Will was dead.

If she didn't step away, she was going to hurl. Despite her distrust in the man and how he'd treated Ingram recently, she didn't wish death on anyone, let alone in this way.

She couldn't imagine how Ingram would handle the news.

"What happened?" The words came out in a croak, and Naya bit her lip.

"Looks like he was shot. I need to call this in." Zack grimaced and pulled out his phone. "This is a crime scene."

"I need a moment." Without waiting for Zack's response, she headed out the front door and paced to and fro on the porch, trying to relieve the sick feeling in her stomach.

If someone had murdered Will, that had to mean he'd known information. But the difficult task would be discovering what that knowledge was.

If Will had been killed over the truth, whoever it was wouldn't stop until everyone who possessed the same information was silenced. That meant no one could be trusted, and Naya hated thinking that way.

It might have saved her in the past, but it was also exhausting believing the worst about people.

Right now, it seemed like this story had led nowhere but to more questions and heartache. Pieces that didn't fit into an ever-growing puzzle, which only added confusion.

In all her years as an investigative reporter, Naya had never experienced such turmoil. Even when she'd had a stalker on her heels after writing the dance instructor's story, the police had resolved the issue quickly.

Raindrops began to splash on her head, and Naya ducked under the awning to keep from getting wet. The skies opened up, and a deluge of rain fell to the ground.

She pinched the bridge of her nose.

Lord, we need Your guidance. Another person is dead, and I don't know how much more I can take. Naya shivered. Everything is so uncertain right now. Hide us in the shadow of Your wing, and bring justice, please.

The police should be here soon.

The door creaked behind her, and she turned to find Zack. He stood silently for a minute, like the weight of the whole situation was too much for words. "You're going to want to see this." He pointed inside.

Naya followed him back into the foyer, and he stopped in the hallway. Several picture frames hung on the wall. One of Will and Ingram smiling near a waterfall was in the middle. Naya rubbed the back of her neck. How had this happened? She'd have to break the news to Ingram soon, who'd be calling shortly if she didn't hear anything.

A few other pictures surrounded the happy couple, all of different travel places and landscapes. Including a map of Pine Crest pinnacle.

A hiker's memorabilia? Or evidence of something more sinister?

Naya wanted to believe the best.

"Notice anything interesting about any of these pictures?" Zack pulled out his phone and took a picture.

"He has a map of Pine Crest." Naya studied the other images, then gasped. "And his hat. It has the same crisscross emblem that the guy on the security footage wore." No, it couldn't be true. She didn't want it to be. Will couldn't be the one who'd attacked her on the mountain or left the note for Zack.

What did he have to gain from it all? She couldn't press charges against Ingram's boyfriend. Now deceased boyfriend. It would destroy her friend.

"I don't understand." Naya shook her head.

Sirens pierced the air.

Zack and Naya raced outside and waved down the officers.

Wilcox stepped out of one car, while Ramble and Tazwell got out of another.

Detective Wilcox walked toward them. "I'm sorry we have to be meeting like this." She frowned. "Where's the body?"

Naya winced at the language. Of course, the detective was doing her job, but the question felt impersonal.

Zack led the way to the kitchen, while Naya hung back in the hall.

"You didn't touch anything here, correct?" The detective pulled out a camera and bent down.

"Nothing," Zack affirmed. "I just checked for a pulse."

"What brought you out to his house?" Ramble stood near the counter and flipped open a pad of paper.

"My friend, Ingram, well, this was her boyfriend." Naya cleared her throat and explained they'd been worried he might be in danger.

Zack filled in his details, then beckoned the officer to the hallway. "I noticed this image. He's wearing the same hat Naya described after someone shoved her. And security footage showed a man wearing this cap dropping off a threatening note in the mailbox at the firehouse the other day."

"You still have access to the security footage?" Ramble asked.

"Yes, I can send you a copy of it," Zack said.

Ramble handed him a business card. "We'll look into it. And I'll check the incident report from Pine Crest."

Naya's mind went numb, and she stopped following the conversation.

The thought of writing this story and publishing the details left a sour taste in her mouth.

When the report came out, Naya needed to be there for Ingram.

"If there's nothing else you need from us, we'll get out of your hair." Zack put a hand on Naya's back.

"I'll be in touch if we need anything." Ramble turned to talk with his partner.

Zack escorted Naya outside, and the rush of the rain and wind brought her to her senses. They headed down the street to her car, and Zack popped open the umbrella.

"I need to call Ingram." Naya sniffled.

"Want me to drive?" Zack opened the passenger door.

"Sure." Naya ducked down into the car. She couldn't concentrate right now, and the last thing they needed was another car accident to add to the nightmare of events.

Zack put his hands on the steering wheel but didn't start the car. "Before you call Ingram, there's something else you should know."

Naya narrowed her eyes. "What?"

"I think Will was seeing someone else." He clenched his lips.

Bile rose in Naya's throat. That was a bold claim to make. One she didn't want to entertain because it was all too familiar. "What makes you say that?"

Zack pulled out his phone and handed it to her. "His phone was on the counter, and a text came in when you were outside. I glanced at the screen, and this is what was on it."

Naya scanned the image of Will's phone screen, and heat rose in her face.

Looking forward to having you all to myself tomorrow night. Love you lots, babe.

It wasn't the heart and winky face emojis that did her in but the name of who'd sent the message.

Naya shoved open the passenger door and hurled. When she was certain she wouldn't be sick again, she slid back into the seat and grabbed a napkin from the glovebox.

"I'm so sorry." Zack's face contorted in pain.

The rain that slid down the windshield was a mirror image of the tears that streamed down Naya's face. "He was seeing..." She hiccupped. "He was with Sylvia."

Zack grimaced. "It seems like that."

"Do you think she was the one who locked Ingram in the office?" Naya's mind swirled with thoughts.

Zack shifted in his seat to face her better. "Officers will need to comb the cameras to determine the cause of the forklift collision and who might've trapped Ingram. But would it really be helpful for her to know that?"

He was right. Although it would serve a purpose in finding out what had gone down and maybe provide insight into why cell service and Will's office phone had been disconnected, it wouldn't do Ingram any good.

But it didn't mean the investigation could stop on Naya's end. For her friend's sake, Naya had to find out who'd killed Will—and the information that had led to his untimely downfall.

"We need to find Will's killer." Naya clicked in her seatbelt.

"Nay." Zack's voice lowered a notch. "We can't play this game anymore. He's dead, and there's no telling who might be next."

"I thought we agreed to be a team on this," Naya cried. "Don't you want justice?"

"Absolutely, but the police have it now. We need to let them do their job."

"So now's when you're going to dip out?" Naya laughed and shook her head. "My friend's boyfriend is dead, and he could have been mixed up in everything. We're so close to finding the truth."

"That's not fair, Nay. I care about you." He sucked in a breath. "Now that you're back in my life, I don't want to lose you again. That's exactly what will happen if you get killed."

Naya swallowed. He had a good point. He was looking out for her. But, "What if someone else gets hurt because the truth isn't exposed? I don't think I could live with that guilt."

"That's not a burden you're meant to carry." Zack's brow furrowed. "Sometimes the best choice is to take a step back."

"When people take a step back, it means they're not going to stick around when the going gets tough. If it's not convenient for them or they don't get what they want, they just up and leave." Naya swatted at the tears, her eyes burning.

They were probably bloodshot at this point, but she didn't care.

Naya said, "My dad didn't want me, so he left me. I could never meet Tucker's expectations, so he turned to love elsewhere. And you..." Naya sucked in a lungful of air.

Zack hadn't moved a muscle. Just sat there, listening.

This last part hurt to say, because it meant what happened was real. But she needed to be completely honest.

Naya looked him in the eye. "You left. You abandoned me. Looking out the window to your grandma's house and knowing you weren't there was a reminder of what I'd lost. I was once again the outcast and unwanted."

"I'm sorry," Zack whispered.

"You were my friend. Or so I thought," she said. "And I was foolish enough to trust you again. To think that maybe I didn't know the whole story. Maybe you'd grown up and there could be something more between us." Except she'd been wrong.

Water pooled in Zack's eyes. "I never meant to hurt you."

Naya wrung her hands. He didn't raise his voice or try to defend himself. There wasn't even a hint of anger in his face. Only a mix of what was, what could have been, and what should be.

If Zack didn't want to help her see this story through, that was his choice. But it meant their paths would probably never cross again this side of heaven. She needed people she could depend on.

If they were going to go their separate ways, she needed an answer to one question she'd lived with for years. "Why did you leave?"

TWENTY-FIVE

ZACK GRIPPED THE STEERING WHEEL.

Now or never.

But the words wouldn't form.

The pounding rain against the hood of Naya's car fell in time to the steady thump of his heart. Each beat more agonizing than the last.

He'd meant everything he'd told Naya. Hurting her had never been part of the plan.

They both had choices to make about what happened next, and either way, someone would get hurt. She wanted to keep investigating the story, but now that someone was dead, he wanted her to forget the story and be safe. He wanted to shake some sense into her and tell her she wasn't thinking clearly.

Had she not seen Will face down on the ground—dead?

This story, the truth, was not worth it if the cost was more lives. If it meant she gave up *her* life.

"Why, Zack?" Her whispered voice pierced through the recesses of his mind and took him back to that day. "Why did you leave?"

When you walk through the fire, I will be with you. The reminder from Isaiah 43 echoed in his mind.

Lord, give me wisdom. Help me speak the truth with kindness. Give me the courage to be honest. Whatever the outcome of this conversation, protect Naya. And may the person behind these attacks be caught quickly.

He leaned his head against the cool glass window and took a deep breath, willing his heart to stop racing. "I didn't have a choice."

He raked his fingers through his hair. He hoped Naya could see through to his heart. "We made a pact that we would always be friends. That we'd stick by each other." Zack threaded his finger under the bracelet and spun it around his wrist. He'd been a freshman in high school, and she'd been in eighth grade.

"I remember." Naya's gaze trailed down to his hand. "We gave each other the red bracelets."

"Then you lost yours."

"I fidgeted with it all the time."

Naya had told him she couldn't find it when they got back from youth group one night.

"*I think it fell off during game time. You won't forget me now, will you?" Tears sprang to her eyes, and her breath came in short pants.*

He knew what it was like to lose people. And he didn't want her questioning their friendship.

"I knew how much it meant to you, so I made a promise to myself to find your bracelet."

In retrospect, he should be able to laugh, because the way he had gone about obtaining her bracelet hadn't been the smartest decision. But it couldn't be reversed now.

"What's that mischievous look for?" Naya narrowed her eyes.

Apparently, he couldn't hide his thoughts, either. "I was the goofy kid that my grandma always had to wrangle in."

"That you were."

He'd always found a way to make the other kids at school laugh. Coping mechanism? Sure. It had done his heart good during those years. But how did it serve him now? It was silly to think he could keep conversations surface level and still have quality friendships. It was past time to be real. Honest. "Naturally, I had to devise a plan that would become a tale that lived on. It quickly turned into a quest, and I got the help of two of the other boys from church."

"You came up with a plan instead of just searching for it next time we were at youth group?"

Now she was catching on.

Zack nodded. "After service the following Sunday, I decided to sneak up to the classroom and look for the bracelet."

The other two boys who'd been part of the plan had been meant to distract his grandma. Just long enough to give Zack time to find the missing bracelet. "I found it tucked in the corner by the snack counter. I had just picked it up when the lights went out."

"No one saw you still in there?"

"They must have had all the lights on a timer to shut off after the service. When it suddenly went dark, I panicked. I stood up and slid my hand along the wall to find a light switch." There'd been no windows in the room, which had made visibility harder because no natural light had peeked through. "I ended up tripping over a trash can, and I grabbed onto something on the wall. Suddenly a siren pierced the air, and a single flashing bulb lit up the space."

"The fire alarm." Naya's eyes widened.

"I'd pulled the fire alarm." And secured his reputation as the goof, the troublemaker. "The sprinkler system was activated, and I was drenched, along with everything else in the room."

"Why don't I remember any of this?" Her foster parents always chatted with people after church, which gave her time to hang out with the other kids.

Zack grimaced. "You stayed home with your foster mom that day with the stomach bug."

"Ohhh." Naya's features softened. "That was a horrible few days."

"I raced out of that room real fast. At that point, the rest of the plan slipped out of my mind, and I forgot to exit out the side door." Zack rubbed his jaw. "I barreled out the front door and ran straight into my grandma. She tumbled backward and fell and broke her hip."

He could still picture her frail arms shaking, trying to sit up. The wrinkles on her face deepening from the pain.

Naya sucked in a breath.

"They called an ambulance for my grandma and after her surgery, she went to a nursing home. CPS took over and with no other next of kin, I was put in a new foster home." Zack sighed. "I was the goofball who caused too much trouble. And my grandma paid the price."

"It wasn't your fault." Naya's voice rose a notch.

Zack's gaze locked with hers, but his expression told her he took full responsibility for the situation.

"That's why no one came home and your grandma's house went up for sale. My foster parents tried to contact her, but they weren't successful."

"My grandma only had a landline." Zack let out a humorless laugh. "And I found myself clear across town in a completely different school district, with a family I barely knew. It felt isolating."

Naya's chin quivered. "I was wrong about the whole situation." She averted her gaze to her lap.

He took his thumb and ran it along her cheek, then lifted her chin. "I never intended to leave you. The last thing I wanted was to hurt you or cause confusion."

"I understand that now."

The unspoken words still remained. It didn't change all the years of wondering. The questions whose answers appeared evasive. The times of bitterness.

Silence lengthened. Zack had shared the truth. Now it was up to Naya to decide how to respond. His muscles were stiff, but there was nowhere to stretch his legs in the car. They were trapped in here together, but only they had the key to the chance of freedom that lay on the other side.

He wanted there to be restoration. But he couldn't control Naya's heart. She had to decide for herself what she wanted.

Zack took off the bracelet and unwound the two pieces of red cord. "I've kept your half all these years." He held out his hand.

"Why?" Naya blinked.

"I made a promise. I guess I hoped at some point our paths would cross again." He'd been about ready to give up when he'd spotted her in the water after the bridge collapse.

"So why didn't you reach out?"

Zack shrugged. "I figured you were better off without me."

"I see." She swallowed. "Can you hold on to it for a little longer?"

She shouldn't feel sorry for her answer. He didn't want to force her to feel a certain way.

He rewound the two cords and slid it back on his wrist. He'd hold on to it for as long as she wanted. Maybe one day he'd earn her trust back, and she'd be able to see the lengths he'd go to stick by her side.

"Zack." His name was a whisper on her lips. "None of that was your fault. You did a noble thing, even if it didn't go as planned." She sucked in a breath. "I'm sorry for what I believed about you."

"You had every right to be upset."

"Given my track record with men and them playing the great vanishing act, it's been hard to trust and depend on anyone." She shook her head. "I should have given you the benefit of the doubt. Regardless, it wasn't an excuse to hold a grudge. No matter whose fault it was, my attitude was still a sinful choice on my part."

"You're forgiven." Zack smiled. "I care about you, Nay. I want what's best for you."

Whatever the future held for them, he wanted her to know she had a friend in him. Although, he hoped he'd become more than that. Someone she could turn to.

He couldn't promise he'd be perfect. More mistakes were bound to happen. But he prayed that even in his failings, he could point her to the One who would never leave her side or hurt her.

"Thanks. I'm grateful for you too, Zack."

He could hear the *but* ready to come.

"I need some time to process everything." She rubbed her eyes, then straightened in her seat. "Can you take me back to the hospital? I need to touch base with Ingram."

"Of course." Zack twisted the key in the ignition and put the windshield wipers on full speed.

The police had a handle on the investigation now, and that was the way it should be. They had the resources to put an end to this mayhem—hopefully sooner rather than later.

When they got to the hospital, Zack parked Naya's car and headed into the lobby, where he could call one of his buddies to come pick him up and take him back to the firehouse.

"Thanks for driving." Naya gave a short wave and headed down the hall.

Zack wanted to run after Naya and put everything behind them. He wanted to move forward, but he couldn't. Knowing someone was willing to kill over the secrets surrounding the water contamination in town added a level of danger Zack didn't want to gamble with anymore.

Maybe after all the events of today, Naya would realize it was better to leave things alone. Surely Ingram would advise Naya to stop chasing the story. With her boyfriend dead, she wouldn't want her best friend to endure the same fate.

If Naya was safe, that was all that mattered. Now he could make good on his intentions to find his parents' killer without worrying about Naya getting hurt. Zack would put the past behind him once and for all.

TWENTY-SIX

SOMETHING FURRY TICKLED NAYA'S CHEEK, AND she opened her eyes to Ingram's cat, Coco, nuzzled up next to her on the sofa. Naya yawned and pushed herself to a seated position.

Her back protested the position change, and she turned to the side to stretch. "Looks like someone else didn't want to be alone either." She stroked the cat's back, and he purred.

Naya picked up her phone to check the time. It wasn't even seven yet. She still had two hours before she needed to be in the office.

After she'd gone back to Ingram's hospital room, she'd broken the news about Will. Ingram had been in shock, and the tears hadn't stopped. After being discharged, Ingram had asked Naya if she would stay overnight at her house. Naya wanted to support her friend however she could, and if that meant having a sleepover like when they were kids, she'd take it.

Naya picked up her duffel bag and moseyed down the hall to the bathroom. Ingram's door was still shut, and no light peeked from the bottom crack.

Naya washed her face and brushed her teeth before starting her makeup routine, mindful not to make too much noise and wake up her friend. The past twenty-four hours had taken a toll on both of them. Naya figured she'd need a whole bottle of concealer to cover the bags under her eyes.

The conversation with Zack yesterday still played in her mind like a broken record. It was a wonder she'd gotten any sleep last night. On one hand, relief filled Naya knowing she finally had the full truth. There was no more guessing. The sincerity in Zack's tone as he'd shared the details had told her all she needed to know.

He hadn't intended to hurt her, and she believed him.

Naya pumped the liquid foundation onto a sponge and blended it into her face.

He didn't want her to continue pursuing leads for the story. But he'd told her how he'd gone back for that bracelet. He hadn't given up on what mattered most, and she wouldn't either. Which was exactly why she couldn't drop this story until she found out what was really happening with Ethos and the Green Warriors.

She zipped up her makeup bag and let out a sigh.

Ingram had pleaded with her through watery eyes last night to let the story go. *God sees what's going on. He won't let justice be lost on this. He won't turn a blind eye to this forever.*

But she needed to focus on what was most important. Truth. Justice. Healing. Not just for herself, Ingram, or Zack, but for everyone involved in this case. These people and their families deserved to know they mattered. That a blind eye wouldn't be turned to their situation.

Lord, I need You to direct my steps. Reveal the truth. Show me what I can do to shine light on the situation.

Naya changed into khakis and a patterned blouse, then made her way to the kitchen. She grabbed a glass from the cupboard and filled it with water. A box of honey oat granola sat in the corner, and she poured herself a bowl, mixing it with some almond milk.

"How'd you sleep?"

Naya turned around at Ingram's question and did her best not to reveal her shock at her friend's appearance. Ingram had her hair in a messy bun, although that was an understatement. The ponytail barely kept the locks in place, and flyaways stuck out in every direction. Black streaks sat just above her cheeks from leftover mascara that hadn't been wiped clean. Her sweatpants and T-shirt told Naya she wasn't about to make an appearance to the world today.

"Coco kept me company." Naya ate a spoonful of cereal.

"I'm glad." Ingram offered a half smile. "I called off work today, even though everyone is working remotely while they clean up the building." She slid onto a barstool next to Naya and propped her elbows on the counter.

"Want me to stay here?" Naya's friend was more of a verbal processor, and all the introspection on top of being home alone might compound the distress she was in. "I can work remotely."

"No, I'll be fine." She waved her hand. "What are you going to do today?"

Naya opened her mouth, then realized what Ingram was asking. She didn't want to know *if* she was working today but rather *what* she was working on.

"I really want to see this story through, Grams." She took another bite of granola. The crunch drowned out the turmoil in her mind over what to do.

"I appreciate you wanting to stick up for me with Will, but the police should be the ones to handle the case."

"And they are," Naya affirmed.

"Then find another story to write. One with less stakes. Maybe a happier one."

"What will happen to whoever has caused all this havoc? They killed Will. They might even be responsible for Zack's parents' deaths. So we just let them walk free without exposing the truth?"

"Will's dead, Naya. And I'm left to pick up the pieces of a broken heart." Ingram pinched the bridge of her nose. "You don't have to write every story that comes your way. Not when you could lose so much. You've got Zack. He cares about you. I don't want to see you throw it away." She swatted at a tear.

Naya swirled her spoon in leftover milk.

"You don't have to prove yourself to anyone, Nay. You're you because of who you are, not what you have to offer to anyone." Ingram went over to the fridge and poured a glass of orange juice before returning to her seat.

Did Ingram realize what she was saying? What Zack was asking of her?

"I could care less about the promotion." She dropped her spoon in the bowl with a clank. What she'd done to build her career didn't matter. "It's so much more than that now. A man is dead, and lives have been threatened." Naya cleared her throat. "I need to head into the office."

She rinsed her bowl and put it in the dishwasher. "I love you, Grams." She hugged her friend. "A shower might also do you some good. Add a fresh smell to the room."

Ingram pinched her lips. "So you can say you love me and tell me what to do to move on with my life, but you won't take advice from those who love you?"

Naya grabbed her purse and a light jacket.

"You lost your family once, Naya. You really want to risk losing those who've become your family again?"

Naya bit her lip. That's why she was pursuing this story. She loved them enough she wanted them all to have closure so they could move on with life. Without a killer on the streets wreaking havoc. "I'll be back after work." Naya got in her car and drove off.

Naya turned the music volume down. *You've given me a second chance at family, Lord. How can I stand by and not defend them? Not fight for them?*

Wasn't that what families did? They fought for each other. Protected one another. Jesus had done that for her on the cross. He'd made a way to bring her into His forever family by laying down His life. *That* was love.

By the time Naya pulled into a parking spot at the Tribune, she'd made her decision.

She took the elevator to the third floor and knocked on Tucker's cubicle. "Can we talk?"

Tucker motioned her inside, and she took a seat across from his desk. She'd only been to his space a handful of times. When they'd been dating, she'd insisted they keep things professional around the other employees, which meant visits to each other in their offices had been few and far between.

The early morning sun streamed through the window and revealed a meticulous area devoid of any dust or stray belongings. Yet it still felt stuffy without any personal touches to adorn the mahogany wood desk and filing cabinet.

"What do you have on the water contamination story?"

Tucker leaned forward in his chair and raised his brow. "You want me to divulge information to get you closer to reaching your goal of landing the promotion?" He laughed. "We have five more days. No way am I doing that."

"This story has already put my life in jeopardy enough times. Yesterday a man was killed." She'd lain awake remembering Will lying on his kitchen floor. "This is bigger than a promotion."

"I already told you I wasn't responsible for any of the attacks. Although..." He squirmed in his chair.

She'd been around the man long enough to pick up on his tics and when he wasn't being completely honest. "What do you know?"

"The note someone put on your car..." Tucker paused. "I didn't write it, but I can tell you who did."

Naya wanted to jump up and say it had been him. Instead, she gripped the chair handles. "And you kept this a secret because..."

"I was planning to tell you I saw it, but the woman acted sketchy when she slid the note under your windshield wiper. Like she wasn't supposed to be there."

Clearly not, when the note was a direct threat.

But if Tucker hadn't written the note, then Will would have been her next guess. Not a woman. Given the likelihood of him being behind two of the other attacks, she'd made all kinds of assumptions. If it was a woman, that meant more than one person might be involved in the illegal activities.

"Yeah. After hearing about the other series of, uh, events, I thought coming clean would put a target on my back too."

Not only had Tucker kept quiet, he'd done so to save face. The confession stung. How could he have been so selfish? Clearly, he didn't have her best interests at heart. He was in it for the job.

You've got a guy who cares about you. Don't throw it away.

Ingram's comment earlier resonated. Zack's disagreement with continuing to write the story had been a hard pill to swallow. Although, now she understood the difference between the two men.

It didn't bother Tucker whether her well-being was at stake. He'd signed on to do a job, and he was going to finish it one way or another. And if she got hurt, it wasn't his problem.

Instead, Zack was willing to risk stepping into the crosshairs alone to keep her safe. Not because he didn't think she was competent—rather, he cared enough to have her back.

"Thank you."

"For what?" Tucker cocked his head.

She hadn't realized she'd spoken the gratitude out loud. "Nothing." She waved her hand.

He'd helped her see what she needed in a friend and a potential significant other. The qualities she'd overlooked before were actually the greatest assets.

She needed to talk with Zack. But first Naya had to finish what she'd come in here for. "Do you know the person's name?"

"No. I never talked with her. Only observed from a distance. But she had short blonde hair." Tucker held up his hands to his ears.

Naya grabbed her phone from her pocket and swiped through pictures until she came to the one she'd been tagged in. "Is this her?" She held up the image of Sylvia.

"Right there. Front and center. That's her all right."

Acid rose in Naya's throat, and she swallowed to push it down. But it didn't ease the burn.

It was time to go to the police with this information. Finally put an end to this mayhem.

"I can't write this piece anymore." Naya stood up. She had the pieces she needed to fulfill her quest for the truth. "I have friends who care about me. For their safety and my own, I'm done."

Tucker leaned back in his chair. "Just like that, you're going to hand over the promotion?"

"It's not worth it." What would the promotion win her if she got injured and couldn't even do her job anymore? "I'll send you the documents I have. I'm going to write a human-interest piece instead. Show people what one of the rescue squad members, Zack Stephens, is doing to help kids in foster care. If Drew doesn't like it, then so be it."

At least she'd still give it a shot. It might not be the piece their boss had asked her to write, but she could still submit something to showcase her work for the promotion.

"May the best writer win." Tucker stood up and tugged on his suit jacket.

Naya walked back to her office and shut the door.

She needed to call the police, then fill Zack in on her findings. If Sylvia was involved in the schemes, it might not matter that Naya had forfeited the story.

The knowledge Naya possessed was enough to kill for.

TWENTY-SEVEN

"ZACK?" NAYA'S EXPECTANT VOICE CAME OVER the line, and Zack's heart skipped a beat. "I'm so glad you called."

He'd missed her call earlier because he'd just gotten home from meeting with Powells again and had stopped for a quick lunch on the way back.

Her profession was something he could get used to hearing. If she let him, he'd strive to be there for her and provide for her. Although, now was not the time to think futuristically. There were other pressing matters to focus on.

"I just talked with Tucker and found out something that puts a whole new spin on this story."

His stomach hardened as he pictured Naya talking with Tucker. Zack rolled his shoulders and stood up from his couch. There was nothing between the two anymore. Naya had made that clear.

"Looks like we both have shocking revelations to share." Zack paced the length of the room but never took his eyes off the box. "Can you swing by my house? There's something I need to show you."

"I'll be there in fifteen."

"Great. And Naya?"

"Yeah?"

"Watch your back."

Zack's childhood had been uprooted like a baby tree caught in the winds of a storm, and he didn't know if he wanted to go back and relive those days. The weight of what could be under the latch of that box sat on Zack's shoulders like a heavy yoke. Did he really want to open it and be transported back to another time and place? On one hand, he ran the risk of remembering too much if the contents held pictures and other keepsakes. The last thing he wanted was a resurgence of jealousy over what other kids had enjoyed with their families that had been taken from Zack too soon.

The next several minutes dragged while Zack waited for Naya to arrive. Thoughts of her being run off the road or tailed plagued him, and although he wanted to do everything he could to protect her, it wasn't possible. Only the Lord could guard her constantly.

A door slammed shut, and Zack raced onto the front porch before she'd made it halfway up the sidewalk.

Her brow was lined with creases despite her head being held high. Even her hair was done in a half updo, and her pink blouse added vibrancy to her professional attire. But Zack saw past the put-together demeanor. Something was bothering her as much as what he'd discovered had stirred him.

Zack wrapped her in a hug. "Any trouble getting over here?" He leaned back, staring at her face.

"All good for now." She offered a half-hearted smile. Naya followed him into the living room. "What's that?" She pointed to the box on the coffee table.

"Powells called me earlier. Said he had a box of my dad's stuff he'd been given for safekeeping. And after hearing a report of the incident at Ethos and Will's death from another firefighter, he wanted to rid himself of anything that could be traced back to my dad." According to Powells, he'd never opened the box to examine the contents, but Zack's dad had told him it had pertinent information that needed to be kept safe. Now it was Zack's choice to do with it what he wanted.

Naya sat on the sofa. "Have you opened it?"

"I'm afraid of what might be in there."

Naya reached out her hand and tugged Zack down next to her. "You told me about the beauty of memories, right?" She turned to face him and laid her hand on his shoulder. "You could remember more good moments so you don't forget."

Zack tucked a strand of hair behind her ear. "Has anyone ever told you that you have a special way with words? Reminding people of the truth."

"Once or twice." She smiled. "Whatever's in that box matters. The contents could help bring closure to their case too. Either way, you're honoring their lives, Zack."

He'd been the one to tell Naya to stop investigating leads for the story. And if the box contained vital pieces of information that tied the loose ends together, he'd be bringing her right back into this mess.

Yet she was here, walking alongside him through the reminders of what he'd lost. Zack didn't want to shut her out. She was a part of his life. And that meant letting her into *every* part of his world.

If the box held some of the missing puzzle pieces, he would simply turn it over to the police and let them add it to their investigation.

He set the box in his lap and turned the latch.

The ticking of the clock on the wall above him amplified the anticipation. His hands shook while he removed the contents one by one.

Sure enough, a few photos of his dad and mom lay on top. There was one of them holding Zack as a newborn and several of different trips and outings they'd taken over the brief years they'd had together. In each photo, smiling faces stared up at him.

Zack collected the pictures and handed them to Naya.

"Are these your parents?"

"Yeah." He stared at the picture. The smell of sunscreen and the rumbling of waves took him back to that day on the beach. "Our last family vacation before the fire."

"Your mom was beautiful." She held the picture up next to his face. "You look just like your dad."

"I always admired him." Zack had wanted to be like his dad when he grew up. A man who loved Jesus and helped people.

"I never knew them, but I'd say you're carrying on the family name well." The gentleness of her words worked to smooth away the doubts.

"Thanks."

Next, he pulled out a folded up piece of old parchment paper. A few yellow stains coated the back, and when Zack unraveled the document, his fingers turned to ice. He stared at an exact replica of the map of Pine Crest Pinnacle that Will had hanging in his hallway. The only difference lay in the red X that marked a location down by the river.

The paper shook in his hand. "Look at this." He gave Naya the map.

He'd send this over to Detective Wilcox to investigate. The information was further proof of why the professionals should handle the case and that Naya had been spot on when she'd proposed that his parents' deaths were connected to the water contamination story.

Naya gasped. Her eyes widened. "This is the same map that was in Will's house."

"Bingo."

"And the river is marked with an X."

"So the rumors of something being dumped into the river might be true." Although there was still the question of how it was happening. "If that's the case, how could it have gone on for so long without anyone growing suspicious?" Zack frowned. "If it started with my parents, then it's been going on for over twenty years."

"It's a slow process," Naya pulled out her phone. "Read this."

She handed him the device, and he skimmed the article she had pulled up.

"PFAs are forever chemicals so they are nearly impossible to eradicate from the ground and water supply because they don't break down. If more PFAs are added to an already contaminated site, they continue to build up."

Zack said, "And it takes years for people to see the effects on their body until it's too late and they find themselves battling thyroid diseases or ulcerative colitis." He scrolled through the long list of health complications the article listed at the end.

"Exactly. If the chemicals have been dumped in increasing quantities and started years ago, no wonder people are now getting sick."

Zack gave Naya back her phone then turned the map over and read the sentence etched in pen. *Rats only go empty'n rivers.* "The silly sentence my dad taught me is on here." Zack read the next line. "Huh. It also says, *It's too important not to tell someone, P.*"

Naya lifted the map and studied it. "You think your dad was trying to tell someone what he knew?"

"There has to be a double meaning to the phrase my dad taught me. Did the investigator on their case know about this years ago?" Zack's mind spun with questions that seemed to trail off without any answers.

"P…P…" Naya tapped her finger against her chin. "What if Powells was supposed to tell someone?"

"It's possible. Clearly it didn't do any good. From what we learned about Powells, he was trying to save his own skin." Zack leaned forward on the couch, his hands clasped.

"No one must have thought to ask more questions. Or they kept coming to dead ends," Naya said.

"Which means the method of hiding the activity couldn't seem totally out of the ordinary."

"Exactly." Naya set the map on the table. "Someone would have to know how to get the job done."

"Without sounding any alarms."

"Like Sylvia," Naya mumbled.

"Will's secret lover?" Zack sat down and leaned forward. "But she's too young to have played a role in this when my parents were alive."

"I know." Naya bit her lip. "Hear me out on this. She's been advocating with Green Warriors but works at Ethos. Ingram knows her. Tucker confirmed she was the one who put the note on my car."

"How do you know Tucker was telling the truth?" Zack narrowed his gaze. Based on what she'd shared about this guy before, he didn't seem to always be on the up and up. And he could have tried to protect himself by finding a scapegoat.

"He described the woman before I even showed him a picture that matched the description. And he seemed nervous to say anything. Like it would put a target on his back."

That guy needed to get his priorities in check. It's a good thing Zack hadn't been around to witness the way Tucker had treated Naya when they'd been a couple.

"That means there's more than one person involved in this scheme." Which made sense given the scale of the situation. "Especially if this has been going on for years."

"How many, though?" Naya sat down on the floor and crossed her legs. "And who's the driving force behind it all?"

"I don't know, but Sylvia would have the means to carry out her role in it at the moment," Zack said. "If she knows Ingram and she was working with Will, the two of them could have easily been behind the current attacks."

Naya put her hand over her mouth and pulled in a breath. "What if she killed Will?"

"All the more reason to hand everything over to the cops." Zack held his breath, waiting for the rebuttal. "We have no idea what set off Sylvia enough she murdered him."

"I forfeited the story."

Zack wasn't sure he'd heard her correctly. "You did?"

She sighed. "I'm sorry for not wanting to see things from your perspective. You and Ingram were right. I was being prideful and thought I had to prove myself. But it's not worth it when so many people have gotten hurt already."

"Hey." Zack held out his hands. Naya placed hers on top of his and they both stood. "You are incredibly talented. The last thing I want is to see that gift go to waste because you got hurt."

"I know." Water pooled in Naya's eyes. "You're a great guy, Zack. I'm grateful to have you in my life." She squeezed his hand. "Was there anything else in the box?"

Zack reluctantly pulled away and picked up the wooden container. Nothing else was visible, so he shook it gently. The wood clanked and separated slightly. He took out what had appeared to be the bottom of the box.

"There's a whole other stack of papers." Zack pulled out one that was a photocopied page with pictures on it.

Naya leaned over his shoulder. "The sandbags."

"That's how they're dumping the waste." Zack couldn't believe it had been that simple. "And I bet the map is the drop-off point."

Zack pulled out his phone. Time to tell Wilcox what they'd found and get a crew to investigate the pinnacle.

Because Zack had a feeling the truth had been hidden in plain sight the whole time.

TWENTY-EIGHT

NAYA'S NERVES TINGLED AND HER HEART RACED like she'd just downed a cup of coffee. She sat in the passenger seat of Zack's rental car on their way up to the pinnacle. They'd already alerted the police to their findings, and Wilcox had said she and Basuto would meet them at the river.

She sent a quick text to Ingram to let her know what they'd discovered and instructed her not to go anywhere near Sylvia. This woman could very well be a wolf in sheep's clothing, and Naya didn't want to envision what a confrontation with her would entail. Had anyone else from the environmental group grown suspicious of Sylvia? Or were there more people working undercover to throw off the trail?

She couldn't believe they were chasing this lead. Given her decision to stop pursuing and writing this story for the Tribune, she almost wanted to laugh at the situation. She and Zack were doing what could very well bring about more trouble. But this time, the police were on the way and, she prayed, one step ahead of Sylvia. And Zack was close by.

Naya peeked over at Zack. His jaw was taut, his eyes glued to the road. On his right arm, the red bracelet was woven around his wrist.

This man had fought for her. And continued to fight for her.

Her own experiences and fears had clouded her judgement of Zack for so long. He wasn't afraid to speak the truth, but he did it with gentleness and grace. And he'd stayed—even when it hadn't looked exactly like she'd envisioned.

She needed to take time to pray and discern her emotions with the Lord's guidance.

One thing she did know for sure. When they weren't fighting to survive to the next day, Naya hoped Zack would initiate an official date. Because she wanted the privilege of saying yes.

"What are you thinking?" Zack broke the silence, and heat crept up Naya's neck.

How had she been so rude to him the first day their paths had crossed again at the bridge, when he'd helped her get the old man to safety?

"Just remembering that day when the bridge collapsed."

"That feels like eons ago." He sighed.

She shuddered at the thought of plunging into the river and wading through the debris to get out. "They were there that day too." Naya turned in her seat.

"Who were?"

"Not who—what. There were sandbags in the water. I assumed they were from a temporary dam someone had put up."

Zack snapped his fingers. "What if that's one way they got away with it? People would assume a barrier had been created to prevent unwanted water flow, when it could have really been about disposing of contaminated waste."

"That is a genius idea. Too bad it's not being used for a good cause."

Zack pulled into the gravel parking lot at the base of the mountain, not far from the service road where his car had almost exploded with them in it. Naya pinched her eyes shut, then opened them. That wouldn't happen again today. No one had followed them here, and with police presence shortly, it would be foolish for someone to make a move.

"You ready?" Zack opened the passenger door for her.

"I suppose so." Naya stepped out and zippered her jacket. The sun shone, and no breeze swirled through the air, but Naya still had the chills.

Zack opened up the map, and they headed for the trees. A paved gravel path wove through the wooded area, which made it easier to navigate despite the brush, rocks, and tall pine trees.

"If the drop-off location is marked by this X, it looks like it's on the east side of the river over here." Zack pointed off in the distance to boulders that lay in a haphazard pile several yards from the riverbank.

They hiked down the trail, and the tree covering blocked out the sun, which made the surrounding area more ominous. But as they got closer to the bank, the sound of trickling water worked to calm Naya's nerves. On an average day, this spot would beckon Naya to come with her hammock to find solitude and enjoy nature.

"I thought Wilcox was on her way." Naya glanced at her watch. Ten minutes had already passed.

"They should be here soon." Zack stopped walking and turned to her with a smile. "They know where to meet us."

Naya appreciated his effort to offer consolation.

They crossed over a bridge and came to a clearing. "Look." Naya pointed. "There's a hut."

Zack quickened his steps, and Naya took long strides to stick close behind him.

Zack peered in the side window of the wooden shack. "It's abandoned. Nothing but empty space."

Naya walked around to the back of the makeshift shelter and froze. "Zack, come look at this." Sandbags were stacked up against the hut like firewood. Brown pine needles created a coating over the area. A few feet away lay an overturned, unmarked white truck.

"This has to be the spot." Zack blew out a breath and tucked the map into his pocket.

The burlap bags appeared identical to the one found in the brush last week.

Zack moved around the area, snapping pictures, and Naya headed toward the truck.

A gunshot pierced the air.

Naya dove for the ground. A choked scream left her lips. Another pop sounded, and a bullet whizzed past her, kicking up the dirt. Her ears rang, and her eyes didn't want to cooperate or focus on her surroundings.

Where was Zack?

"Don't shoot! It's Zack and Naya." Zack's voice echoed through the woods.

Another round of bullets sprayed the air and pinged off the truck.

Now was not the time to freeze. Naya pulled in a shaky breath and army-crawled closer to the covering of the hut, where Zack's voice had come from. Footsteps sounded in front of her, and Naya froze.

Zack barreled around the corner and dropped to the ground next to her. "Are you okay?" His eyes widened, and he gripped her arm. "Naya?"

She fought through the panic. "I'm okay."

He glanced over his shoulder once more before turning his attention back to her. "Stay here."

Naya gulped. "That is definitely not the police."

"I'm going to see who it is." Zack pulled a handgun from an ankle holster.

She stared at him, her mouth open. "You brought a gun?"

Zack let go of her arm. “Didn’t know what we’d encounter. Thought it was better to be safe than sorry.”

“You can’t confront them!”

Zack stood up. “Call 9-1-1. I’ll be back.” He kept his body flush against the hut, then disappeared around the corner.

No more gunshots rang out for the moment, but Naya didn’t know whether that was a good or bad thing. She held down her phone’s side buttons to activate emergency services.

“9-1-1, where’s your emergency?”

“Pine Crest Pinnacle.” Naya tried to whisper, but her voice sounded too loud in her own ears. “Someone’s shooting down by the river.” She slowly inched back against the shack and kept her gaze roaming.

“Is anyone hurt, ma’am?” the man asked.

“Not yet.” Naya curled her toes. *Keep us safe, God. Put an end to this evil before someone else gets hurt.*

“Officers and medics are en route.”

A gunshot ricocheted through the stillness, and a few birds burst out of the trees and flew away. Naya squeezed her eyes shut and curled into a ball. She opened one eye but didn’t see any bullets nearby.

“Ma’am, are you still there?” The dispatcher’s voice echoed once more.

“I need to go make sure my friend is okay.” Naya disconnected the call and pocketed the device.

A motorcycle engine roared to life, and Naya’s chest tightened. Had they hurt Zack? She couldn’t just sit here if he needed her help. He’d been the one to come to her aid more times than she could count.

Out of love.

Love.

Yeah, she was going after him. She wasn’t about to lose him for good.

Naya crouched and shimmied her way to the side of the building. She scanned the expanse in front of her, studying the trees for any movement.

Sirens rang through the air, now coupled with the revving of the motorcycle.

The threat didn't appear to be near her anymore, so Naya darted from her covering to the bridge. She ducked by the base of the crossing along some boulders so that her knees almost touched the muddy dirt by the water's edge.

Her breath came in pants, and she strained to listen. No other footsteps followed. She stood up and tore across the bridge and up the incline toward the parking lot. She wove in and out of the trees, following a zigzag pattern, and stayed off the main trail.

Another gunshot boomed, and Naya froze.

"Police. Drop the weapon." Shouts ensued.

Naya peered around the tree trunk and spotted Zack fifty yards away, near the parking lot, hands held high in the air.

She made her way up to the main entrance in the lot, mindful to keep her hands in front of her. Basuto stood next to Wilcox, who had a tight rein on someone she was handcuffing.

A motorcycle lay on the ground near the three of them, and when Wilcox turned around with the suspect, Naya gasped.

"Sylvia." Naya balled her hands into fists by her sides. "You could've killed us!"

Wilcox began reading the woman her rights.

Sylvia glared at Naya and Zack. "Don't think for a minute I'm going to talk."

"Let's go." Wilcox escorted her to the back of the patrol car.

"Are you okay?" Naya hurried over to Zack's side and wrapped him in a hug.

"If you're safe, that's all that matters," he whispered into her ear.

She pulled back and examined his face for any sign of injuries.

"I'm fine. Really. You're shaking." Zack rubbed his hands up and down her arms. "Do you need a blanket?"

Naya shook her head. Her teeth chattered, but she clamped down on her lips. How was this man so selfless? Even in the face of danger, he continued to look out for her needs first. The gesture made her want to reciprocate.

Basuto walked over to them. "Do either of you need medical assistance?"

"We're good." Naya didn't want a big fuss right now. Not when she wanted to find out what was in that truck.

"You guys came in the nick of time," Zack said.

"All right." Basuto radioed in to cancel the ambo. "I'm going to need to take your statements."

Zack relayed the information, then Naya filled in her parts of the story. "There's also an overturned truck down there by the pile of sandbags."

The three of them headed back down the path while Wilcox stayed with Sylvia.

They crossed the bridge and came to the truck's tailgate. "My hunch says the back is loaded with sandbags," Naya said. "There is also a stack by that shed."

"We think the bags are where they're hiding the chemicals that are causing the runoff in the water," Zack said.

The lock was already open, so Basuto pushed up on the rolling door. Sure enough, mounds of burlap bags were piled into the bed of the truck. Basuto's radio squawked.

The police lieutenant grabbed his radio and replied, "Bring the forensics crew down to the river base."

Basuto walked around to the passenger side door and opened it. A body lay slumped in the seat. Gray peppered the brown locks, and fine lines etched the forehead.

Naya stepped closer to get a better look.

"And bring the coroner," Basuto radioed and let out a sigh. "We've got..."

Naya tuned out Basuto's conversation. Her eyes were plastered to the man in the front seat. His face was pale, but his clean clothing indicated he hadn't been here long. "No, no. Oh, God. No," she mumbled.

It couldn't be. She must be hallucinating.

"This can't be real." Naya squeezed the skin on her forearm between her fingernails. The pain that followed told her she wasn't dreaming.

"It's all my fault." She went to take a step forward, but her legs wouldn't move.

"Nay." Zack's voice echoed somewhere in the recesses of her mind, and strong arms wrapped around her.

Former fire chief Ricky Powells stared back at her with lifeless eyes.

TWENTY-NINE

SWEAT DRIPPED DOWN ZACK'S SHIRT AND THREATened to drown him in a pool of heartbreaking loss. He stared unseeing at the wall in the firehouse weight room.

It's all your fault. That's why he's dead.

It wasn't Naya's admission from yesterday; it was Powells's. Back when Zack was a kid staring at the flames consuming his parents' house.

Don't leave meeee. The cry of his eight-year-old voice reverberated in his skull.

They're gone, kid. You were too late. The fire chief's curt tone pierced his eardrum.

Now Powells was dead.

The weights on the shoulder press clanked over and over with each repetition. But no matter how many sets he did, he couldn't silence the echo of that voice.

Zack pulled the weight toward his chest once more, then let it drop back into place on top of the pile with a thud. He let out a grunt and fisted his hands. Too bad they didn't have a boxing set in the firehouse gym. He could use a good couple of lunge punches.

Instead, he dropped to the floor and started a speed round of push-ups.

"With a routine like that, you're going to be sore for the next couple of days." Eddie swung a towel over his shoulder and sat on the bench, setting his water bottle next to him.

"At least I'll be ready for a callout." Zack pushed himself off the ground, breathing hard. He moved to the bench and grabbed a towel. After he wiped the perspiration off his brow, he took a swig of his water. "I can't get yesterday out of my mind, man." Zack shuddered. If he could take the guilt from Naya and shoulder it himself, he'd do it in a heartbeat. "It never gets easier."

"We see tragedy too often." Eddie's low voice carried the weight of the reality. "But it's a good thing it's not getting easier. Or else we'd be calloused. And that's a problem."

"The emotions are hard to swallow at times." Zack gritted his teeth. He'd already shared all the sordid details with his friend yesterday over the phone after he'd gotten home. "All I see are my parents. And Powells. So much loss."

Zack sat with Eddie in silence for several minutes. Nothing could be said to change the outcomes or take the pain away.

"When we walk through the fire, we're not alone. You're not alone." Eddie pointed a finger at Zack. "You've got the Lord and this crew."

"I was just reading those verses in Isaiah the other day." Zack gave a short laugh. Nothing like hearing the same truth in different ways.

"The Lord has a good way of reminding us what we need to take to heart." Eddie smiled. "Naya's gonna need people surrounding her too," he said. "Reminding her it's not her fault."

"It feels like being back in the system some days. One loss after another, you know?"

Eddie grimaced.

"How many more need to leave, disappear, or die before one stays?"

"Jesus. Remind her of Jesus." Eddie took a swig of water.

You are mine. I am with you. The words the Lord spoke in Scripture whispered an assuring response.

Eddie added, "Just be there for her. Sit. Listen. Pray."

Yes, that's what he'd do. However he could help her, he'd do it. "I called her this morning to check in, but she didn't answer."

"Is she by herself?"

"No. Her friend came over to stay with her." Zack slung his damp towel over his shoulder. "That scene yesterday is haunting me. I kept telling Naya the danger was reason enough to give up finding the truth. But now I almost understand the need to get answers. This killer has taken too many lives."

"Right now, Naya needs you." Eddie stood up and closed the distance between them. "Don't get wrapped up in more trouble when you can support her with your presence." Eddie slapped Zack on the shoulder.

Eddie was right. Zack didn't need to go out and find the killer. Or make Naya think this was all her fault. Not when he understood the blame game all too well. Sitting in the shame wouldn't change the outcome. She needed him to be there to listen. *Lord, watch over Naya. Remind her of the truth in the midst of this heartache. Encourage her heart with the reality that You will never leave her nor forsake her.*

A rap sounded on the gym door. Trace popped his head in. "Lieutenant wants to see you in his office, Zack."

"I'm going to change real quick, then I'll be in." Zack headed to the shower stall to rinse off.

Five minutes later, he put on a fresh uniform, then made his way to Bryce's office. He paused in the doorway when he spotted the chief, Macon James, and city liaison, Allen Frees, in conversation with Bryce.

He pivoted on his heel, ready to give them space to finish up whatever they needed to discuss.

Instead, Bryce paused midsentence and waved his hand. "Come on in. Have a seat."

Zack eased himself into the chair next to Macon, across from the lieutenant's desk. Already his muscles protested the movement.

"What's going on?" He drew the words out while making eye contact with each man. Whatever had happened must be significant. Allen never came to meetings unless it impacted the town.

Zack didn't want to entertain the idea of trouble from the get-go, but having all the bosses in one room made his spine tingle.

"Have you kept up with the news over the past few hours?"

Zack's mind kicked into overdrive, and his heart rate sped up. Had something new surfaced he didn't know about? "Not really, why?"

Frees cleared his throat and spoke up. "An article was published two hours ago and has already gained an immense amount of traction and comments."

Bryce spun his computer around.

Zack scooted to the edge of the seat and skimmed the glaring headline.

Firefighter working to cover up dad's missteps puts department reputation at risk.

At the top of the article, a picture of Zack in the woods, glancing over his shoulder, was positioned next to another photo of him by the pile of sandbags and truck yesterday.

"Take a minute to read this, then we can chat." Bryce handed him the computer mouse.

Zack scrolled down the page and couldn't believe what had been written, never mind published. His throat tightened. He wanted to shout that none of this was true.

The author built an argument stemming from the water contamination situation.

Local firefighter Zack Stephens has known all along that the fire extinguishers and foam on the market were poisoning people. He was caught at the dumping ground, where sandbags concealed chemicals discarded in the river. His work at the fire department is putting people in jeopardy. Thanks to his hazmat training, he has all the knowledge needed to concoct the chemical reactions causing the water threat in the first place.

Blaming the entire problem on Zack.

But what had him ready to jump up and demand answers was the snippet about his time in foster care. *Zack Stephens is a troublemaking goofball who is passing along those same qualities to teen foster boys—grooming them for a life of illegal activities.*

Heat burned at the base of Zack's neck, and he gripped the mouse tighter. He scrolled back up to the top in search of the person responsible for this news piece. Except he couldn't find one. It only showed the Last Chance Tribune's logo and banner at the top.

"Who wrote this?" Zack's gaze flitted between the men.

"That's what we're trying to figure out." Allen rubbed his face.

"Is any of the information in the article true?" Bryce steepled his fingers.

Zack clamped his mouth shut. How could they accuse him of any of *that*? Surely they knew him better. Did they really doubt his integrity?

The walls in Bryce's office closed in around him. Like interrogators, the three men waited in silence for the accused to fess up and admit his guilt.

Except Zack was innocent. It was all a lie.

Well, not the fact that his dad was a former chemist who'd known information about the fire foam. Or how Zack helped with the foster kids. But the truth had been twisted, given a wicked ending. Designed to degrade his credibility.

"You really think I'd do something like this?" Zack rubbed the base of his neck.

He didn't know what else to say. How could he? This crew was supposed to have his back. He thought they were family. And family stuck up for each other. Believed the best until proven otherwise. He'd been trying to prove himself for a long time.

And for what?

"We're simply covering all our bases. We want to get all the details we can. And hear your side of things." Macon leaned back in his chair.

Zack turned to Bryce. "I thought you'd know my character by now. But if I need to defend myself..." Zack took a sharp inhale. "Yes, my dad was a chemist."

Bryce blinked but didn't say anything.

"Thanks to the cold case you gave me, Lieutenant, I recently found out he had information about a chemical in firefighting foam and extinguishers that could pose a hazard. He tried to stop it from going to the market and was murdered because of it. Given the recent events and near-death experiences I've had, I'd say there's a pretty good chance someone wants me and Naya out of the picture too."

Zack paused, searching for any kind of regret or apology on the men's faces. Instead, they sat there with blank expressions, waiting for him to continue. "I mentor some of the boys that friends of mine are fostering, but I can assure you I want to see them succeed in life as upstanding citizens. They've been to the firehouse several times." He turned to Bryce. "You've seen how I interact with them."

Zack pointed to the screen. "Whoever wrote this story took defaming liberty on the other details, which are far from the truth."

"I see." Allen jotted something down on a notepad. "Thank you for those details."

"Did you call the Tribune?" Surely someone had to have authorized the article going live on their site. They had to know who'd written it.

"That was the first contact we made," Bryce said. "But they seemed clueless about the origin of the piece."

"Well, something needs to be done about this bunch of lies." Zack flexed his fingers to release the tension. These three men could throw around a lot of weight if they were so inclined. They had influence in town.

The sooner someone got to the bottom of this, the better.

"We already told the Tribune they needed to pull the article until facts could be verified and a proper statement made," Allen said. "We do not want any allegations made prematurely."

Bryce propped his arms on the desk and frowned. "I wish you had told me the case was your parents'."

Zack swallowed. "I considered it. But I wanted to follow through on the task you gave me. Given it was a cold case, there wasn't any conflict of interest."

"Since we need time to sift through the information to get to the bottom of things, we're giving you a two-day leave of absence." Bryce pinched his lips.

"What?" Zack shot out of his seat.

"Don't take it personally." Macon rose from his chair.

How else was he supposed to view it? Zack had worked so hard to fit in with this team. To not be a hothead that caused trouble but a team player whose skills were needed.

Allen turned his wheelchair to face Zack. "It's to protect all of us. And to give time for the rumors to die down."

"Let us do our jobs and get to the bottom of this." Bryce stood up and opened the office door. "We will see you in two days."

Zack blinked. The flames of this fire threatened to set him ablaze. What was he supposed to say? Zack gave a curt nod, then shut the door. His footsteps pounded down the corridor, echoing in the empty space.

THIRTY

NAYA'S SHOES HIT THE SIDEWALK PAVEMENT. Her lungs burned with exertion. Just one more circle, then she could take a leisurely stroll back to her house. She pumped her arms harder. Running was the only thing that cleared her head when she needed an escape. Thanks to her ankle and trying to survive all the attacks thrown her way, she hadn't been able to decompress like usual.

Powells was dead. And she was to blame.

Naya scanned her surroundings, the pepper spray clipped to her belt loop bouncing in time to her steps. A car drove past her and around the corner. She passed a few kids playing basketball on their driveway. The earbuds she wore played no music and were merely a sign for anyone else out at the moment not to bother her.

Despite the sunny spring morning and the redbud trees in full bloom, her eyes were tired and heavy from the tears she had shed all night and the lack of sleep.

She should have listened to Zack. Stopped the hunt for the truth while they were all ahead.

Now Will and Powells were dead.

Who would be next?

Lord, I'm exhausted and I can't see how this will get easier.

Naya rounded the cul-de-sac, then paused to catch her breath. She stopped at the curb and stretched out her right leg before moving to her left. Then she rolled each ankle in a slow circular motion to relieve the tension. At least her injured foot had healed enough that the weight on it today didn't hurt.

A bruised reed I will not break. I will not snuff out a smoldering wick. In faithfulness I will bring forth justice.

The truth from Isaiah 42 was a balm that brought comfort to her heart.

Naya lifted her head toward the clouds.

Powells had warned them that whoever was behind the attacks would find out they were talking with him. He'd been reluctant to share information, and she'd pressed him for it.

And for what?

Had his life been worth the truth?

Naya wanted to scream, but the ache in her heart weighed down any opportunity to voice her anguish. She didn't know what to do anymore. Someone was still one step ahead of them, and Naya wasn't sure how to keep those she cared about safe.

Naya headed back toward her house, her shoes dragging against the pavement.

She clocked her workout on her watch and made a left down her neighborhood street. A notification told her she'd missed a call from Zack earlier.

He'd been the strong one yesterday, someone she'd been able to lean on. Who had tried to remind her that none of this was her fault. For that she'd been grateful. She wanted to tell him that.

When she got closer to her driveway, Zack's car was parked along the curb. *I guess I'll get to do that now.* Her heart skipped a beat, and her lips curved upward despite the grim reality of Powells's death.

She slid her earbuds in her pocket and peered in the car window, but the interior was vacant.

She unlocked the front door and stepped into the foyer. "Grams?" Naya's voice echoed down the hall. Ingram had come over to her house last night and hadn't left.

"In here," Ingram called out, and Naya walked into the kitchen.

Zack straddled a stool at the kitchen island. Two cups sat on the counter next to an empty vase. One she really needed to put to use with a bouquet of fresh flowers. It would make both her and Ingram feel better, even if only a little bit.

Ingram gave Naya a knowing look and pointed her thumb behind her before picking up her purse. "I'll go run some errands. I'll be back." A few seconds later, the front door shut.

"I got a mango smoothie on my way over. Figured it might help." Zack picked up the cup and handed it to her.

Naya took a sip. "Mmm. These never get old." She loved the tropical fruit that was an ode to her native country. Her heart thudded at the realization of what Zack had done. The small gesture spoke volumes. "Thank you. For more than just this." Naya closed the distance between them and wrapped her arms around Zack's torso.

Zack rested his hand on her head and tucked her into his embrace. She let her shoulders sag and closed her eyes. Being around Zack felt like home. A place of safety where she could be herself. No frills attached.

With a sigh, Naya pulled back, and cool air intercepted. If she didn't create distance, her feelings would push her to do something she'd regret.

Zack squeezed her arms. "How are you doing?" His eyes searched hers, willing her to open up and confide in him.

Silence lengthened, and Naya bit her lip. What could she say? Every thought brought with it a well of emotions.

"Anytime you need to talk, I'm here. I want to be a safe place for you." His voice deepened.

"You've been that for me, Zack. I..." She offered him a watery smile and used the back of her hand to hold the tears at bay. "I don't know what to say without a waterworks display starting."

"I happen to enjoy the splash zone." Zack wiggled his brow, and Naya let out a belly laugh, which brought a steady stream of tears with it.

Zack used the pad of his thumb to wipe a tear from her cheek. The gesture sent nerve impulses ricocheting through Naya. He grabbed a tissue from the counter and handed it to her. "Here."

Naya dabbed at her eyes, very well aware of their close proximity. "Thank you. For being available."

Zack's eyes darkened. "I'm here for you." He took Naya's hand in his and rubbed it. "So is the Lord. I prayed He would remind you how near He truly is."

Naya's breath hitched. Zack had prayed for her? His admission sent waves of delight through her. The fact that he pointed her closer to Jesus made her attraction for this man grow.

"Thank you. I—" Naya swallowed.

"What is it?" Zack cocked his head.

"Never mind." She wasn't ready to make any type of profession.

She might love his devotion to the Lord, but that couldn't equate to a love for Zack—yet. She cared for him. But the best relationships deepened over time.

Even though she wanted to explore the possibility of a relationship with him, she had to trust that God would give them time to do that. She didn't need to rush it.

Guide me in Your wisdom, God. Not my will but Yours. Make it clear if this is the man You would have for me or not. Give me patience with Your timing too.

"Thank you for stopping by." Naya picked up the smoothie cup. "This was a much-needed distraction."

Zack's brow furrowed. "Unfortunately, I have another distraction. This one is, well, less than ideal."

"What is it?" Naya slid out another stool at the counter and sat down.

Zack pulled out his phone. "There was an article published this morning. About my supposed involvement in the water contamination schemes." He handed her the device.

Her jaw dropped at the headline, and she quickly clamped her lips shut. She scrolled through the rest of the article, then set the phone down. Had Tucker taken liberties with the content she'd given him for the story? Would he really have stooped so low and twisted what she'd said about Zack helping the foster kids?

"This article is a bunch of baloney." Naya huffed.

"It was published by the Tribune. Who knows how many people have seen it?" Zack's shoulders slumped. "Do you know anything about it?" His gaze never wavered from hers.

"Are you asking if I can find *out* information or if I had a say *in* the information?" Naya had relinquished the story. Surely Zack wouldn't be insinuating that she'd had something to do with the publication of false details.

Zack ran his fingers through his hair. "I thought you might know something."

He hadn't answered her question.

"Not many people know me as the troublemaking goofball kid," he whispered.

Naya grimaced. "And you think I told someone?"

For a second, Naya pictured them in school and in the backyards of their houses, practically growing up together. She understood his fear. Most people thought foster kids were trouble. Or that they instigated trouble out of enjoyment, which was rarely the case.

Troublemaking was a symptom of a heart that desired to be noticed and loved. A child that needed to know they were valued. Of all people, Zack should know Naya wouldn't want him painted in that light.

"I don't want to be that person anymore." Zack sat stick straight on the stool.

The person Zack had once been was a far cry from the man he was now.

Didn't he know?

"That is not who you are." She wanted to take his hand in hers, but her trembling fingers wouldn't allow her to. "I don't see you that way."

"How do you see me?" His Adam's apple bobbed.

"You are a child of God. Your past does not define you. You have been made new and now live in the Spirit, producing good fruit." Naya poked her finger at Zack's chest. "You love Jesus. You're patient, respectful, funny. You encourage me and are servant-hearted in everything you do."

"I want to be that man."

"You *are* that man." *Oh Lord, help Zack see where his identity lies. Give him confidence to live it out.* "You're a hero, Zack. Not just to me. To a lot of people."

He stared at her, his eyes red.

Naya picked up Zack's phone and pointed at the headline. "And I can assure you I had nothing to do with this piece."

"I believe you. But someone wrote it. And whoever it was put my job in jeopardy."

"What do you mean?"

"I have a two-day suspension. While things are sorted out." Zack shoved his hands in his pockets. "I want to know who took the pictures. Sylvia couldn't have sent them from a jail cell." Confusion laced Zack's tone.

He was right. On the surface, the evidence incriminated her. She was the only one who'd been with Zack when he found the truck.

Naya pinched the bridge of her nose. "Someone must have been hiding in the shadows."

"Would Tucker have known there was evidence on that trail?"

"It's possible." She blew out a breath. "Although, it hurts to think he'd do that to you after I told him he could have the story. I gave him all my files, but there was nothing in there about that box Powells gave you. You showed it to me after."

She tried to think what Tucker might have discovered.

"It's okay if you can't remember everything, Naya. You've had a lot going on. I'll take care of it. You should rest."

Naya didn't want to leave Zack to figure this out alone, but her mind was foggy from the past twenty-four hours and the stress her body was under. "I'll call my boss."

"Promise me you'll get some rest too." Zack stood up and pocketed his phone.

"I don't think rest will come until we get to the bottom of this." Naya shrugged. The side-eye Zack gave her told her he wasn't buying that answer. "I'll try."

"I'll let you know what I find out," Zack said, then he headed out.

Naya grabbed her laptop and sank onto the couch. No matter how hard she tried, she couldn't escape this story.

Right now that was a good thing, because Zack's reputation was on the line.

She might not be able to change the past, but she could work to change the future.

For all of them.

THIRTY-ONE

ZACK FOUND A PARKING SPOT AT THE TRIBUNE'S office site and climbed the steps to the third floor. A large sign with the paper's branding and logo sat above the entrance. The overhead bell chimed at his entrance, and the receptionist glanced up from her computer screen.

"How can I help you?"

"I'd like to speak with Tucker. He's a reporter here."

"His cubicle is down on the right." The woman pointed with a manicured finger.

Zack took long strides through the hallway. For Tucker's sake, he prayed he hadn't been the one to publish the story. Zack's fingers cramped. He hadn't even realized he'd had them balled up. He opened and closed his hands to relieve the tension.

That's not how I see you. You are a child of God. The past does not define you.

He could have sworn Naya's words had been coupled with a glimmer of hope in her eyes. How he wanted to be the man she believed in. But how could he measure up?

Of course, it didn't matter that he wasn't perfect. Because he'd never attain that on earth. The posture of his heart was what was important. Zack knew it. But it was another level to believe the truth and live in it.

Naya had affirmed all the qualities in him that only God could have worked out. Yet it still didn't feel like enough. Not after the conversation with Bryce, Macon, and Allen. They had their doubts, and Zack didn't know when he would be able to stop proving himself. When others would stop pegging him as a troublemaker.

The thought of people whispering behind his back, questioning if he should be allowed around the foster boys, or even questioning his ability to stay on rescue squad threatened to send anxiety bubbling to the surface.

Thank You, Lord, for making me into a new man. Help me live out my new identity. May others see it too.

He stopped in front of the cubicle with Tucker's name plate on the wall and rapped on the divider.

"Tucker, it's—" Zack walked around the corner and froze. An array of papers littered the man's desk. A mug lay overturned, and coffee dripped off the edge onto the floor. Where was he? The five-by-five area wasn't big enough to hide in. And why leave in such a rush?

Zack grabbed a tissue and wiped up the puddle of coffee. He slid a few papers over to keep them from getting more wet. Maybe Tucker's boss was in and he could talk with the man. Zack crumpled the tissue, and the words on an index card caught his attention.

I'm sorry. I can't do it anymore. This mistake is too big to fix. I deserve to die in that river where this whole mess started.

River.

Wats only go empty'n wivers.

Now was not the time to think about his dad's silly game.

Zack snatched the note and raced back down the hall.

Had Tucker played a role in the scheme this whole time? What if he'd lied to Naya about his involvement?

Zack bounded down the steps two at a time and sprinted to his car. He wasn't about to let a man die on his watch. Even if the guy had played a role in publishing the article.

While one hand turned the ignition, Zack dialed 9-1-1 with the other.

"Where's your emergency?"

"The Penn Bridge. By the river. I have reason to believe someone is making a suicide attempt." Zack pressed down harder on the gas. The speedometer climbed. The bridge was ten minutes away, but Zack would make it five.

"Medics and rescue are on their way."

Zack couldn't let Tucker kill himself.

The car tires squealed to a stop by the curb, and Zack shoved open the door. He bolted past the park entrance. The bridge, or what was left of the structure, stood in view.

Please Lord, don't let me be too late.

Zack scanned the area. A few kids played on the playground nearby. A couple walked their dog on the path that wound past the river.

Tucker had to be here somewhere. Zack just hoped he wasn't already in the water.

Movement to his right caught his attention.

The man had one leg wrapped over the side of the bridge.

"Tucker. Wait!" Zack tore through the caution tape blocking the area and bounded up the bridge. This side of the structure seemed sturdy enough. The last thing he needed was the rest of the bridge collapsing. "You don't have to do this."

Tucker braced his arms on the railing. He glanced back. "It's too late."

The brief moment of hesitation gave Zack enough time to close the distance.

Tucker let go of his hold and leaned forward.

"No!" Zack reached over the edge and gripped the back of

Tucker's jacket. He yanked with one hand and wrapped his other arm around the man's torso.

"Let me go," Tucker yelled.

Zack pulled the man over the railing and tackled him to the ground. The bridge groaned under the sudden force of added weight.

Sirens pierced the air.

The structure shifted, and Zack braced his hand along the wood, his back on the ground.

"You should have let me die alone." Tucker's chest heaved.

"Why'd you do it?"

"I didn't have a choice." Sweat beaded on Tucker's brow, and he lay on the bridge and leaned his head against the slats.

"Your life is worth more than this choice."

The bridge jerked. Zack scrambled to a crouched position and braced himself. He peered over his shoulder. The paved walkway that led to the bridge was only a few feet away. They could make it to solid ground.

He wasn't going to let them die. They were too close to the truth.

Zack wedged his arms under Tucker's and grunted. The man held on to the railing, not making it easy for Zack. "You've got to let go." Zack used all his weight to pull the man backward.

The bridge creaked and wood snapped apart. Splashes resounded. More pieces broke apart and threatened to pull Zack and Tucker with them.

"I don't care what you wanted. I'm not going down today," Zack said through clenched teeth.

Tucker released his grip from the railing and pushed against the wood with his feet, creating more distance between them and a deadly descent. Zack dragged Tucker a few more steps, and the two collapsed on the dirt.

Zack shifted to his side and exhaled—right when the rest of the bridge splashed into the water below.

"You all right, hero?" Eddie loomed overhead and extended his hand.

"Could be worse." Zack gripped his friend's hand and stood up.

Trace and Kianna hovered over Tucker, ready to take his vitals.

"I'm fine," Tucker huffed. "No thanks to that guy." He stood up and shooed off the EMTs, but Trace and Kianna stayed nearby.

The rest of rescue crew worked to clear the area of bystanders.

"What were you thinking?" Zack clenched his hands.

"The money isn't worth it. Not when my career is now destroyed."

"Because of the story?"

"I should have never taken the information Naya gave me."

Zack pulled in a breath. "So she wrote it, then?" He would not let this guy use Naya as a scapegoat. "That's the excuse you're going with?"

Tucker's face went slack. "You have no idea what you're dealing with."

Zack stood to full height. "Telling the truth is easy. Either you wrote it, or you didn't." Bryce stood nearby talking to Ridge, who pointed to the river. "And my boss should hear what you have to say. In case you didn't know, defamation is a serious offense."

Tiny beads of sweat broke out along Tucker's hairline. "I was coerced into publishing that piece. They're not even my own words, dude." Tucker's eyes widened.

Zack ground his teeth. "You submitted a story you didn't even write? Why?"

"He promised me money. Said he could help me get the promotion. He'd make it look like Naya wrote the story."

"Who put you up to the task?"

"Some guy from Ethos."

"Who?"

"I dunno, Hudson something. I don't remember his last name."

Of course Hudson would have had knowledge of Zack's childhood problems.

Why meddle in Zack's life now? So many years had gone by since that season of teenage angst and all those dumb fights. Why did the guy still hold a grudge?

Zack waved to get Detective Wilcox's attention.

"What are you going to do?" Tucker's eyes darted around.

"I'm going to have a talk with Hudson." Zack shoved his hands in his pockets. "And let the police handle you."

"Whoa." Tucker held out his hand. "I'd be careful with that dude. He's not someone to mess around with."

"And neither are people's reputations," Zack said.

"C'mon, man." Trace walked up to Tucker. "You need to get checked out. Protocol." Trace, Kianna, and Wilcox escorted a resistant Tucker away.

Zack walked off to the side and leaned against a tree. The rescue crew followed orders to secure the scene. The team he *should* be on right now. Zack pulled up the phone number for Ethos. It was time to put an end to all of this for good. He'd dealt with Hudson many times before and nothing had changed; the guy was still a bully. But Zack could handle him.

"Thank you for calling Ethos. How may I direct your call?" A woman's voice came over the line.

"I'd like to speak with Hudson Callahan."

"I'm sorry. He's currently in a meeting. I could set up a three o'clock appointment."

"That's fine."

Zack had an hour to spare. He walked over to the truck just when Eddie closed up the side compartment.

"How are you holding up?" Eddie leaned against the truck.

"Glad it was just a close call today."

"You and me both, man."

"There're so many moving parts to all of this. I turn one way and there's a hurdle. I look the other direction and there's a boulder. It's like being pushed to the sidelines, unable to do anything."

"You don't give up easily, though."

That he didn't. One of the worst feelings was inadequacy. Being unable to do something worthwhile. Zack fought against it like a firefighter breaking down a wall. He wanted to be useful. Zack rubbed his forehead. "Tucker fessed up about the story. One of the guys at Ethos got him to write it."

"That better speed up the investigation. Get you back on Rescue with us."

"How're the guys?" Zack shifted his gaze. The rest of the crew gathered their equipment and headed up from the river. Did any of them really miss him? Even notice he was gone?

"About ready to stage a coup if you aren't back in forty-eight hours." Eddie smiled.

"Really?"

"Heck yeah. You're an asset, man, and anyone with two eyes can see it."

It was good to know the crew missed him. He'd had a lot of people in and out of his life growing up, but he'd been around the firehouse long enough that the guys and gals had become like family.

"How'd you figure out Tucker's plan?"

"His note mentioned dying in the river."

Wats only go empty'n wivers.

Zack rubbed his temple. So Tucker hadn't been behind everything. But he wasn't sure how Hudson fit into all this either.

"I can't get this silly saying from my dad out of my head, either."

"What is it?"

"Rats only go empty'n rivers." Zack laughed. "My dad was adamant that *r* was the most important letter in my vocabulary. So important he said he'd told other people how necessary it was too. I found the phrase in the box with the other evidence my dad had.

Including a note for P to tell someone." Zack scratched his head. "I think P was for Powells. But now he's dead, and any information he had is long gone with him." Zack blew out a breath.

"Maybe the phrase is a secret message. Like each letter is connected to a number or something." Eddie pulled out a pen from his turnout jacket and wrote it on his palm.

"It definitely points to the sandbags being dumped in the river." That part made sense. Although Zack wasn't sure what else it would allude to—except how adamant his dad had been that other people know how important the *r*'s were.

"Let's pack it up. I want us back to the station in fifteen." Bryce shouted the order.

"I'm going to head out." Zack slapped Eddie on the back. "I'll let you have fun with that riddle." Zack headed back to his car.

When he arrived at Ethos, Zack checked in with the receptionist, then took the steps to the second floor. The hallway was quiet, and he followed the signs until he found Hudson's office.

His phone rang, and a glance at caller ID showed it was Eddie. "Yeah?" He stopped walking.

"It's *Roger*. The first letter of each word spells out the name."

Zack scanned the hall. No one was present, but he still turned and faced the wall to keep his voice from projecting. "That's the CEO, Eddie. Roger Callahan." He clenched his hand and sucked in a breath.

This whole time, the company had been covering up dangerous actions with lies. Instead of creating products for the good of the community, they were dealing silent blows.

He had to warn Naya. "I've got to go, Eddie. I'll be out soon."

He hung up and texted Naya.

Roger is behind it all. Keep an eye out. I'll be at your house soon.

He turned around to head back to the stairs when an office door opened.

"You're early." Hudson grinned. "Trying to be punctual?"

"Didn't want to miss the chance to clear the air between us." Zack plastered on a smile and stepped into Hudson's office.

"Want something to drink?"

"Water's fine."

Hudson turned around to retrieve a water bottle from a mini fridge, then handed it to Zack. "I'm glad you thought this meeting would be profitable."

Zack twisted open the cap.

"It's finally time you get what you deserve." Hudson whipped out a small aerosol container, and a stream of liquid pelted Zack's face.

Zack didn't even have a chance to respond before the water bottle fell from his hand and he collapsed on the ground.

THIRTY-TWO

ROGER IS BEHIND IT ALL.

The text had lit up Naya's phone screen five minutes ago, and she hadn't been able to check the locks on the doors enough times. Zack was on his way.

He'd get here before Roger could think of sabotaging her in her house again. Right? She redialed Zack's number, but it went straight to voicemail.

She called Ingram, but her friend's voicemail came over the line too.

What if something had happened to them?

Naya rolled her shoulders. "Stop it. Overreacting is not going to change the situation." She might have only been talking to empty air, but the confession slowed her heart rate.

Lord, I need Your direction.

If Zack really was in danger, she needed a clear head. The thought of anything happening to him sent a wave of nausea rolling through her stomach.

Naya wanted to be honest about her feelings. She wanted to be part of Zack's life.

Permanently.

To make that desire a reality, she needed to find Zack first. Naya pulled up the Eastside Firehouse number with a quick Internet search. One of Zack's buddies might have seen him.

The garage door whined in the background and Naya paused.

Ingram was home.

Thank the Lord. She'd be able to help.

Naya hung up. She'd wait until she filled Ingram in on the details, then they could go to the firehouse in person. The door opened and Naya hurried to the kitchen. "Thank goodness you're back. I think Zack's—"

Naya rounded the corner and skidded to a stop in the entryway. Ingram stood by the counter with a gag over her mouth. Her pupils were dilated, eyes wide. Her hands were tied behind her back.

Naya's focus flitted between her friend and the man who closed the door behind them. He turned around with a scowl plastered on his face. "Mr. Roger Callahan."

His gray hair was spiked, and his eyes narrowed. The dark blue suit he wore was pressed in all the right places. His appearance was much different than the distraught man outside his house, worried for his wife.

"So we meet again." He moved to Ingram's side, and Naya caught sight of the gun he held snug to her friend's back. "It was really nice of Ms. Chacko to drive me here for our meeting."

So he was using his employees. Naya balled her hand.

"Throw that phone over here. Now!" Callahan swung the gun.

Naya couldn't afford to make a wrong move. Not when Ingram's life was on the line. Naya flicked her wrist, and the phone skittered across the floor. "We have friends who will notice if we disappear."

"Not if it's an accident." Roger slammed his heel against the device, shattering the screen.

Naya studied the pair. "What do you want?"

"Ingram here was trying to get into Will's office. It's a shame all his work stuff is confidential information." Roger pushed Ingram farther into the kitchen.

Did anyone else besides Zack know Roger was behind the attacks? She should have stayed on the line to talk with someone at the firehouse. Now she was trapped in her own house with a madman. She needed to find a way to get herself and Ingram out of here.

She scanned the kitchen counter. A block of knives sat by the stove. If she inched to the right, she could snag one, but the weapon would only be useful up close.

And against a gun?

Naya shuddered.

"One wrong move and she's dead." Roger slapped his free hand on the granite.

"What are you going to do?" Naya stood straighter, proud that her voice didn't crack.

"Put an end to your investigation." Roger leered. "Some secrets are better buried."

"Like Will?"

Ingram let out a cry.

"Please," Roger scoffed. "You ruined it for him. You and that good-for-nothing firefighter. Thanks to your research, you were about to bust open the empire I've worked hard to build."

Naya blinked, trying to process what this guy was saying and his twisted way of seeing people. "So you killed Will?" Naya challenged.

"My partner did." Roger huffed. "He could have had it all, but it all got messed up. Love over money. Such a shame."

"Because of Sylvia?"

"Because of this lady right here." Roger pointed the gun at Ingram. "The guy grew a conscience. Felt guilty for cheating on his girlfriend and putting her in harm's way. Said he was going to come clean." He scoffed. "Now I have to take care of things myself."

Where was Zack? He'd said he was on his way to her house.

Ingram whimpered.

"Enough." Roger slapped Ingram. "Be quiet."

Naya lunged forward. "Don't treat her like that," she yelled.

"I said don't move." Roger's elbow collided with Naya's cheek.

The gun exploded close to her ear.

Naya screamed.

Ingram dropped to the ground.

Gunpowder filled the air, and Naya choked back a cough.

Her ears rang.

Roger wrapped his arms under Ingram's shoulders and dragged her across the kitchen.

"Let her go." Naya raced after them.

Roger pushed her out of the way, and Naya stumbled and fell into the cabinets. The handles dug into her spine. She held back a groan. Her back pulsated with pain. She crawled on her knees, her clammy hands sticking to the hardwood floor.

Roger shoved Ingram into the guest bedroom and slammed the door shut.

Tears soaked Naya's face, and she swatted at fresh ones that spilled down her cheeks. "Just take me and let her go." She closed the gap between her and Callahan and stood up, ready to throw a swing. She wasn't going down without a fight.

"That's my plan."

Naya swung her fist, prepared to hit Roger in the jaw.

Roger's hand shot out and latched onto her wrist. He yanked her injured arm down, then twisted it behind her back.

Needlelike pain shot through her elbow.

She bit down on her tongue, refusing to give him any sense of victory.

"Hold still," Roger whispered in her ear. He used his other hand and pulled out a black stun gun. Before she could react, the flash-light shone in her eyes, and she blinked.

He thrust the device into her waist. The zap followed by the surge of electricity coursed through her muscles.

Naya's body convulsed. Pain tore through her abdomen, and she doubled over.

"I've got a surprise for you." Roger loomed over her.

Her legs twitched, but she couldn't get her body to move away. A cloth covered her nose and mouth. Naya jerked her head, trying to get away from the sweet-smelling concoction. A minute later, Naya's world tilted on its axis, and everything went blank.

Fogginess pricked at the edges of Naya's consciousness. How long had she blacked out?

A door slammed shut, and the force reverberated through her body.

Loud voices echoed from somewhere, and her head throbbed. She slowly opened her eyes and took note of the area. Naya squinted against the harsh lighting.

Where was she?

The space was large. There was a small wired window cut into the only door that led out of the room. White industrial walls surrounded her, and paint supplies and chemicals were stacked in the corner along the concrete floor.

A stale, dusty smell filled her nostrils, and Naya wrinkled her nose.

Gross.

Naya tried to lift her hand only to be stopped by something strapped around it. Her arms were fastened with rope behind her back and tied to the chair.

She didn't know where she was, but she needed to find a way out.

Where was Roger?

And Zack?

Was Ingram...

Tears pooled in Naya's eyes, but she couldn't wipe them away with her hands tied.

A shadow passed by the room, then the door swung open. Naya pushed her feet back and the chair squeaked.

Callahan and Hudson shoved Zack into the room. His hands were tied too, and his knees collided with the ground.

"Zack!" Naya started forward, but the ropes tied around the chair behind her back held her in place.

"Glad to see you're both awake." Roger grinned.

"It'll make the last part of the adventure entertaining." Hudson shoved his hands in his pockets. "Too bad it won't end well for you both."

So Hudson was Callahan's partner. But why? What was in it for him?

The two men turned to leave.

Zack pushed himself up off the ground and nodded his head to her.

"Wait." Naya's heartbeat thrashed in her ears. She needed to stall them. And if Zack had an idea, she'd help.

Zack barreled toward Hudson. The guy went to turn around, but Zack sideswiped him. Hudson took a step back to regain his footing before shoving Zack.

"One last fight for old time's sake, eh?" Hudson tackled Zack to the ground, and a series of grunts followed.

"You're not going to get away with this," Zack snapped.

"We don't have time to waste, son," Callahan yelled.

"Shut up, Uncle Roger. I've got it."

Naya gasped. She and Zack had gone to school with this kid. And the whole time, Hudson's uncle had been in the background, hiding the truth. Now he'd trained up his own flesh and blood to follow his lead. To cover up what was really happening at Ethos.

Hudson stood up and wiped his hands. Zack went to get up, but he took one glance at Naya and stayed put. Blood dripped from his nose.

Naya couldn't let Callahan and Hudson leave. Not without all the answers. "I thought your company helped people."

"We do. We *help* the firehouses put out fires with our foam. And families stay safe with our fire extinguishers. Each time they buy our products, we make the big bucks. And I can't lose out."

"You *help* people at the expense of their health." Naya narrowed her gaze. "Why not change the chemical formula?"

"None of you nosy reporters know when to stop asking questions." Callahan gripped the door handle.

"If you're going to kill us, why not let the truth go down with us?" Naya sucked in a breath to keep from shaking.

Callahan paused, and a sly grin formed. "If you must know. I can share the brilliance behind this mind." He crossed his arms. Hudson moved to his uncle's side, his frame blocking the doorway.

"It's too expensive to change the ingredients. We had a profit margin goal to secure."

"Even when the chemicals would harm the people you're supposed to be helping?" Naya asked.

"There's too much money on the line. One employee learned that the hard way and invested unnecessary time inspecting the chemical formula. And it cost him."

"My dad." Zack's jaw twitched.

"Douglas couldn't keep his hands out of *my* business. I bought out the company he used to work for. He forgot who his boss was."

"You were his new boss?" Zack's brow creased.

Roger grinned. "Securing that business deal, taking over ProEco Plant, and climbing the corporate ladder to CEO of Ethos was my shot at making it big in the industry. Such a shame that Douglas couldn't see the payoff in the end. Instead, he tried to thwart *my* success. And you thought you could do the same." Roger pointed at Zack. "I should have killed you in that fire too."

Naya gaped. How could anyone think such evil?

Her knees trembled.

Naya wanted to grab one of those paint cans and chuck it at the two men. But she couldn't do anything with her hands tied. And in the wide-open room, any attempt to escape would be foiled. She hated being the victim.

Zack sat in a crouched position, like he too was debating what move to make.

They had to find a way out.

Zack's dad and Powells had died because they'd gotten mixed up in this mess, and she couldn't let their deaths be in vain.

Roger and Hudson would not win.

Evil could not win.

Naya tugged at her restraints. "Why don't you—"

"Enough," Roger bellowed.

"You're wasting our time here." Hudson stepped into the hallway.

"I did you a favor by having that note put on your car. Too bad you didn't listen." Roger walked out behind Hudson and slammed the door shut.

THIRTY-THREE

ZACK GRITTED HIS TEETH AND YANKED ON THE ties around his arms. Instead of loosening, they only dug into his skin. He walked over to Naya, strapped in the chair.

"We need to find a way out of here." Her voice rose.

"And we will. I won't let us pay the price for the trouble they've caused." Zack crouched down next to her. "Are you okay?" A bruise had formed on her cheek, and Zack swallowed hard. If Roger or Hudson had done that...

He ground his teeth.

Naya nodded. "Callahan shot Ingram." She pinched her eyes shut and a tear fell. "I don't know if"—she gulped—"if she's alive or not."

Zack wanted to wipe the tear and console Naya, but each second that ticked by narrowed their chances of escaping.

"Let's get out of here. Then we'll find her." He offered a smile for her sake, then inspected the ropes around her wrists. Roger had used rope, unlike the plastic restraints Hudson had fastened on Zack. It made it harder to undo, but not impossible.

"Can you twist your way out?"

Naya tried to work at the ropes, but with her arms behind her back, the ropes didn't budge. "I can't."

"Hang on." Zack stepped back and lifted his hands high in the air, then yanked them down and out in front of him. His bonds snapped, and he tossed the zip ties aside.

Zack scanned the room for a sharp object that would cut Naya's ropes. He opened a metal standing cabinet in the back corner of the room.

A stack of papers, cans, and office supplies occupied the shelving. A quick spin of the desk organizer on the top rack revealed pens, paper clips, and…

Bingo.

An X-ACTO knife was mixed in with the writing supplies.

"I'm going to help you get out of this chair, but I need you to trust me."

Naya's wide eyes stared at the knife in his hand. "Okay."

Zack circled around behind her and knelt. He tugged on the rope, pulling it away from her wrist to create a gap. He slid the knife down and out toward him. With the swift motion, the fibers frayed, then snapped.

Naya rubbed her wrists and stood up. "Thanks." She brushed her matted and tangled curls away from her face. "Let's get out of here."

"You go check the door. I'm going to see what's back here." Zack raced over to the supplies against the wall. A few empty paint cans sat on a tarp next to a water jug and aerosol containers. He picked up the gray aerosol can.

Butane.

That could get them out of here.

He shook it.

Empty.

"The door won't budge." Naya yanked on the knob. "And the window's got wiring in the glass."

Zack picked up the other aerosol can and pressed down on the valve. Liquid hissed from the top. "I've got a plan!"

Naya raced back over to Zack. "Do you smell that?"

He sniffed. "Smoke." There was no way to tell where the fire was coming from. If his idea backfired, they'd be dead.

He needed to be honest with Naya. In case they didn't make it out of this room alive, she deserved to know how he felt.

She must have sensed his hesitancy, because she grabbed his hand. "Whatever happens, you didn't cause this mess, Zack. You're the hero. My hero." Her lip quivered.

Lord, help me get us out of here. You brought Naya back into my life. Please don't let this be the end.

"Naya, I love you. I don't know what's going to happen, but I needed you to hear that from me." He wiped a tear off her cheek with the pad of his thumb.

"I love you too, Zack." She pulled in a breath. "Tell me what to do. I'm ready to fight this till the end."

"One of the many reasons why I love you." He pulled away and handed her the gallon jug of water. "Dump half of this out. We're going to make a rocket."

The smell of smoke continued to intensify, and Zack coughed.

Zack took the lid from the water bottle and used the X-ACTO knife to make a small incision.

Naya held the half-empty water container and Zack twisted the lid back on before pouring the butane in. Then he uncapped the jug.

He had no idea what room they were in, and if he sent this off in the direction of the fire, the explosion would be lethal. There was nothing he could do to control the situation. No way to calculate the odds of staying out of trouble.

This is in Your hands, Lord. Only You can save us. One way or another.

"Back up, Naya. I'm going to shoot this off into the ceiling."

She moved to the door.

Zack flipped the bottle over and let go. The container sizzled and shot up into the air, then catapulted into the ceiling.

Zack twisted his body and shielded his eyes. Liquid sprayed him, and plaster rained down around them.

"It worked." Naya jumped up.

"Let me help you." Zack bent down on one knee and held out his hands.

Naya placed her foot into his hold, and he hoisted her up. She pulled away some of the remaining plaster so she could squeeze through then grabbed hold of a beam in the ceiling and swung her leg.

A cry escaped her lips.

"You okay?"

"It's my elbow. I'll be fine." She cradled her arm. "I'm in." Naya coughed. "The smoke smells stronger up here."

"Hang on." Zack backed up against the opposite wall, then sprinted to the other side of the room. He pushed off the wall and stretched out his hand to grip a beam from the exposed ceiling. With one hand wrapped around the wood, he used his other to push up.

The weight crumbled the plaster, and he lost his grip. His arm dangled and he dropped back to the ground. Dust flew in his eyes.

"Zack," Naya screamed.

"I'm fine." He wiped his face, then ran across the room and jumped once more. He swung his legs up and over and gripped the beam.

He'd made it.

He lay there for a minute staring at the floor below. His chest heaved.

"Which way do we go?" Naya shifted in the enclosed space, and her arms brushed his.

Minimal light filtered into the space, and it took a second for his eyes to adjust. They could go forward or backward. "Let's try this way." Zack pointed straight ahead and inched his way through the space first. If they ran into any obstacles, Zack wanted to take the initial hit.

More light streamed up ahead.

"We're getting closer to something," Naya said.

They crossed over a thicker beam into what was probably another room. The light grew, and Zack quickened his pace. "Just up ah—"

Zack's words were cut off by a rush of heat and flames.

"Watch out!" Zack shouted and ducked his head. This wasn't an exit. They'd just walked straight into the landmine. "We need to go back. Go. Go." Zack spun on his knees.

Naya was already turned around and a few paces away.

The heat nipped at Zack's ankles, and he dug his hands into the beams, moving faster.

"We can't just drop back into the room we were in or it's over," Naya yelled over her shoulder.

"Keep going the other way." Zack coughed. "Let's try to break the ceiling of another space." His lungs burned.

Smoke filtered through the enclosed duct work. Each particle cut off more oxygen. Zack pulled his shirt up over his nose.

"I can't see much," Naya wheezed. "It's so hazy."

They crawled past the gaping hole above the room Roger and Hudson had trapped them in. The second the fire filled that space and collided with any traces of butane, they'd be burned to a crisp.

"I can't go…much…more." Naya lowered her head and expelled a cough.

Zack glanced behind him. They had minutes before the fire caught up to them. He scooted past Naya in the space and sat back on the beams.

He lifted his legs up, then shoved his feet against the ceiling.

The heels of his shoes broke through. "Help me push through this plaster."

Naya slid next to him and stomped her feet.

They made a hole big enough to maneuver through. Zack peered below. No obstacles stood in their way. "Let's go." Naya dropped to the floor and Zack followed.

"Where are we?" Naya spun around.

A shout slipped from Zack's lips. *Thank You, Lord.*

He grabbed Naya's hand and bolted around the conference table. "Follow me." They'd landed in the room the forklift had driven through the other day when they'd been called to Ethos to get the employees out. The hole he and Eddie had created in the wall was boarded up. There was no time to plow through it.

They raced for the door and tugged it open.

Zack turned left in the hall, Naya on his heels. A boom resounded in the space behind them and shook the area.

Zack stumbled, and he lost Naya's grip. He turned around, ready to pick her up, when she stood. "We're almost there."

A painting on the wall fell to the ground, and debris and dust flew through the air.

Flames ripped through the hall.

Sirens whined around them, but he'd welcome the loud cries any day. Help was on the way.

Zack and Naya ran past the receptionist's desk and pushed through the doors out onto the front lawn.

Naya braced her hands on her legs, her breaths coming in pants. "We're alive." She turned back to the building, and he followed her gaze. Smoke poured from the windows and roof.

Fire trucks screeched to a stop, and the police sped in behind them.

More tires squealed on the pavement, and a figure ran down the sidewalk. "Hey! Don't let them leave," Zack shouted, then raced after Hudson. He was not about to let Hudson or Roger get away.

Hudson froze for a split second, checking both directions.

"You idiot. Get in the car," Roger bellowed.

Zack's footsteps pounded against the cement.

Hudson opened the door and slid inside, then grabbed the handle.

Zack took another step and gripped the corner of the door, yanking it open. "Not so fast," he grunted.

"Watch me." Hudson put one foot on the curb and threw a fist.

Zack grabbed Hudson's wrist and pulled it behind the guy's back.

Hudson let out a shout.

"Zack, watch out," Naya called.

He looked up, right into the barrel of Roger's gun.

"Police! Stand down!" Basuto yelled.

Roger backed away from the vehicle, then he swung his weapon and fired.

Zack dropped to the ground with Hudson.

More shots rang out, and officers swarmed the area.

Roger bolted back to his car and yanked open the driver's door. Ramble hopped over the hood of the car and tackled Roger to the ground.

Hudson was yanked from Zack's grip. "I've got him." Tazwell pulled her cuffs and snapped them on Hudson's wrists.

"Uncle Roger is to blame. He made me do it." Hudson shouted and writhed in Tazwell's grasp. "Told me I had to kill Will and take out this nosey hooligan." He stared at Zack.

Zack took a step back and held up his hands. Lights flashed and people raced around.

Ramble pulled Roger up from the ground and restrained him. Then the officer escorted him over to the sidewalk.

Zack's buddies raced back and forth to the building with hoses spewing water.

Where was Naya?

Zack spun around and nearly toppled over when Naya wrapped her arms around him from behind. "Are you okay?" She turned to face him.

He gulped. "Yeah. And you?"

Tears poured down her face. "I will be."

Zack wrapped her in his arms and tucked her head to him. Her heart beat a steady rhythm against his chest. They were both alive and unharmed. He never wanted to let go. Never wanted her to leave.

"That dirty reporter is going to write lies. None of it's true," Roger snapped. His face was a dark shade of red.

Naya stepped out of Zack's embrace but wrapped her arm around his.

"It's over. Give it up, man." Zack shook his head.

Ramble and Tazwell put the two men in the back of their cruisers, and Basuto walked over to Zack and Naya.

"I've got evidence from my dad that Roger is behind everything," Zack said.

"I don't doubt it. We got prints back from the abandoned truck by the cabin, and Sylvia confessed too. Said she was the one behind the shooting that day and had been ordered by Roger to take care of Powells after Roger killed him."

"She was willing to confess to everything?" Zack raised his brows.

"Once she learned about Will's death, she said she was done working for Roger. She didn't want the money he was offering. Not when her chance at love was gone."

Naya gasped and raked her hands through her hair. "Ingram. Roger shot her. She's at my house." Naya took a step toward the sidewalk.

Basuto held out his hand. "She's alive. They took her to the hospital."

Naya's shoulders dropped. "Thank You, Lord. But how?"

"She's the one who called 9-1-1. Apparently, Roger thought she was dead and mumbled something about going to Ethos. She overheard it and told us you guys were here."

"So it's really over?" Naya turned to Zack, then back to Basuto.

"I'm going to need your statements, but yeah."

When they finished giving Basuto the rundown of what happened, Naya said, "Are you able to confirm who was behind my attack at the mountain?" She rubbed her arms.

"We have a copy of Will's secret files, and they share everything." Basuto grimaced. "Will executed the attack at the mountain and started the brush fire. Even wrote the note on your car and had Sylvia plant it."

"So they all had different roles in Roger's schemes?" Zack frowned.

"Seems that way." Basuto nodded. "The files say Hudson was responsible for shooting at the fire truck during the parade. And the attempted gas leak. He even helped start the fire at Roger's house and the chemical leak at Ethos to shift suspicions to Green Warriors."

"Unbelievable." Zack shook his head.

Naya sighed. "Thank you for everything."

"Just doing my job. You two should go get checked out now." Basuto pointed to the ambulance.

Zack walked hand in hand with Naya over to Trace and Kianna.

The Lord might be giving him a second chance with her after all these years, but he wasn't sure he could say the same about his job on Rescue.

Amelia shouted orders, and everyone worked together to battle the blaze.

Zack wanted to be one of them. Wanted to belong at the firehouse. But he didn't know how he could make that happen.

THIRTY-FOUR

NAYA SAT IN HER CAR PARKED BY THE FIREHOUSE and refreshed her email inbox. The spinning circle stared back at her.

"Any word?" Ingram's voice echoed through her phone speaker.

Today was Thursday. Two days after the fire at Ethos and Roger's and Hudson's arrests. Today was also the day she'd find out who her boss had selected for the promotion.

Drew had told her to take a couple of days off work to recoup, and she'd spent the past forty-eight hours sleeping and rearranging her office space at home, thanks to the painting Zack had helped her do last week.

Naya squeezed her eyes shut, then opened her left eye a smidge. The blurry phone screen came into focus.

She opened both eyes and skimmed the list of emails with the blue dot next to them—a reminder of all the to-dos she had to check off her list.

She scrolled through the list once more.

"Nada."

"It's early. Maybe he's still making his pick."

"After everything that's happened, I don't think I want the promotion." Sure, the story her boss had originally assigned them could make headlines. Given the people involved and the impact on the community, it probably would. But she'd forfeited that information and handed it over to Tucker. Would the human-interest piece she had submitted instead be compelling enough? It certainly wasn't what Drew had originally assigned her. "So why am I holding my breath for this decision?"

"You're a gifted storyteller. You want hope to shine through, and you do it by sharing people's journeys."

"That's exactly what I want to do, but that goal hasn't been my focus so far." She'd pursued enough stories where her life was on the line. It had meant discovering stories that would keep people's attention. And people tended to focus on bad news. No wonder the search for truth had grown exhausting.

"The Lord will show you the way forward. Keep praying and trusting."

"Right back at ya. How are you doing with everything?" Naya glanced in her rearview mirror, and the sun gleamed off the glass.

The urge to watch her back lingered, and it would be a while until a sense of safety became the norm again.

"Every day gets better. The hardest part is reconciling the Will I want to remember from the good times while we were dating, and the Will who was involved in the massive cover-up and affair."

"However I can help, I'm here. And so is Jesus. He'll show you the way forward."

"I actually just submitted an extended leave of absence from Ethos." A smile filled Ingram's voice.

"You deserve it, girl. What are you going to do with all the time?"

"Buy a plane ticket and go visit relatives in India. It's been too long. I need to get away from the memories here for a while."

"That sounds like a great idea." Naya still hadn't worked up the nerve to drive by Ethos for fear that it would trigger the memories of what she'd almost lost.

Who she could have lost.

The firefighters had worked hard to contain the blaze at Ethos, but the repairs would take months.

The Lord's grace had been evident over the whole situation. He'd taken the trials and the tragedy of the past and brought something good from them. He'd kept them safe. He'd shown her how to stand up for the truth. And He'd brought Zack back into her life.

She still couldn't believe Zack had worked to get them out safely and even put his own life on the line to protect her. They'd even worked together.

As a team.

One more scenario that confirmed the kind of man Zack was—selfless, humble, and courageous.

A man she could see herself loving and building a life with.

It might have only been two days since she'd seen Zack, but she couldn't wait to spend time with him and talk.

"Let me know when that trip is booked, 'cause I need to give you a giant hug. If Coco needs a place to stay too, I have the space." Naya got out of her car. She grabbed two bags from the backseat and slid them on her arm.

"So, you like my cat?" Ingram chuckled.

"He's cute. We've bonded." Thanks to the few nights she'd stayed at Ingram's place in the past week.

"I'm sure he'd be happier with you than boarded up somewhere."

"Then it's settled." Naya ended the call and headed into the firehouse.

Zack wasn't due on shift for another hour and a half, so that should give the crew plenty of time to pull off their celebration plan to welcome him back. Thanks to Tucker's and Hudson's confessions about the article, everything had been cleared, and Zack's suspension had been lifted.

Naya couldn't wait to see his reaction when he came into work today. She'd even parked in the alleyway so he wouldn't spot her vehicle when he arrived.

"Let me grab that." Eddie met her at the front door and took a few of the bags.

"Thanks for helping me put this together," she said. They made their way into the common room and spread out the supplies. A "welcome back" banner, streamers, photos from different events at the firehouse, and cupcakes.

Izan made his way into the room. "Just tell us what we can do." He clapped his hands.

"Right there with you," Ridge and Bryce said.

The girls followed in behind and nodded their agreement.

Even the foster kids, Karson, Carlos, and Andrew, were here and ready to jump in.

Naya gave instructions for the setup, and within an hour they had everything finished. She stood in the entryway and assessed the display. "This looks great, guys. Now for the last step." Naya walked over to her purse and pulled out markers and cards. "I thought it would be fun for everyone to write down something they admire about Zack."

"With all due respect," Izan held up his hands, "you're basically asking us to throw away our man cards."

"A man card?" Karson puffed out his chest. "I want one of those." He took a card from the stack and sat at the table.

"Me too." Andrew snagged a marker and paper. "Real men share their feelings. That's what Zack does with us."

The crew chuckled and their faces softened. "I suppose I'll take one." Izan walked over to sit next to the teens. This was what Naya wanted Zack to witness. The admiration and respect everyone had for him. Not only did he make an impact each day, but he was part of this family.

Ten minutes later, the front entrance chimed.

"Places, everyone," Naya whispered and waved her hand.

Zack stepped into the room.

"Surprise!" everyone shouted. A few whistled.

"What's all this?" Zack glanced around.

Eddie crossed the room first. "You're an essential part of this team, man. We're glad you're back." He slapped Zack on the shoulder and guided him over to the table.

"Does this mean we can dig into those desserts now?" Ridge darted past the rest of the crew.

Amelia swatted at his hand. "Not so fast."

"There's something else we want to give you." Bryce stepped up and handed Zack a frame. "Congratulations."

Zack scanned the words and his eyes widened. "Really? I passed my hazmat training?"

"You completed all your training hours. And you certainly applied what you learned with your quick action to get yourself and Naya out of Ethos with that butane rocket." Bryce slapped Zack on the back. "There's no one else I'd want on my crew overseeing the hazmat unit. You're officially the team leader."

Karson, Andrew, and Carlos walked over to Zack and handed him a patch. "This makes it legit too." Andrew slapped his own chest. "For your uniform."

"I don't know what to say." Zack's Adam's apple bobbed.

"Say we can celebrate with dessert," Ridge piped up.

Zack laughed. "Go for it, dude."

Amelia gave Ridge a side-eye, but he shrugged. "You heard the man." Ridge picked up a cupcake.

"Let's bring it in." Eddie waved people over. The guys and girls circled around Zack and wrapped their arms around each other. Ridge laughed at something that was said, and Eddie smiled.

Naya stepped back to give everyone space. Zack had found his place among the team, and she couldn't be happier. He deserved this. After all the loss, he'd found his home.

A few seconds passed, then Zack separated from the group and headed in Naya's direction.

His eyes locked with hers, and even in the midst of a crowded room, he still managed to make her palms sweaty. Everything dulled to a hum around her, and Naya held her breath.

"Who do I have to thank for this surprise?" A smile tugged on his lips, and the new stubble along his jawline added an extra dimension Naya liked.

Naya couldn't take all the credit. "It was a joint effort."

"Thank you, Nay." The way her nickname rolled off his tongue made her mind go blank. She cleared her throat. "I, uh, have a card for you. Although," she winced, "I was told those are a serious offense to one's man card."

Zack laughed, then his face grew serious. "Looks like I'm about to take a hit then."

This man had a way of making any situation memorable.

He tucked the card in his pocket, then took her hand in his. "Come with me for a sec." He guided her out of the room, through the hall, and outside into the parking lot.

Naya turned her back to the sun so she didn't have to squint.

"Ah, much better." He gave her a hug, and Naya breathed in his fresh pine scent.

She leaned back but kept her hands clasped in his and looked up. "What is?"

"You. Me. With a moment to ourselves."

Despite all the excitement inside, Zack had still seen her. Naya wanted to melt in his embrace and forget about all other responsibilities. "Thank you for not forgetting about me."

"You're pretty unforgettable." Zack tilted her chin and ran his finger along her jaw. "In all the best ways. The thought of losing you again..." His forehead creased. "Thinking I might lose you again is terrifying. I don't want that to happen."

Naya squeezed his hand. "Neither do I."

Zack rocked back on his feet. "Do you have any plans tomorrow?"

Naya's breath caught, but she told herself not to jump to conclusions. "Depends on why you want to know. I've had enough excitement to last me the rest of my life."

"I suppose I could figure out how to make a date extra boring." Zack cocked his head. "Let's see. We could—"

"A date?" Naya interrupted him. Giddiness coursed through her head and brought with it the most pleasant lightheaded sensation. "That's some excitement I'm willing to have."

"Well, in that case, can I pick you up tomorrow afternoon at four?" He winked.

A month ago, Naya would have had reservations about saying yes because of the way Tucker—and Zack, or so she'd thought—had treated her.

Zack had changed her mind and shown her that godly, and attractive, for that matter, men still existed.

"I'd be honored." Naya grinned and wrapped her arms around Zack's neck.

"I was hoping you'd say that." Zack lowered his head and sealed his lips to hers, light and unhurried.

Naya leaned into his frame and closed her eyes, letting everything else fade into the background.

Zack had fought for her, and she was ready to return the favor. She wasn't going to let him walk this path alone. Whatever the next several months brought, Naya wanted to stick by him. And she prayed tomorrow would just be the start.

THIRTY-FIVE

ZACK'S STOMACH TWISTED IN KNOTS. HE TUCKED Naya's letter back in his pocket and grabbed another water from the fridge. The number of callouts today had been enough to distract him.

Until now.

In fifteen minutes, he'd be heading out on a date with Naya. The best way to spend a Friday afternoon. A normal day without running for his life, thanks to the arrests a few days ago that put Roger and Hudson behind bars.

Still, Zack rubbed the base of his neck and moved his head side to side.

This was Naya he was seeing. She'd seen all the good and ugly, so why was he panicking?

Because this was *Naya*.

One of his closest friends from childhood. A girl who'd turned into a beautiful woman, who somehow saw enough in him that she'd been willing to say yes to a date.

Her kindness and willingness to see through his flaws to who he was becoming stirred his heart. He didn't deserve a chance with her. But somehow, her once-calloused heart had opened up to him of all people.

He'd read her letter a few times just to make sure this was real.

She might have been the girl who got away once, but he didn't want to do anything to mess it up now.

Lord, guide our time together today. May our conversation be honoring to You. Show me how I can love and respect Your daughter.

Zack spun the red bracelet on his wrist. A reminder of where he'd been and how far he'd come. He prayed he could show Naya today how much she meant to him. That he wouldn't take her for granted—ever.

He capped the water bottle and headed to his locker to grab his belongings.

Eddie walked out of the locker room and stopped in the hallway. "Let me know how things go."

"You bet, man." Zack gripped his friend's hand and pulled him in for a slap on the back. "Thanks for everything."

Zack gathered his belongings, then headed out to his car.

Two kayaks sat perched on his car roof. He had no idea if Naya enjoyed kayaking or had even gone before. It was a gamble, but there was intention behind his choice.

The sun shone, and the unseasonably warm spring temperatures made it a perfect day to enjoy the outdoors.

On his way to pick her up, he passed Ethos. Crime scene tape surrounded the exterior, warning people to stay away from the unstable structure. A few shingles littered the ground, and shards of glass reflected rays of the sun's light. The gaping hole in the wall where they'd escaped just the other day was boarded up.

How quickly life's circumstances changed. Yet their lives had been spared, and justice would be dealt.

Ever since their meeting with Wilcox, he'd slept better, knowing Roger and Hudson were locked away. Sure, emotions would threaten to kindle a blaze in his heart. Especially knowing the role

Roger had played in his parents' deaths. But right now wasn't the time to dwell on that. He and Naya weren't running for their lives anymore, and Zack didn't have to worry about trouble following her because of him.

He wanted to stir a different—better—kind of fire with the girl who'd left her mark on his heart. And he intended to make it more permanent than the bracelets they'd exchanged years ago.

Zack stepped up onto Naya's front porch, and the door swung open before he could knock.

"Are those for us?" Naya pointed at his car, her mouth widening.

"Figured we hadn't had enough adventures yet." He winked.

Naya slung a drawstring bag over her shoulder and followed him back down the sidewalk.

He'd told her to wear something comfy, more athletic. Even in sneakers, a T-shirt, and shorts, she stole his breath. And with her hair in a high ponytail, her long black curls cascaded around her shoulders in an elegant fashion.

Zack opened the passenger door for her. "After all the excitement we've had, I didn't want to make today too boring and risk you running off to get caught in the crosshairs of another life-or-death story again."

Naya laughed. "You can rest assured that won't happen. I'm ready to live the quiet life for a while."

"Hopefully this will be a good mix between exciting and peaceful." Zack grinned.

Fifteen minutes later, he parked by the lake. Zack went to get out of the car but paused when Naya didn't make a move to unhook her seatbelt.

"You okay?"

She stared out the front windshield, which had a direct view of the body of water. "I don't exactly have the best memories when it comes to water."

Given how her brother had died and the situation at the bridge when they'd met again, her hesitancy was understandable. "I thought we could make some new ones. But I don't want to force you to do something you're not comfortable with."

Naya turned to him, her eyes glistening. "Making memories with you seems to be a recurring theme lately."

One he wanted to continue for a long time.

The tension that had been prevalent a few seconds ago erased itself from her features, and the lines along her forehead disappeared.

"Having a better mindset around this," she waved her hand in the direction of the lake, "would be wonderful." Naya unbuckled her seatbelt and pushed open her door. "Let's go kayaking."

Zack worked to unhook the kayaks from their perch. They carried them in tandem down to the loading dock.

A few people were out on the lake in their canoes and paddleboards, but the area was quiet overall. Zack hoped the fewer people and distractions would lend itself to good conversation, because he had some important things he wanted to share with her.

Naya waded down the embankment, splashing up water behind her. She climbed into a kayak and Zack followed suit. They both used their paddles to push off the landing.

"Want to race to that island over there?" Naya grinned.

Zack shrugged his shoulders. "Depends on if you're going to let me win."

"Not a chance." Naya dug her paddle into the water and took off.

"Hey, you didn't say go." Zack sped after her, following her giggles all the way to the other embankment.

Naya tilted her head back and narrowed her eyes. "You just let me win."

Zack wiggled his fingers. "No way." He feigned being out of breath. "You just cheated and left me in the dust."

Naya gasped. All the while, her eyes gleamed. "I would never."

They pulled their kayaks out of the water, then sat down on the grassy hill and let the silence lengthen.

Zack fingered the red bracelet on his wrist. He was ready to share what was on his heart.

Naya broke the silence first. "You know I would never leave you in the dust. Or tell lies." Her expression grew earnest.

"I don't doubt you. You are a truth seeker. In all the best ways." Zack clasped his hands together. "I didn't mean for my comment to come across that way."

Naya shook her head. "It didn't." She sucked in a breath. "My boss asked if I would write a story on your parents' case. Since I have firsthand information."

Oh. Was he ready to have his family's life and the pain of the past become public knowledge for all to talk about? Did this mean she'd gotten the promotion? He'd been so caught up in the celebration yesterday that he'd forgotten to follow up on her boss's decision. "Are you going to write it?" he asked.

"I didn't take the promotion," she said as if she'd read his mind.

"You gave up the offer?" Zack's eyes widened.

"I don't want it." Naya propped her hands behind her. "I gave my boss an alternative offer though. One that reworks my job description but still meets the needs of the paper. Especially since Tucker was fired."

"So what are you going to do?"

"I've spent enough time searching to expose the truth." Naya glanced down at his wrist, and Zack stopped fidgeting with the bracelet. "I have an idea for another hope-filled story. One that has been playing out before my very eyes."

Zack propped his arms on his knees. "Does this said story involve you sticking around?"

"There's nowhere else I'd rather go." Naya bit her lip.

Zack still couldn't believe this was actually happening—being here, with Naya. Now was his chance.

"We've both had lots of people come and go from our lives." Zack swallowed. Although there was truth to those words, he couldn't dwell on the past. Not when the present moment glimmered with the prospect of a future reality he didn't want to risk losing. "And I don't want us to go separate ways. I want to be someone you can lean on. Someone you can trust and count on to stay."

Zack reached into his pocket and pulled out the box that held the one keepsake he'd waited years to give back to her.

He opened the lid and held out her red bracelet.

Naya looked at him, then the ribbon, then him again. Tears gathered in her eyes. "Zack, what's that?" She pointed to the silver diamond infinity band tied to the bracelet.

"We made a promise to each other as teens that we would stick by each other's side. There may have been some mishaps along the way," he chuckled, "but it would be an honor to pursue you. To love your fiery, yet compassionate heart. I can't promise I'll be perfect, but I'll point you to the One who is." Zack pulled out the red ribbon from the box and held the ring. "This is a promise of what's to come. I love you, Naya."

"Thank you for showing me what it means to stay." Naya held out her hand. "I love you, Zack. There's no one else I'd want by my side."

Zack unhooked the ring, then slid it on Naya's finger before clasping the bracelet around her wrist. He leaned in and enfolded his fingers over hers. Then he cupped her cheek with his other hand and sealed his lips to hers.

Naya deepened the kiss and wrapped her arm around his biceps.

He could get used to this unhurried pace with her so close. She gave him strength and reminded him how to fight for what mattered.

Naya squeezed his arm, then pulled back.

Zack used the moment to catch his breath.

"I think this could make a great story." Her eyes glimmered.

"Oh yeah? How so?"

"Legend has it that those who carry a red ribbon will find their forever family. Though the ribbon may be tangled, twisted, or lost, it can never be severed. And you have shown me where true family lies." Naya scooted closer to Zack and leaned her head on his shoulder. "It doesn't matter if our family is related by blood or not, because we're part of a bigger family."

Zack stared out at the expanse of the lake. He didn't deserve any of these blessings. But it was all "Because of Jesus," he whispered.

"Exactly. His crimson blood has made a way."

Zack imagined his heavenly Father smiling down at him. Sure, his biological dad would be pleased with him too. But it was what the Lord said of him that mattered most. Zack wasn't a trouble-making kid but a man with purpose. "What are you going to title this story?"

"I think I'm going to call it Rescued Duty."

"That has a nice ring to it."

Zack rested his head against Naya's and stared at her finger. One day very soon they'd share the promises they'd make to each other with their family, who'd stand by their side.

The rhythmic lapping of the water against the shoreline reminded him over and over of the beauty all around him.

Indeed, he and Naya had been rescued from the fowler's snare. Now he had the wondrous duty of spending his days showing Naya how much she meant to him.

Zack prayed he could do so for a lifetime.

BONUS EPILOGUE

Thank you for reading *Rescued Duty*. We hope you loved this story. Find out what happens next for Zack and Naya with a **Bonus Epilogue**, a special gift, available only to our newsletter subscribers.

This Bonus Epilogue will not be released on any retailer platform, so get your free gift by scanning the QR code below. By scanning, you acknowledge you are becoming a subscriber to the newsletters of Laura, Lisa, and Sunrise Publishing. Unsubscribe at any time.

Read on for more from the

Last Chance

FIRE & RESCUE

series

Gear up for the next Last Chance Fire and Rescue romantic suspense thriller, Rescued Faith by Lisa Phillips and Michelle Sass Aleckson.

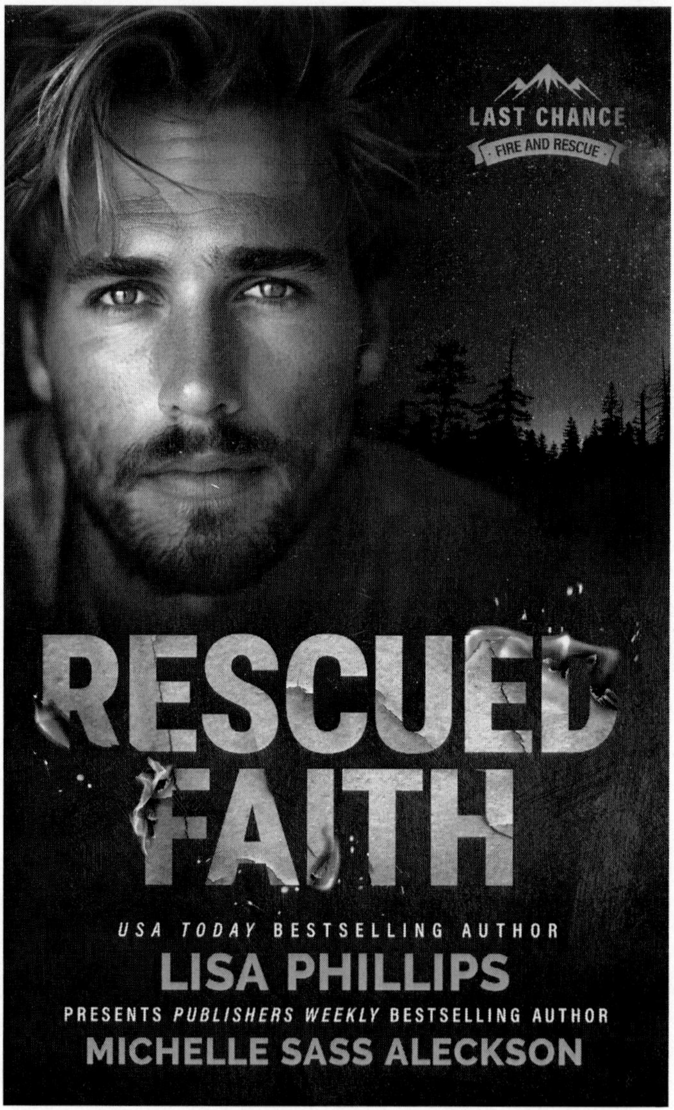

Dive back into the danger—and the romance—of the bestselling Last Chance Fire and Rescue series...

When private detective Penny Mitchell's latest case takes her right back to the last place on earth she wants to go, she must make a choice—continue running from her past, leaving Last Chance County for good, or stay and ensure that her sister and her kids are safe. Even if that means running into her ex.

Rescue firefighter and notorious playboy Bryce Crawford is supposed to be a different guy now that he's come to faith, but he isn't exactly sure how to do that—especially when the woman who broke his heart comes back to town. As if seeing Penny isn't dangerous enough, they have to work together on a new task force to find the criminals responsible for the recent string of explosions and epidemic of dangerous new weapons on the streets.

Together, Penny and Bryce must set aside their past and race against time to uncover the criminals' end game...and stop them before it's too late.

Dive into this heart-pounding romantic suspense where danger lurks around every corner and second chances come at a price. Rescued Faith is a thrilling tale of redemption, forgiveness, and the unbreakable bonds of family in the face of adversity.

Pre-order from the Sunrise Shop to get your hands on it early, or later from your favorite retailer.

Keep reading for a sneak peek...

ONE

FAVORS WERE A DANGEROUS CURRENCY TO DEAL in. Too many hidden costs. As a private investigator, Penny Mitchell knew better. People got sucked into all kinds of trouble from helping out a friend. Which was why she liked her solitary life back in Denver. Less blowback. Less entanglements. Less complications.

And yet, here she was, in the last place on earth she wanted to be, all because a former coworker had given her those Bronco tickets for her nephew's birthday and now he was cashing in the favor.

Man, she needed to get this job done and get out. Before anyone knew she was in town.

She killed the engine of her Ford Edge, reached over the almost-empty coffee cup and half-eaten bag of sunflower seeds for her camera in the passenger seat. She held it to her eye, focused across the street at the red Nissan Rogue and the woman behind the wheel. The curly dark hair and round face with glasses came into sharp focus. Penny snapped a few pictures.

She should've turned down the job ATF agent Ben Freeman had begged her to take as soon as her target had headed west from Denver. He'd assured her that Emma Kemper wasn't a criminal mastermind like her bomb-making brother Vince. Which meant tailing her and snapping some photos should be an easy assignment.

But there was nothing easy about being *here*. The sooner she could get the heck out of here the better. Because if Penny didn't run into someone she knew, the memories themselves would drive her away.

All right, Emma. What are you doing here?

Last Chance County's little warehouse district wasn't a travel destination. There was no hotel in this part of town. No Airbnbs or cute rentals. Just some old metal-sided buildings and dilapidated brick storefronts from an era gone by. And Emma was simply sitting in her driver's seat. This felt more like a purposeful destination. Like she might be here awhile.

Penny used voice commands to make a call.

"Freeman here. Whatcha got, Mitchell?"

"Does Emma Kemper have connections to Last Chance County?" If he knew, he was cunning to have kept it from her when he'd asked for this "itty bitty favor."

"We haven't been able to find much about her. That's why we hired you. Why? Is that where she is?"

"Believe me, I wouldn't be here if she wasn't," Penny ground out. She shouldn't be so snippy. But...Last Chance. Really?

"Huh. I woulda thought she was heading for Nevada or Arizona, where she grew up. But that's good that it's Last Chance. With Jude Brooks there, you'll have some backup if you need it."

"I don't need backup." She needed to get out of here as soon as possible. "Are you sure she doesn't have known associates here? I could capture her tonight and bring her in." Then the job would be done. Favor fulfilled and she could move on with her life and not worry about running into her past.

"Nice try. Emma flew under the radar while we focused on her brother. She has no record, but she might have been sent by Vince to do some of his dirty work. I need you to keep your distance and gather intel, Ms. Private Investigator. No formal charges yet."

Penny switched the camera to one hand and downed a swig from her cup.

Ugh. She almost spat out the cold dregs of her gas-station coffee. Instead, she forced herself to swallow it. She needed the caffeine.

"You *still* haven't gotten anything out of Vince Kemper?" Ben Freeman was sharp and had a rather intimidating presence with his tall, beefy frame. The scrawny explosives expert hardly seemed like a formidable opponent. "I would've thought by now you would've cracked him."

"He may be a pasty scrap of a man, but he's not saying a thing. And he covered his tracks well. We haven't been able to untangle much here. It's up to you now to make sure Emma isn't involved in his bomb-making agenda. And if she is, then maybe we'll be able to figure out what the endgame is, cuz we're getting a whole lot of nothing."

Gee, no pressure. Penny blew out a long breath. This meant staying longer.

"What's the matter? She get away from the great Penny Mitchell?" He chuckled.

But there was nothing funny about this. Penny was barreling straight toward a disaster if she spent any more time in the area than absolutely necessary.

"I have her in my sights. I just didn't think this job would bring me to Last Chance County." She snapped a few more pictures as Emma turned toward the window, giving Penny a better angle of her face.

"Jude can bring her in for questioning or take over if you want to be done. Which, by the way, if you get tired of the wandering lifestyle, he's requested more staff for the satellite ATF office there in Last Chance."

"You suggesting I come back to the dark side?" Jude Brooks, her former coworker, had followed a case to LCC, where he'd spent his childhood summers, and reunited with Andi Crawford two years ago. Little had he known then, when he brought Penny in on the case to help capture Diego Ruiz Sosa, the series of events he would kick off. It had been nice to be a part of a case for a while, the thrill and adventure of tracking down a cartel leader. Something different than finding cheating spouses or gathering intel on criminals for the lawyers, or the private security she did for the rich and entitled. Now Sosa was dead, and Jude and Andi were married.

She, on the other hand, was still single—just the way she liked it—and in danger of getting sucked down a rabbit hole if she stayed any longer than necessary.

"Being a federal agent isn't all bad. Jude has a great thing going there."

And Jude deserved all the good things life had to offer. Including the tightly knit family he'd recently married into and a place like Last Chance to put down some roots.

So yeah, she'd given up a few things for the sake of being in business by herself. And at times like now, it would be really convenient to have the authority to bring Emma Kemper in. But no way did she want to give control over to someone else. Because those jobs came with bosses. Bosses who led people on, made promises they didn't intend to keep.

No, thank you.

"That's great for Jude, but I'm happy where I'm at. Charging the big bucks. You sure this is worth my hourly rate?" Because she wasn't sure there was any compensation worth the risk to her heart of being back here.

Maybe she *should* let Jude pick it up from here. He could keep an eye on things. She could get back to the open road. Freedom.

But her bank account balance flashed through her mind. She might not be in dire straights yet, but she needed the work. And she did have a professional reputation to consider. If she couldn't complete this job, who knew if Ben would give her another? She liked to stay near Denver so she could see Libby and the kids more often.

Of course, she always talked her sister into coming to see *her* so she could avoid this kind of thing. But with Libby's family living here, Penny should be the one to make sure there was nothing dangerous going on. She groaned again.

"Do you want me to contact Jude? If you really don't want this job—"

Her father's voice echoed from the past. *Buck up, Pen.*

"Nah, no need to bother the newlyweds. I'm just whining."

"Hey, that reminds me. Why didn't you make it to the wedding? You missed seeing Jude do the Macarena. Those Crawfords sure know how to throw a party."

Yes, they did. Memories of country music, learning how to two-step, and a certain masculine beachy fragrance floated through her mind.

"I...had a job I couldn't get out of in time. But I sent Jude and Andi an obnoxiously expensive gift, so all was forgiven."

The hefty price tag hadn't made *her* feel any better though. No one had to know that she'd specifically taken a job that'd meant she would be gone that day. And no need for Jude or *any* of his in-laws to know she was in the vicinity now.

Especially Bryce.

The handsome rescue firefighter, one of Andi's brothers, probably hadn't given her a second thought since the last time she'd hightailed it out of the county a year and a half ago.

And it was better for everyone if it stayed that way. Even if there wasn't a day that went by that she didn't see something that reminded her of him. Try as she might, it was hard to forget those passionate brown eyes.

"You missed a good reception." Freeman obviously wasn't going to let it drop.

Movement on the sidewalk across the street grabbed Penny's attention.

"I need to go. Someone else is coming. I'll let you know when I find anything."

"If Emma ends up sticking around, contact Jude."

Not unless she absolutely had to. "Bye."

The high desert sunset softened to a lavender haze behind the mountains outside of town. She had to give it to Jude, he'd picked a beautiful place to live. Something like a sigh escaped as she watched the street. Some things just weren't meant to be.

She sat up and watched two men park a truck and approach Emma's car. One stocky and tall, the other average height and thin. Penny took pictures as they came closer. Both had darker hair and olive skin tones that could be from a variety of ethnicities. The lighting wasn't great, but hopefully she could still identify them later.

Emma got out and opened the back of the SUV. She pulled a couple duffel bags out and handed them to the men. Then she grabbed another. They turned down an alley between two of the buildings and were out of sight.

Penny checked her Smith & Wesson Equalizer and quickly ran across the street to follow them just as the streetlights turned on. Her black leather jacket helped fight off the spring chill in the air and blend her into the night shadows. Too bad it didn't have a hood to hide her blonde head. She picked up her pace and approached the alley between the warehouse and the empty store next to it. She peered around the corner.

Empty. Just scraggly weeds growing in the cracks of the asphalt between the buildings, and trash scattered against the wall.

They had to be close. Penny jogged down the alley. There. A door in the warehouse hadn't quite closed.

With gun in hand, she toed the door open a smidge, testing it to see if the rusty hinges would squeak. It opened quietly.

Good. She peeked in first, then slipped into the dark building, letting her eyes adjust. Voices carried from deeper within the space.

Penny crouched by a pile of pallets just inside the doorway and scoped out the area. Tall metal shelves were mostly empty, although some held boxes. An old forklift off to the side looked like it hadn't been started in decades. But the tables in the middle were bright white plastic, like the kind one could find at the nearest Costco. Those must be new. And the folding chairs didn't look too worn either.

There was nowhere else to hide in the cavernous space. Emma spoke to a tall man, but in the dark there was no way Penny could distinguish any features. Not even the color of his hair. His bright flashlight shone down at the table between them. Where had the other two guys gone?

"Did you bring them?" the new man asked.

"I've got them here." She dropped the duffel bag on the table and wrapped her arms around the man's neck. "I've missed you." Pulling him close she gave him a lingering kiss.

"Me too." He kissed her back. "But everything is in place now. So let's see what you brought."

She opened the duffel to show him.

"Good." The man reached in and grabbed a smaller bag out of the duffel. "And your brother? He was able to finish his work?"

"Of course. The devices are here." She unzipped a different pocket. "He showed me how to set them."

So much for the theory that Emma wasn't involved with Vincent's agenda.

Penny tried to move closer and get a better look, but there was no cover. She used her phone to get a couple of pictures. However, she couldn't see one distinguishing feature of Emma's boyfriend in the dark. The hooded sweatshirt he wore kept his face shadowed.

"And you're sure he won't—"

Emma huffed. "He's not going to rat us out. My brother understands how important this is. Now, can we get out of here? I want to see the new—"

"Boss, we're set." The thin guy from out front jogged over from a door on the wall across from Penny. It must've been an office of some sort. "We need to go."

Boss handed the duffel with the hidden device to his cohort. "You know where to put it." The man snatched the bag and ran up the metal stairs in the back of the warehouse while Emma and her guy headed straight toward Penny and the alley door.

Penny quickly moved to the back of the pile of pallets. If she opened the door now, they'd see her. As soon as they left she could follow and find out who—

"What do you think you're doing?" A dark and ominous voice sounded behind her. But it was the click of the safety being switched off that immediately put Penny on edge.

Cold metal pressed into the back of her head. "Drop the gun now."

"Who's there?" Boss Man asked.

Penny tensed her grip on the gun. She could make a move and take out the guy behind her, but the boss pulled out a gun of his own. If he came closer, maybe she could ID him, but it was still too dark.

She needed more time. She tried a little chuckle. "I was lost, I was just looking for—"

"I said drop it. I have no problem putting a bullet in you," the man behind her said.

And from the hardness in his voice, Penny didn't doubt it.

"Al, get outta here. I'll take care of her." The man spoke to Emma's boyfriend.

"Stick to the plan. Let the blast take care of her and get out." He led Emma out of the warehouse.

Clearly Emma was no innocent bystander. That girl was in this up to her eyeballs and apparently didn't care about leaving a fellow female to the mercy of whoever had a gun to her head.

Penny was on her own. "Look, I was just trying to find—"

"This is your last chance. Put. Down. The. Gun."

She slowly lowered her gun to the ground. The pressure of the man's weapon against her skull didn't give her a choice. Before she could stand up, he yanked her arms behind her and dragged her toward the back. He had to be tall. And big.

Penny was no lightweight, but his grip had no give to it whatsoever. She fought, pulling away from him, but her shoulders screamed as they were trapped against his chest.

Trapped. Again. With no one to rely on for a rescue but herself. No surprise there. If she believed like she did when she was a little girl, she might've prayed. But that never changed anything.

Buck up, Pen.

Penny tried throwing her head back, driving it into what she hoped was his nose or another soft body part. Nope. His chin was as hard as her head.

He shook her and squeezed tighter. "You're feisty, I'll give you that. But this will not end well for you."

Not if she had anything to say about it. "People are looking for me. They'll be here any—"

The other minion came barreling down the metal stairs. "It's set. We have two min—who's that?"

Two minutes? Penny's mind raced.

"Doesn't matter. We gotta go." The hulk man dragged her farther.

"Shoot her and let's get." The skinny twerp said it like it was no big deal. Real upstanding friends Emma had.

"Shooting leaves a bullet in her. A bullet they can trace. We should find out who she is, but we don't have time. Help me get her to that closet back there."

Closet? No way!

The man in front of her went for her legs. Penny kicked and flailed. Her black combat boot connected with his jaw. He staggered away for a moment but then shook his head and came back. He wrapped two vise-like arms around her thighs while the brute behind her picked her up, squeezing her arms against her chest.

"Let me go! I can help you." She tried to use her weight to throw them off-balance.

It was useless. They dragged her to the back of the room as Penny's mental countdown kept going.

The guy holding her legs let go and opened a door. She was thrown in, and her head bounced off the cement. The door shut before she could even open her eyes. No!

Her head swam, waves of agony pounded. Thoughts jumbled together except for one clear truth. She was trapped.

"It's not a basement. I'm fine." Her voice wasn't very convincing, even to her own ears. Too breathy. Too small. But if it tricked her brain into forgetting that she was alone, she would keep talking to herself. "Not a basement."

She crawled to the door in the pitch black, too dizzy to stand. The knob didn't budge. Her fingers felt the lock. Maybe she could pick it. But her pulse quickened. Her hands trembled. She couldn't see a thing in the thick darkness, and her gas-station coffee and sunflower seeds were about to make another appearance.

Penny pounded on the door. "Let me out of here. I'm serious. I can help!"

One of the men laughed. Footsteps on the concrete floor grew quieter as they moved away. And then...silence.

They'd left her here to die. In the dark. Alone.

Penny tried the knob again, but it was useless. Her scream of frustration ripped through the darkness.

Her phone!

With shaky hands she pulled it out of her pocket. No reception. But she could use the flashlight. Maybe—

A huge boom shook the building. Dust rained down. A paint can from the shelf above the door fell.

This was why she didn't do favors.

She never should've come back to Last Chance County.

ACKNOWLEDGMENTS

Susie, Lindsay, and the whole Sunrise team—Thank you for believing in me and my story idea. Your willingness to provide expert guidance through the publishing process has been invaluable.

Lisa Phillips—Thank you for championing my characters, letting me step into the world of Last Chance County, and mentoring me each step of the way. All the frantic questions I had, Discord chats, Zoom meetings, brainstorming sessions, and behind the scenes work has shown me what it truly means for writing to be a community of authors supporting each other.

Megan Besing—Thank you for being my writing buddy, prayer warrior, and friend. This writing journey is sweeter with you!

Jonathan Al-Khal—Thank you for taking time to answer all my hazmat and special ops questions! Your expertise helped me make sure the situations in this story were authentic.

Lisa Hoppe, Katie Harley, and Pamela Berger—Thank you for your valuable insight into the world of foster care and answering all my questions. This story would not be possible without your guidance. All of you are truly living out what Zack and Naya experience—true family is not in blood but in the love of Christ.

Family and Friends—If I took the time to list each one of you, I'd write another novel! Thank you for your prayers and giving me the space to write this story. Even if that meant a pile of dirty dishes and laundry, rearranging plans, and bombarding you with fictional ideas.

My Lord and Savior—Nothing in life is possible apart from Your saving grace and bringing this sinner from death to life. You placed the dream to write in my heart. May the words on these pages point people back to Your Word so that Your name is glorified. Thank you for writing the most beautiful redemption story. From now and into eternity, may my life and the words I write be focused on an audience of One.

Laura Conaway is a Publishers Weekly bestselling and Selah Award-winning author who resides in Pennsylvania. She creates stories with a healthy dose of suspense and happily ever afters while her characters discover triumph through trials. As a former librarian, she's always searching for the next best read and loves solving mysteries like Nancy Drew. When she's not inhaling sweet potato fries to motivate writing, Laura spends her time playing guitar and sharing about the Greatest Story ever written.

Connect with Laura at www.lauraconawayauthor.com

Lisa Phillips is a USA Today and top ten Publishers Weekly bestselling author of over 80 books that span Harlequin's Love Inspired Suspense line, independently published series romantic suspense, and thriller novels. She's discovered a penchant for high-stakes stories of mayhem and disaster where you can find made-for-each-other love that always ends in happily ever after.

Lisa is a British ex-pat who grew up an hour outside of London and attended Calvary Chapel Bible College, where she met her husband. He's from California, but nobody's perfect. It wasn't until her Bible College graduation that she figured out she was a writer (someone told her). As a worship leader for Calvary Chapel churches in her local area, Lisa has discovered a love for mentoring new ministry members and youth worship musicians.

Find out more at www.authorlisaphillips.com.

LAST CHANCE COUNTY

• LAST CHANCE FIRE AND RESCUE •

Expired Return

Expired Hope

Expired Promise

Expired Vows

Rescued Duty

Rescued Faith

Rescued Heart

Rescued Dreams

• LAST CHANCE COUNTY SERIES •

Expired Refuge

Expired Secrets

Expired Cache

Expired Hero

Expired Game

Expired Plot

Expired Getaway

Expired Betrayal

Expired Flight

Expired End

Get your romantic suspense fix from Sunrise!

Elite Guardians: Savannah

Safety. Secrets. Sacrifice.
What will it cost these Elite Guardians to protect the innocent? Discover the answers in our Elite Guardians: Savannah series.

A Breed Apart: Legacy unleashed!

Get your hands on all of Ronie Kendig's A Breed Apart: Legacy series.

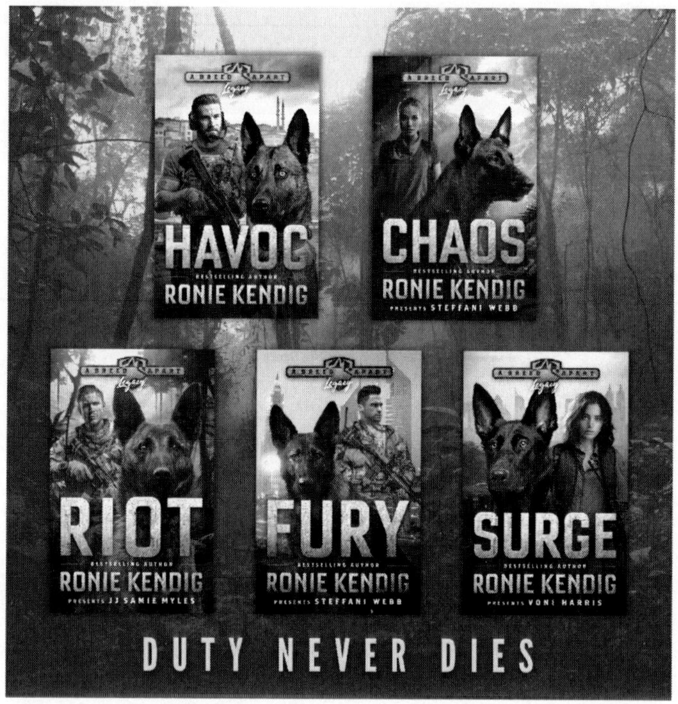

Available Now!

RESCUE. DANGER. DEVOTION

THIS TIME, THEIR HEARTS ARE ON THE LINE…

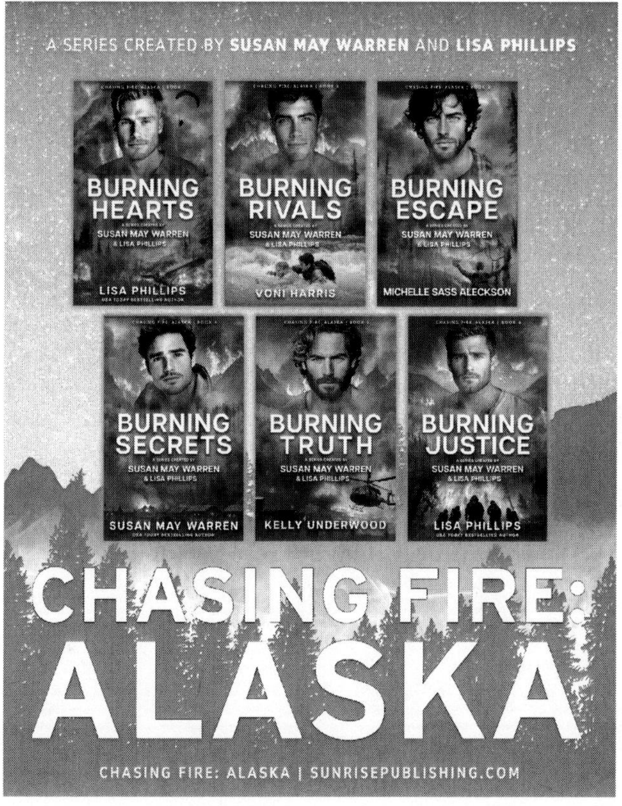

The skies over Alaska's vast wilderness are ablaze, not just with wildfire but with the flames of a dark and dangerous conspiracy. Join the Midnight Sun Fire Crew in another heart-pounding adventure as they find themselves fighting not only fires…but for their lives. Old romances reignite and new attractions simmer, threatening to complicate their mission further. Now, the team must navigate their tangled emotions and trust in each other's strengths as their fight for survival becomes a fight for justice in another epic, best-selling series created by Susan May Warren and Lisa Phillips.

Connect With Sunrise

Thank you so much for reading *Rescued Duty*. We hope you enjoyed the story. If you did, would you be willing to do us a favor and leave a review? It doesn't have to be long- just a few words to help other readers know what they're getting. (But no spoilers! We don't want to wreck the fun!) Thank you again for reading!

We'd love to hear from you- not only about this story, but about any characters or stories you'd like to read in the future. Contact us at www.sunrisepublishing.com/contact.

We also have a regular updates that contains sneak peeks, reviews, upcoming releases, and fun stuff for our reader friends. Sign up at www.sunrisepublishing.com or scan our QR code.

Made in United States
Cleveland, OH
16 March 2025

15200860R00194